TAKEN

Willow Danes

TAKEN
by Willow Danes

©2015 Here be Dragons

Cover Design: Steven James Catizone

Published by Here Be Dragons

ISBN-13: 978-0692377734
ISBN-10: 0692377735

Also available in eBook publication

PRINTED IN THE UNITED STATES OF AMERICA

ONE

Coldness snaked through Hope's belly as Keri's silence dragged on.

"Did you know?" Hope asked again. Her cell pressed hard to her ear, her heart in her throat as she waited for her friend's answer, she had a sudden urge to open the car window and hurl the damned thing into the road before Keri *could* reply. "Did you know about Brian and Megan?"

Through the phone she heard Keri sigh and Hope's grip tightened on the steering wheel, the center diamond of her engagement ring sparkling in the sunlight.

Parked in front of the diner where she was to pick up the rental's keys, Hope blinked out at Brittle Bridge, North Carolina's quaint Main Street. Outside her car, people strolled about on their Friday morning errands, enjoying the May sunshine and the sweet mountain air, chatting and laughing.

Inside the car, Hope's breath had the quick shallow pant of an animal caught in a trap.

"Look," Keri began, a little impatiently. "It wasn't my job to tell you. Megan—Brian really—should have."

"You're my *friend*. You went with me to look at venues, at wedding gowns. You bought a bridesmaid's dress." Hope's throat tightened. "*Megan* bought a maid of honor dress!"

"I didn't actually buy the dress," Keri mumbled. "I called the boutique after we left and asked them to cancel my order."

But that was back in March!

"How long?" Hope asked, her voice high and tight. "How long has it been going on? How long have you known?"

Keri sighed again. "I went to Gable's with some people from work back in January and I saw Brian and Megan in a booth in the back and they were—It's probably been going on longer though."

"*January?* But—" Hope began, her tone pleading now as if she could argue this away, as if to point out the faulty logic of it would cast a spell and make everything right again. "But we got engaged on Valentine's Day! He asked me to marry him on *Valentine's Day.* If he and Megan were—" Her eyes stung. "He broke our engagement by text, you know. He sent me a *text* today to tell me that he and Megan were together and how very, very sorry he was. Megan texted to say she's sorry too—Oh, and since she's not coming for the weekend she's not going to pay her third for the rental."

"Oh, that is shitty," Keri said.

Shitty as letting me plan a wedding when you knew all along Megan was fucking my fiancé?

But the great burden of red hair was everyone expected you to have a bad temper and a sharp tongue. Hope had spent most of her twenty-seven years showing the world how even-keeled she was, how she could handle anything with a cool head, not raging or weeping even in the face of heartbreak and grief, not letting anyone know how bad she hurt.

Those walls went up when she was eight and were so thick now that nothing—not the death of her parents, not the humiliation of her fiancé screwing her maid of honor—was going to bring them down.

"Yeah, it is," Hope said instead. "So when were you going to get around to telling me that you aren't coming for the weekend either?"

"Look, I just thought if you and Megan were alone— maybe the truth would finally come out. Being with the two of you and pretending I didn't know sucked."

"Wow." Hope nodded even though Keri couldn't see her. Even a determined redhead had her limits. "That must have been really rough on you."

Keri went silent again.

Hope put her hand over her eyes, blocking out the cheerful spring sunlight. "I lost my job this morning."

"What?" Keri sounded startled for the first time during their conversation.

"They made the announcement today. They sold the company to the Hindle Group last week and they had one too many graphic designers so they let me go. They made me drive all the way to Asheville to give me the news. My fiancé ends it in a text but my company had to tell me in person."

"Jesus . . ."

"They gave me three months' severance. And they shook my hand too. Apparently someone in the D.C. office did me the favor of clearing out my stuff while I was driving to Asheville yesterday so I'm all packed up. They'll have everything delivered to my apartment by the end of the day."

"So you're driving back to D.C. tonight?"

"What for?" Hope asked bleakly. "Brian and Megan are at his place, making the most of the romantic curtained bed I bought. I don't have work on Monday. No fiancé, no best friend, no job. My apartment lease is up in ten days and now I won't be moving in with Brian. Maybe I'll just move up here to the mountains. Take up wood crafting or something."

"Call me when you get back," Keri urged. "I'll take you out and get you drunk. We'll find you someone new."

"No. I'm cursed." Hope shut her eyes. "No one on the planet has worse luck with men than I do."

Keri was smart enough not to argue that point. "I really am sorry."

"Yeah, me too," Hope said and hung up.

She turned off the car and sat there, the cell cradled in her lap. The invitations hadn't gone out yet so she didn't need to work through the guest list; with her parents both dead and no siblings there was no one left to call.

No one at all.

She sat there until the air got stale inside the car and she couldn't bear the stuffiness anymore. The car door sounded too loud when she closed it behind her, the sunshine outside too bright, the laughter and chatter of those around her grating.

It shouldn't be like this; the whole world should be as silent and dark and cold as the inside of her chest felt right now.

It was three quick steps up the concrete stoop and then she was pulling open the door to Dolly's Diner, grimacing against the happy jingle of the bell over the door.

The diner was pretty typical: a long bar with high chairs fixed to the floor, blue vinyl booths lining the windows, the air heavy with the smell of fried food and old grease. The worn linoleum floor looked like it had been put down in the eighties, the music from the ceiling speakers also from that era. The place was slow now at ten-thirty, too late for breakfast on a weekday, a bit too early for the lunch crowd.

Hope made her way to the end of the bar where the old-style cash register sat, ducking her head against the patrons' curious looks. Her hand automatically went to her carrot-top hair, smoothing it down, a habit she'd picked up when she'd started dating Brian. He'd poked fun at her mad curls and not always in a kindly way; she'd even booked an appointment to have it straightened next week, intending to surprise him with a new, tamed look. Maybe that was why he'd chosen Megan. Her ash blond hair was always perfectly highlighted and shiny as silk . . .

The waitress looked about sixteen or so, a slim girl with short dark hair and a cute rabbit-like overbite. Her name tag read "Rachel" and she met Hope at the end of the bar, already reaching toward the neat stack of laminated menus next to the cash register.

"How many?"

Hope shook her head. "I'm not here to eat."

Rachel's eyebrows rose and her glance took in Hope's wild hair, her business casual clothes; the sensible heels that made Hope, at five-eleven in bare feet, over six-one.

"I'm supposed to—Is Dolly here? I'm supposed to ask for Dolly. To get the keys."

"Oh, you're a renter!" Rachel took her hand off the menus. "Sure, Dolly's in the back. Have a seat, I'll fetch her up. You want some coffee, ma'am?"

I'm not a ma'am! I'm not getting *married! My—ex— fiancé just ran off with my maid of honor!*

Hope wet her lips. "No, just the—I'm fine."

"You renting one of Dolly's places?" The woman asking occupied a booth close by. She looked to be in her mid-fifties, blond with good cheekbones, her round face friendly and open. The man with her had salt-and-pepper hair and a good sturdy look to him except for the still reddened scars on his face. That and the way he held his body taut, his posture odd. He was turned a bit in the booth, his back against the wall, as if he felt unsafe here, unsafe anywhere.

"Yeah," Hope mumbled.

"You moving here to Brittle Bridge?" the woman asked. "Or up for the summer?"

"Neither." Hope glanced at the doorway Rachel had just vanished through, praying the owner would show up to save her from this conversation. She just wanted to get the goddamn key and hole up in Dolly's three-bedroom-with-Jacuzzi-and-way-too-big-for-one-person place so she could fall apart in privacy. "I'm just renting a cabin for the weekend."

"Which one?" the man asked sharply. "Which cabin?"

The other diners were shifting in their seats, looking ill at ease, and at least one sent a dark look the man's way.

"Which one?" he demanded again.

"I don't remember," Hope stammered. It had some stupid, touristy name—"Skylands Hideaway maybe?"

His lips went white. "The one near the McNallys'."

"Bill—" the woman began but he cut her off.

"She can't go up there." His fists clenched on the table, his dark brown eyes wild under bushy salt-and-pepper brows as they fixed on her. "You can't go up there!"

"There he goes again," one of the men muttered.

The woman quickly put down her coffee cup. "We should probably get a move on, Bill. Lots to do this morning."

"I know you don't believe me!" Bill speared the other diners with a look, his mouth trembling. "I know don't none of you believe what I saw!"

"Bill . . ." the woman pleaded.

"They're going to find her someday, Riley," one of the other men, seated at a table near the back, returned with a scowl. "Jenna McNally. Everybody's gonna know what really happened to her."

"What really—! Goddamn it, I've told you! Jenna got between me and that . . . that black-haired demon-eyed *thing*! I fired at it and it attacked me!" The man pointed to his face, to the reddened scars that marred his cheek. "I've told you all a thousand times—that creature picked her up and ran off with her!"

Creature? Hope edged away. The guy was clearly nuts.

"'Cause we all done believe an alien attacked you, Bill," the man sneered.

"'Course we do!" Another man, seated at the same table, pushed his worn ball cap back and smacked his meaty palm on the table. "Why, we got us a regular Area 51 right here in Brittle Bridge!" He looked around at the other diners and spread his hands. "And who else would them aliens come to but Sheriff Bill Riley?"

"It wasn't *human*!" Bill's face reddened as the other diners snickered. Spittle showed at the corner of his mouth, making him look every inch the town crazy. "Big as a damn bear with eyes that glowed!"

Another woman, stout, with a helmet of pineapple blond hair, pushed through the swinging doors, swiftly moving to place her bulk in the aisle and block the men's hostile stares.

She leaned over as if just casually clearing the plates off the table and murmured, "Best take him home, Sarah Jane."

Sarah Jane gave a quick nod, already pushing her way out of the booth.

"It was *real*!" Bill exploded.

Clearly everyone else had heard this from him before but Hope scooted back, pressing against the counter to give the pair plenty of room to pass.

"Come on, honey," Sarah Jane pleaded, urging him toward the exit.

With a final, frustrated look the man muttered a curse. The bell gave a cheery jingle overhead as he yanked the door open and stalked out to the sidewalk, his hands balled into the pockets of his jeans.

Sarah Jane paused to send an apologetic glance at the other woman. "Sorry, Dolly."

"Maybe you should keep him out of here for a couple days." Dolly laid her hand on the woman's shoulder for a moment. "They just get him riled up like anything."

Sarah Jane's face pinkened, her lips pursing for a moment as if she intended to argue, then she gave a stiff nod and followed Bill out. As soon as the door shut behind her one of the men made a comment that didn't carry to where Hope stood, but the others at his table burst into loud laughter.

Dolly sent them a sharp glance with her mouth drawn downwards, but she let the comment—whatever it was—go unchallenged and waved Rachel over. "Bus the table, will ya?"

Then Dolly turned and hustled toward Hope. "Sorry to keep you waiting, sugar," she began brightly. "Now, you're Miss MacGowan, aren't you? Come to fetch the keys to the Skylands cabin right?" The space between her thin penciled-on brows puckered. "Oh, I meant to ask—are your friends going to need their own keys? Only that's an extra twenty-dollar deposit, per set."

"Hold on—What the hell was that?" Hope asked, indicating the door the pair had exited through.

"Oh." Dolly's pudgy cheeks flushed. "Bill Riley used to be town sheriff but he had himself a breakdown a while back. Nothing to worry about. Sarah Jane'll take care of him."

"And who's Jenna McNally?"

"Just a girl that used to live hereabouts." Dolly circled to the other side of the counter and started rummaging around. "She used to waitress here during the summers, a real sweetheart too—her and her granddaddy both. Probably the biggest funeral this town ever saw."

"Wait a minute—" Hope took a quick step forward, her hands on the countertop. "Those people were killed at the cabin I rented?"

Dolly straightened instantly. "Oh, goodness, no! Nothing like *that*! This is one of my cabins, not the McNally place. You see, Pap—Mr. McNally, that is— passed on last year and his granddaughter Jenna was clearing out the house to sell, had it listed and everything. She was moving back to Asheville, I think. Anyway, she left town without saying goodbye and Bill got it in his head that—Look, the job got to him is all. He thought he saw someone pick her up and carry her off."

Hope glanced at the other end of the room, at the rough men who'd been laughing at the former sheriff. "And by 'someone' you mean an alien?"

"That's just Bill talking nonsense," Dolly said impatiently. "Jenna must have had herself a boyfriend in Asheville and just wanted to get back quick, is all. Believe me, nothing carried Jenna McNally off."

Rachel, breezing past with dirty dishes in hand, stopped at that. "My sister Susanna's a nurse at Mission

Hospital," Rachel confided to Hope. "And she was there when they brought Bill in. Susanna said he was screaming like anything about how we had to get the army into Brittle Bridge, that we was all in danger from aliens. 'Course *Susanna* thinks it was a bear what attacked him and Bill was just in shock or something on account of losing so much blood. *I* think it might have been a werewolf. That's what it sounded like to me." Rachel paused, considering. "Or maybe one of them Sasquatch things—only not so furry."

Hope's frown deepened. It was a seven-hour ride back to D.C. She probably wouldn't make it before midnight but it might be worth the drive if everybody in Brittle Bridge was this bonkers.

"Hush yourself," Dolly hissed at the girl. "Get that table wiped down and get busy with refills at table six. Can't you see Lester Mills holding up his coffee cup over there?"

As Dolly handed the coffee pot past her Hope pressed her palms hard against the cheap countertop. She'd gotten up extra early every morning for months and left Brian sleeping to creep into the living room, a mug of coffee tucked into her hand. She'd sit there, curled on the sofa, sipping from her cup and gaze contentedly at the wonderful ever-changing chaos of wedding things spread out over her coffee table, imagining her perfect day, the perfect family the two of them would create when they exchanged those rings.

She'd left the table still covered with all that wedding stuff when she'd gone to Asheville—copies of *Brides* magazine, venue brochures, sample invitations printed in silver and gold. Brian's clothes might still hang in the closet—or not. He might have cleared his stuff out with

Megan's help but Hope doubted those two would be thoughtful enough to strip the bed. The sheets would smell like him. And possibly of Megan's Hermès perfume too.

Having to walk into that living room tonight, alone, and see all those broken hopes waiting for her, the model brides smiling up from their big glossy pictures, the scent of optimism and anticipation gone sour, that cold, lonely bed—

Dear God, I think I'm actually better off here with the crazy mountain folk . . .

"Ah! Here you go, sugar." Smiling, Dolly held up a key ring and jangled the keys before Hope. "Let me just run in the back and get you the rental packet."

Still rubbing her eyes, Hope dragged herself onto the screened-in porch that ran the length of the cabin's front. She'd managed to fall asleep last night but she still felt tired and raw. Dressed in jeans, T-shirt, and hiking boots, her favorite sweater and a cup of tea proof against the chill, Hope sank into one of the rustic rocking chairs to look out on the Smoky Mountain morning.

Fog blanketed the woods surrounding the cabin and gave the mountains a peaceful, otherworldly air. Hope wrapped her hands around the cup's warmth and hunkered down, holding the teacup against the frozen lump where her heart used to be.

From Dolly's helmet hair and polyester clothes Hope wouldn't have expected the woman to own such a beautiful, well-appointed cabin, but this place was even better than the pictures. Three bedrooms—all with king-sized beds—a two-story windowed living room with stone fireplace, gourmet kitchen, hot tub; the place just rocked.

Maybe I'll just stay here. Use my severance to rent the cabin out for the whole summer and learn how to fish or make preserves or even do some real art again. Maybe by September I'll have some clue what the hell I'm going to do with myself.

Brian was just the latest in a lifetime of crap taste in men but she had good luck with vacation spots, at least. This place was just perfect for a girls' weekend away. Good place to talk and unwind, to make cocktails and stuff save-the-date envelopes, to strategize about the wedding with her two best friends, it was even nice enough for a honeymo—

"How about a walk," she muttered.

Hope put down her untouched tea, the steam curling above the delicate blue and white patterned china cup, and yanked her sweater tighter.

The polished wood rail was smooth and cool under her hand as she headed down the cabin stairs. The ground was soft after last night's rain, her footsteps silenced by the dampness as she headed into the woods. North Carolina pines towered over her head and the mountain air smelled richly of growing things.

Yep, this is better.

A mourning dove's plaintive coo sounded through the trees. Hope quickened her pace, letting the cabin and the mess that was her life vanish into the fog. In no time she was enveloped by cool, clean forest with all the hurt and heartache and pain left far behind.

I'll walk for a while then head back and drink my tea. I'll make pancakes for breakfast and I won't think about—

Hope broke into a trot, determined to outpace all those memories, all those nagging feelings insisting that something wasn't right, all those red flags waving right in her face.

Like the tiny tuck of smugness at the corner of Megan's pink mouth whenever she saw Brian. How Brian was always suggesting she invite Megan to join them for drinks or dinner when it really should have been just the two of them alone. How he was a bit too proprietary with Megan, a bit too suspicious of her dates, how he always insisted on walking Megan to her car after dinner, his hand at the small of her back—

Hope stumbled, catching the front of her boot on an exposed tree root in her hurry, and fell hard, scraping her palms.

Her knees and hands throbbed as she knelt there, her head hanging, a wail rising from her chest to stick and catch in her throat before it finally broke.

"Never again," she sobbed to the solid silence of the mountain beneath her. "Will never be so fucking . . . *stupid* again . . ."

She stayed like that, her red curls blocking her vision, tendrils sticking to her face, her weeping the only sound in the fog enveloped little clearing.

Finally, wrung out and trembling, Hope slumped back to sit on the damp ground. She brushed her hands onto her jeans to get the dirt off and then wiped at her wet face.

I should have known. I did know. Give me a room full of men and I'll pick the first lying, cheating, son of a—

The soft crunch of a nearby footfall brought her head up.

Out of the grey mist dark shapes moved toward her and Hope froze as they took on recognizable forms.

Oh my God!

No more than ten feet away now and already well into the little clearing where she sat, the large black bear swung its head in her direction. At the same moment, Hope spied two young bears toddling behind their mother.

A mama bear with cubs.

Hope had grown up within walking distance of the metro's Red Line but even *she* knew you stayed the hell away from a mother bear and her cubs.

The fur on either side of the big bear's snout was a light tan and the black fur of her body gleamed darkly in the fog's muted light. The sow sniffed at the air and her inky eyes locked with Hope's.

Hope's fingers clenched, digging into the damp earth at her sides as the bear lumbered closer. The bear's claws gleamed against her black fur—white, long, deadly.

The bear paused, her wet nose twitching, then suddenly slapped her feet on the ground in challenge. The sow made a loud huffing noise, somewhere between a moan and a growl, her eyes fixed on Hope.

An *angry* mama bear with cubs!

Hope risked a darting glance around. There wasn't even a branch or a rock nearby to grab. She'd left her cell back at the cabin. Even if she could shield herself from the bear long enough, she couldn't call anyone for help. Like an idiot she'd just blundered blindly into the woods; she didn't even know which direction the cabin was from here!

The bear huffed, clacking its teeth.

What the fuck am I supposed to do? I can't remember what I'm supposed to do! Play dead? Run? Climb a tree?

A scream tore from Hope's throat as the bear charged—

A huge snarling blur shot past her to throw itself against the bear. Hope scrambled backwards as the force of the man's impact knocked the bear off its feet, his powerful arms wrapped around the sow's neck to wrench it away from her. Then the two—bear and man—went tumbling, rolling over, the bear moaning, her cubs making high-pitched cries as they pawed at the ground.

The big bear gripped at the ground with her claws and gave a sharp shake of her powerful body to throw the man off. He twisted in the air, nimble as a cat, to land in front of Hope in a crouch, his back to her and balanced on the balls of his feet.

The sow swiped at him and the muscles of his broad back tensed as he dodged the bear's claws.

The man growled and a chill ran up Hope's back as the sound rose to an inhuman snarl. The bear's large head reared back at his roar, her black fur rippling in alarm as she backed up toward her cubs.

He angled his body to stay protectively in front of Hope even as the bear nudged her cubs and fled with them, the three lumbering over the crest of the hill to disappear into the mist.

His broad back still toward her, the man stood, showing himself ungodly tall—six feet seven or eight inches at least. His brown leather clothes had the oddest look to them—as if they had been wrapped around him—but Hope wasn't much for the outdoor life. For all she knew, *all* hunters were dressing like that now, and this guy must spend most of his time outside; his skin was very tan for a blond.

His golden hair, long and gathered at the nape of his neck, had picked up a few pine needles and a tiny leaf during his tussle with the bear. He kept his attention fixed on the spot where the bears had vanished and shifted his weight restlessly in those big boots of his, his broad hand flexing beside the gun holstered at his hip.

"Thank you!" Still sprawled out, her jeans cold and damp from the wet ground, Hope pressed her hand to her chest, her heartbeat thundering in her ears. "Thank you so much! God, if you hadn't been here that bear wou—"

The man turned toward her and Hope broke off, her mouth parting in horror.

For a moment, all she could do was stare up at those glowing, green eyes. His eerie gaze bored down at her from beneath thick blond brows; his brow bone was heavy and his forehead bore inhuman raised ridges.

"You're—" she gasped. "You're not—"

His full lips drew back, his fangs flashing, terrifyingly sharp even in this soft light. Hope screamed, her hands flying to her ears to block the earsplitting sound of his roar.

Still screaming, Hope twisted to push off with her hands, propelling herself forward and onto her feet. His movements were a blur and she managed only a few stumbling steps before she stopped short, he in front of her. Instinctively she spun to flee in the other direction, choking into petrified silence at seeing him in front of her again, cutting off her escape.

Fucking nobody moves that fast! No human can!

Hope shook her head, her hands held out to hold him off, backing away as he drew his weapon, his snarl rising to another roar.

But he's not—!

It was the last thought she had before he shot her.

Two

Hope stirred, wincing against the ache in her head.

Where—?

The light was dim, the familiar feel of a mattress and pillow beneath her. The room was very quiet, the bed big and soft, the air touched by the warm, comforting scent of cinnamon.

Oh, right, the cabin in North Carolina.

After the long day of driving and heartache it was no wonder she had headed upstairs and fallen right to sleep in this comfy bed.

But . . .

She *remembered* being out on the cabin's porch, seeing the mist curling through mountains, the warmth of that pretty blue and white china cup in her hand, steam rising from the milky tea—

And this sure didn't look anything like the inside of a vacation cabin. The walls were smooth, smoky colored, not rough wood like that rental.

Where the hell am I?

Her arms felt funny, too heavy, but it wasn't until she tried to sit up that she realized she was handcuffed.

She stared in astonishment at the bindings holding her wrists and panic slammed into her chest at the realization that she wasn't alone in that room.

The same man—that same *creature* from the woods with the inhuman face—stood there, just beside the doorway, his back to the wall, so unnaturally still that at first she hadn't noticed him. His eyes glowed in the room's dim light and he was every bit as alien and dangerous looking now as he had been in the woods.

Something about his stance told her he'd been standing there for a while, watching her.

That guy in the diner—the crazy ex-sheriff—raving about an alien carrying off that girl—

The alien's lips drew back to reveal his fangs. His low snarl sent a jolt of adrenaline through her veins that instantly cleared the muddiness from her brain.

Gasping, made clumsy by her bindings and whatever he'd knocked her out with, Hope threw herself toward the other side of the bed, rolled and staggered to her feet, putting the big bed between them.

"Oh my God, you're not—" It may have been the most obvious, possibly even the *stupidest* fucking thing in the world to say, but she simply couldn't stop herself. "You're not *human!*"

As suddenly as the bear had charged, the alien was around the bed reaching for her. Hope, still lightheaded, backpedaled from his grasp so fast she lost her footing. With her hands cuffed Hope couldn't break her fall and she cried out, landing hard on her backside.

He made another grab for her and she scrambled back, whimpering, to curl into a terrified ball in the corner of the room.

"Don't hurt me!" Hope pressed herself back against the cold walls. "Oh, God, please don't hurt me!"

He towered over her, his square-jawed face half in shadow, his glowing green eyes fixed on hers, holding so still he didn't even seem to be breathing. Hope's lips trembled as she craned her neck, forced by his great height to look up at him.

Then in a move that left Hope blinking, he knelt.

He stayed like that, a few feet away from her, his legs folded under him, his hands resting lightly on his thighs. He bent his head, silently gazing up at her from under his heavy blond brows.

This isn't happening! This can't be happening!

Because the alternative was she was actually looking at an intelligent being who not only wasn't human but who was looking right back at her.

Maybe I'm crazy, a breakdown or something from the stress. Any minute a doctor or nurse will show up and say that no, of course there isn't a huge, blond alien right there!

But wondering if she was crazy probably meant that she wasn't.

He was less terrifying this way, certainly, this alien creature, without all that bulk looming over her. They were nearly at eye level this way, although even kneeling he was still taller.

As time stretched on and he didn't lunge at her, his gaze steady and his fangs not showing, Hope's racing heart started to slow a little.

She'd been pulling against the cuffs blindly, trying to work herself free, and now she risked a glance down at them. Her bindings felt slightly warm and appeared to be completely smooth metal, as if they had been custom formed to her wrists. Attached by a thick cord between them, there was no catch or hinge she could see. The cuffs were so fitted she couldn't twist them on her skin either.

The alien hadn't moved. Still kneeling, he regarded her with his steady, luminescent gaze. Hope wet her lips, her glance darting around the room. She couldn't remember a damn thing after he leveled the stun gun—or whatever it was—at her but it was pretty obvious he was the one who'd brought her here.

A lifetime of striving not to come off as the stereotypical redhead, of forcing herself to calm, clear thinking, served her well. Hope was proud that she managed a couple of really useful thoughts.

Okay, I'm handcuffed but I'm not helpless. I've got a brain and a mouth and eyes. I'll find out whatever I can and I'll go from there.

"Where am I?" she demanded. "Why did you bring me here?"

The alien's head came up. He growled again, but softly this time, and odd to think it but those seemed like gentle, even reassuring, sounds rumbling from his throat.

But however he meant them, those growls sure weren't shining any light on her situation.

"Um." Hope cleared her throat. "Can you talk?"

He leaned forward, reaching for her again, and she flinched away. He stopped short, his hand still outstretched, his rippled brow creased. After a moment he eased his weight back and took up his former nonthreatening posture, his hands resting on his thighs again.

Holding her gaze with his brilliant eyes, he growled in that soothing way. The tones of his rumbles rose and fell, each melding so completely into the next she couldn't tell if it was supposed to be one long snarl or a bunch of short snarls, one after the other.

"Wait, is that what you're doing?" Hope asked, eyeing him warily in case all that pleasant rumbling was intended to distract her from a new attack. "Are you—are you talking right now?"

He was watching her mouth as she spoke. When she stopped he met her gaze again and jerked his chin toward her.

What the hell does that *mean?*

Hope shifted her weight. Her butt and back hurt from her fall and her shoulders ached with tension. "Is that how you talk? Those growls?"

He jerked his chin toward her again.

His way of nodding, maybe?

"Okay," Hope muttered. "I'm going to say that's a yes."

The alien tilted his head, the soft light making his hair a halo of gold, but he didn't try to grab at her again and Hope risked another glance around the room. A bedroom, obviously, and something about the items, how they lay in their places as if put down a bit carelessly, bespoke of an occupied, lived-in place.

His.

She suddenly wondered just how long she had been lying there on his bed, how long he had been watching her sleep, why he'd dragged her here at all . . .

"Did you bring me here to"—she swallowed back the word *kill*—"to hurt me?"

His eyes widened and he instantly gave a sharp snarl that couldn't be anything other than a no.

"I can't believe I'm saying this," she allowed finally. "But I actually believe you." She chewed her lip for a moment. "There was another girl—I don't remember her name—Jenny, maybe? Did you take her too?"

Hope was rewarded with a sharp headshake, his golden hair catching the light at the movement. Back at the diner that nutso—well, as it turned out, *not* so nutso—ex-sheriff said Jenny had been carried off by a black-haired creature with demon eyes.

And my demon-eyed creature is definitely blond.

If the ex-sheriff saw Jenny carried off into the woods and it hadn't been this alien who'd taken the other girl, then it stood to reason that another of his kind *had*.

Hope's hands clenched. Was this an invasion? Or just random kidnappings?

She wet her lips and glanced toward the smooth, fitted door. Was this a spaceship then? If that girl, Jenny, was here too—wherever *here* was—she might have some idea what was going on.

"But Jenny—Is she here?"

He gave another growl but no chin jerk. From his tone she thought that was also definitely a no.

"Is there anybody else here?" she asked, then added hopefully, "Anyone who speaks English?"

Another shake of that blond head.

Okay, I've been abducted and handcuffed by a growling, snarling creature who doesn't speak English any more than I speak "Growl" but he seems to be able to understand me at least.

Hope shifted again and her engagement ring caught the light.

And you know it's been a bad week when being kidnapped by a huge, fanged alien isn't the worst thing that's happened to you . . .

She raised her arms, holding out her manacled wrists a little. "Did you do this to me?"

With a sudden flash of white, squared-off teeth and wicked-looking fangs the alien gave a boyish, proud grin.

The change was astonishing. His smile was warm, his alien eyes alight with intelligence and mischievous good humor—

Hope gave herself a mental slap.

Worst taste in men. Ever.

"Well then, think you could take them *off* me now?"

He watched her mouth again.

"Oooofffff," he growled.

Progress! Hope extended her hands toward him. "Yes, *off.* I'd really like you to take these cuffs *off.*"

Unexpectedly the alien pushed himself up to stand and Hope straightened to peer over the bed, watching as he crossed to the other side of the room. He had his back to her so she couldn't see what he was doing but she heard the clink of glassware, the scrape of metal.

The alien turned back, an elegant tray held in front of him, his expression solemn and absorbed now, intent on his task as he carried it toward her. He stopped a few feet away and knelt again, then placed the tray on the floor between them.

The tray was black with elaborate swirling inlay that resembled mother of pearl, and on it sat a decanter and a delicate-looking crystal glass. Next to the glass was a round plate of the same crystal with some white, square things that looked a bit like cookies.

Hope glanced between him and the tray. "I don't want anything to eat." She held her bound hands out toward him again. "I want you to take these off."

He slid the tray toward her. He scooted closer himself in its wake, close enough now that she realized that warm cinnamon-like scent she'd noticed earlier was his.

With care, the alien took up the decanter and goblet, the delicate crystal looking unbelievably fragile in his huge hands as he poured some of the liquid into the cup.

He put the bottle down and held the cup to her mouth.

Hope leaned away. "No, I don't want a drink." God knew what was in that stuff anyway. She held her cuffed wrists nearer to his face. "What I *want* is for you to take these cuffs *off,* please."

He studied her for a moment then growled, "Cccuufffs*ooooffffff*plllleeasse."

He held the goblet out to her again and she turned her head to evade it. Just why he wanted her to drink that—and willingly, since at his size he could hold her with one huge hand and force her to it—wasn't clear.

Problem was, she wasn't seeing that she had much choice either. She wasn't getting past him; he blocked the way to the door and he could move faster than an attacking mother bear. It didn't take a genius to figure out her chances of escape were going to be tons better if she were free of the restraints.

"So I drink, uh"—Hope glanced at the cup—"*whatever* that is and you take the cuffs off?"

The alien gave what seemed to Hope's ears like an agreeable rumble and held the glass toward her.

"Look, you might have grabbed me from the middle of nowhere but I'm no backwoods hick, you know." Hope threw a narrow look at the cup he held. "You first."

The alien settled back on his haunches to regard her with puzzled, glowing eyes. After a moment he lifted the glass and, making certain she was watching, took a drink.

He offered the cup to her again. "Cccuufffs*ooooffffff*plllleeasse."

Hope narrowed her eyes at him, considering. He hadn't hesitated to taste it himself, which meant it wasn't drugged or poisonous. Or, if it was, he was confident it wouldn't harm *him* anyway.

"One sip," Hope agreed finally. "And then cuffs off, right?"

His green gaze was bright, eager, as he held the cup to her mouth. Her hands came up to steady the glass but she realized she probably hadn't needed to; he moved closer, his palm coming to rest lightly at the back of her head as he carefully tipped the cup to allow her to drink.

She was thirsty but took the tiniest of sips possible. It was light, fruity, and sweet and really very pleasant stuff. She licked some off her lips, almost wishing she could have more.

His full mouth curled into a faint smile and his long fingers brushed her forehead, unexpectedly tender as he smoothed a curl away from her eye.

He put the glass down and picked up one of the white square cookie things. With an air of ceremony he broke off a corner and held the morsel out to her.

"Oh, hold on!" Hope protested as he pushed the bite at her mouth. "I take a drink, you take these things off—that was our deal!"

His brow furrowed, his fingers following her mouth as she twisted, trying to elude the morsel he held.

"Stop it! I don't *want* it!"

The flash of hurt in his glowing eyes took her by surprise but Hope kept her lips stubbornly together and finally he lowered his hand.

He drew a deep breath and growled. His voice rose and fell with solemn, gentle tones and when he finished his glowing eyes searched hers.

Damn it, why is this so important to him anyway?

Hope took a cautious glance at the bite he held. He raised the morsel hopefully.

She wet her lips and gave a nod at the biscuit he held. "You first."

Instantly he put the bite in his mouth, chewed and swallowed.

From the same biscuit-like thing he broke off another piece, offering it to her. "Cccuufffs*ooooofffff*pllllleeasse."

"You'd *better* take the fucking cuffs off this time," Hope warned and opened her mouth to let him feed her.

It was pretty tasty actually. Sweet but not too sweet, with the crumbly texture of shortbread and man, did his face brighten to have her take it.

Hope held her hands up. "Cuffs. Off. *Now.*"

In response he put his hands over her wrists and in the next moment the bindings melted away into his grip and she was free. She'd never seen anything like it.

"How did you do that?"

He was already twisting to toss the cuffs aside. When he turned back, his eyes were warm on her, his mouth pulled up at the corners as if he were struggling to contain another kid-like grin. With a sweep of his large hand he shoved the tray aside and moved closer to her.

Caught with the wall behind her, Hope couldn't retreat. The feel of him, his sheer nearness, the warm cinnamon scent of him, sent every nerve of Hope's body tingling.

His palms felt hot, dry, a little rough against her skin as if he were used to manual labor, but his touch was gentle as he took her hands in his. He was looking down at their hands clasped together and Hope saw that the size and strength of his made hers look positively delicate then he gently tugged her toward him.

Hope expected her body to tense up, to steadfastly resist the pull of this half-beast, but to her own astonishment she nearly melted into him. With Brian, with other men too, she'd had to work at relaxing into their embrace, but as the alien slid one hand around her waist she felt soft, supple, yielding easily to him.

God, this must be what a moth feels going to the flame . . .

He bent his head toward her, close enough that she felt the warmth of his breath against her mouth. He made a soft sound then, a rumbling purr that seemed to radiate right through her to tighten her center as he bent his head toward her. He gently rubbed his nose up one side of hers then tilted his face to nose-rub down the other side and his rumbling deepened.

Hope's breath quickened, her breasts suddenly heavy, her clit vibrating along with the sound he made, her mind reeling in astonishment at the sensation. Her mouth parted. She'd never in her life been so instantly and powerfully aroused; if he merely brushed his fingers against her cleft he'd have her coming.

His head dipped, his warm breath mixing with her own for an instant, and then his lips were against hers.

His kiss was light at first, almost shy, but the rumbling never stopped and Hope softened against him as his tongue touched the inner part of her lip, filling her mouth with the cinnamon-sweet taste of him as he deepened the kiss.

Instinctively Hope wound her arms around his neck to draw him closer and returned that heat with her own. This was nothing like kissing Brian, like other men, where she'd held so much of herself back, not wanting to scare them off, to let herself get too vulnerable.

This time, with his mouth on hers and with that rumble-purr thrumming through her, she had no choice but to yield.

His glowing eyes were half-shut, heavy with desire as he drew away a little to look at her. His mouth curved into a half-smile as he held her palm to his face. He closed his eyes then and rubbed his cheek against her hand, rumbling in contentment. His skin was completely smooth. She fleetingly wondered if he grew a beard at all but then his mouth was moist and hot against her palm and Hope groaned, suddenly imagining that rumbling kiss pressed to her clit.

His rumbling caught, stumbled and stopped.

Hope watched through the haze of desire throbbing inside her as he pressed his nose to her palm, breathing deeply, then again. His thumb ran over the bump of her ring and he drew away a little, his brow furrowed. He turned her hand and the diamond caught the light, sparkling in the dim room.

"Oh." Hope cleared her throat, trying to think past the insistent heat at her center. "Yeah, that's, uh, my engagement ring."

He lifted her hand, till the ring itself was under his nose, and drew in his breath deeply. When the alien raised his head he had the most curious expression on his face. If he'd been human she would have said he was square between stunned and annoyed.

His jaw hardened and he stood. With his great height and her wrist now firmly in his grip she didn't have any choice but to stand too.

"Are we going somewhere?" she gasped as he pulled her along with him.

The bedroom door slid open at their approach and Hope squinted against the bright light flooding in from the adjoining room. A long row of light gray padded seats lined the space; deep and comfortable-looking, they appeared oversized to Hope's eyes but were probably perfectly suited to someone like him. A table and four large chairs, all fixed to the deck, were located on the far end of the room. Hope's glance darted around, despite what he'd said—or rather *growled*, half-expecting to see the black-haired alien or even the missing Jenny, but the room was unoccupied.

Her alien clearly wasn't interested in lingering here though, quickly crossing the room and pulling her along with him into an equally brightly lit—and equally empty—hallway. It was clean and well lit but the walls and deck plating were metallic, rather utilitarian really, and not at all what she would have imagined a space ship to be.

He had firm hold of her and she was forced to a trot to keep up with his long-legged strides.

"Damn it, where are we *going*?"

It occurred to her then that at some point, alien that he was, she'd clean forgotten to be afraid of him. That fear came roaring back when they reached the door at the end of the corridor; it slid open at their approach and he pulled her along inside.

The alien abruptly let go of her and headed to the far side of the room, already rummaging around for something. The room had an antiseptic tang to it and Hope, her mouth dry, shrank back in horror.

Unfamiliar equipment and scary-looking alien instruments were neatly arrayed along the walls and counters. A large padded surface dominated the center of the room; with bright lights directed down on it and actual straps hanging down its sides, it had the unmistakable look of an operating table.

If someone had set out to design a nightmare especially for her, he couldn't have done a better job. Since she'd had her tonsils out at age eight she'd had a morbid terror of anything medical and her phobia had only gotten worse as she'd grown older. Now, at age twenty-seven, only a combination of Xanax and deep breathing exercises got her through even the most rudimentary physical. The last time she'd gotten a flu shot Brian had to drive her to and from the doctor's office and he'd grumbled darkly about the crescent-shaped nail marks she'd left on his skin from gripping his hand.

The alien turned back, his inhuman gaze fixed on her, and gripped in his huge hand was a very sinister-looking metallic cylindrical instrument—clearly intended for her.

He was across the room and had hold of her arm in a heartbeat, already bringing the instrument toward the base of her skull. Hope screamed and with a desperate, hard push against his chest she managed to break his hold, retreating so fast she slammed into the wall behind her, rattling some of the equipment there and bruising her shoulder.

He stared at her, his brow creased. He gave an annoyed huff and Hope recoiled at his approach, intending to flee into the corridor only to find the door wouldn't open for her.

"Stay away from me!"

He gave an impatient snarl and she darted to the other side of the room, putting as much space between them as possible.

"Goddamn it! I said stay *back*!"

Hope put her hand behind her, feeling along on the counter at her back for anything she could use to fight him off. Fumbling blindly she got hold of something cold, metallic, and hopefully dangerous. It wasn't very impressive looking when she brought it around, no bigger than the screwdriver she kept at home for simple repairs.

She held it in front of her defensively and whatever it was she'd managed to grab, it made the alien hesitate.

Hope wet her lips and brandished the thing a little. "Don't come any closer."

His glowing gaze met hers and narrowed. From the way he shifted his weight, his broad shoulders tensing, she knew he was calculating how he could get hold of her.

"I'm serious!" she warned, her voice cracking. "I *will* hurt you! I'll kill you if I have to!"

The alien's glance went again to the thing in her hand. She tightened her hold on it, readying herself for his rush.

Finally he gave a frustrated *snorf* and lowered his own weapon.

Hope's heart was hammering in her chest as he took a step back. She watched him warily just in case he suddenly changed his mind but he simply crossed the room and returned the cylinder to its place among the other alien equipment.

Empty-handed now, he turned and leaned back against the counter. He folded his massive arms, regarding her with his unnerving, alien eyes.

She adjusted her hold on her new weapon carefully, wondering just how lethal what she'd grabbed *was*.

"Okay." She gestured with the instrument. "Open the door."

The alien's eyes narrowed again but he stayed where he was.

"I said, open the door!" She took a step toward him and hefted the weapon threateningly. "Now!"

He sent an annoyed glance at the instrument she wielded. In the next moment he gave a low grumble and pushed off against the counter. Hope skirted back as he stalked past her, his footfalls heavy against the deck plating in those big boots of his.

With a quick pass of his hand the door opened. He paused and looked over his shoulder at her, his thick eyebrows raised as if to say *well, what now?*

She had no idea, but she knew if this spaceship could land on Earth once it could land there again. She would take her whatever-it-did weapon with her and get the hell out of here.

Hope's glance darted to the hallway. She'd already asked this but she wanted to be sure. "*Is* there anyone else here? Anyone besides us?"

He gave a sharp headshake.

"Okay." Hope wet her lips. "Okay," she said again. "Where are we? Where is this ship? I want you to show me *exactly* where we are."

He glanced at her hand again. She narrowed her gaze and raised the weapon.

"I *will* use this if I have to," she warned, hoping if she had to do anything with it she would be able to figure out how in time.

She suddenly realized she still had to force him to take her back to Earth, back to North America, in fact. An image of herself calling from Australia and begging Keri to overnight her passport and plane fare home flashed through her mind—

The alien's nostrils flared a bit then he gave a short growl. She followed him into the bright corridor again, careful not to get too close to him.

Her glance darted about as she followed him through the ship's corridors, seeing a number of empty rooms as they passed. There really didn't seem to be anyone else on board.

At the door at the end of one passage, the alien hesitated.

Hope narrowed her gaze. "Go on, open it! Show me where we are."

With a low snarl he waved his hand to activate the door, then stepped through. Blinking in astonishment, Hope followed.

It was the cockpit of the ship, with two seats in the front—presumably for the pilot and co-pilot—and two seats behind. A control panel curved along the perimeter of the space, set within easy reach of the pilot and co-pilot's seats. Various lights and indicators were active on the panel but Hope's gaze was riveted to the view through the windows.

"Oh my God!" She took in the greenness and the golden light streaming into the cockpit as she came to stand beside him, lowering the weapon a little in shock. "We never left! We're still on Earth!"

The alien moved so fast she didn't even have time to cry out. He plucked the weapon from her hand and spun her to catch her against him, his massive arm around her chest to hold her immobile.

Cold metal pressed to the skin of her throat; there was a stinging burn, then her legs gave way and the world went dark—

THREE

Hope groaned as she came to.

Opening her eyes brought forth another pained sound as blinding light pierced her vision. She tried to raise her hand to shield her eyes and couldn't.

She was strapped down.

Gasping in terror and revulsion, Hope struggled against the restraints binding her wrists and ankles, running across her legs, abdomen, and chest to hold her pinned to the table. Only her head was free; raising it a little and squinting against the blinding light, she saw she was indeed back in the same nightmare of an operating room.

A huge shadow suddenly blocked the lights above the table. The alien's face came into focus, watching dispassionately with his glowing gaze as she strained against her restraints.

Hope shrank away, too frightened even for tears. "Let me go! Oh God, please—!"

"When you have given your word you will not threaten me again!"

Hope's mouth parted. He was still growling, she could *hear* snarls, but in her mind she heard *words*.

"What the hell . . .?" She shook her head a little. "I can understand you! How come I can understand you now?"

He held up the cylindrical instrument he'd wanted to use on her earlier. "I have placed your linguistic implant." He touched the base of her skull, lightly peering at the spot, and then gave the chin jerk that was his version of a nod. "It appears to be functioning properly."

"*Implant?* Wait, what the fuck have you done to me?"

"I did not *do* anything to you. A nano-translator has been attached to the language center of your brain."

"You—God, *why?*"

His brow creased. "So that you are able to understand me now."

Hope glanced at the silver instrument. "That's what you were trying to do before? Implant me with something that would let us understand each other?"

"I could already understand you," he corrected. "But *you* could not understand *me*."

Damn, that was disorienting! Hearing growls, hearing words at the same time . . .

"What else does it do?" she demanded. "Does it tell you what I'm thinking?"

"That would be very useful." He put the instrument down. "But I do not possess that technology. This implant provides translation only."

"Will it—" She glanced at the cylinder. "Is there any danger to me having it? I mean, will it hurt me?"

"No, but it is just as well I placed it while you were unconscious. Apparently humans find the implantation unusually painful."

"Humans—?" Her glance darted about seeking signs of other, past captives. "You've done this before? To other women?"

"No. Just you."

His tone was mild but Hope gritted her teeth. "Well, I'm honored."

His rippled brow furrowed. "I do not think you mean that."

"Look," Hope began, forcing her tone to evenness against the terror of being strapped down, "I can understand you now." She pulled against the restraints. "So *now* you can take these off me."

His gaze narrowed. "I am a g'hir warrior. I have been trained to defend myself and in doing so I may injure you. I cannot allow you to attack me." He shut off the bright lights over the table and the room's illumination fell to a far more comfortable level. He folded his arms. "You will promise not to."

"Attack *you*? *You* attacked *me*! You have me strapped down like—like a—"

But she couldn't think of anything known for getting strapped down a lot and the frustration and fear and medical smells were choking her. Hope clenched her hands into fists and turned her face away from him, mortified at dissolving into helpless tears.

Her sobs echoed in the room and the alien growled something under his breath that her brand new brain implant didn't catch. The straps holding her prisoner slackened. As soon as he released the restraints she sat up and brought her knees to her chest, too shaky to attempt getting down off the table. Hope wiped her tears away but more just kept coming and she couldn't seem to stop.

His alien gaze was puzzled. "Why are your eyes watering like that?"

"It's called 'crying,'" she hiccupped, wiping impatiently at her face with the back of her hand.

"I *know* what it is called. They told me humans did that."

"You mean you never cry?"

"My eyes will water when they are irritated. But why are you doing the crying now?" His glowing glance swept over her. "And why so *much*?"

"Are you kidding? Why the hell do you think?"

He gave a frustrated huff. "A human's eyes water when they are in pain, frightened, unhappy."

Hope pushed her hair back. She hated to cry, especially in front of anyone. Her nose got all swollen and her face got blotchy, and between that and her freckles and her wild red hair it was *never* a good look.

"Yeah," she agreed, sniffling. "I'd say that about sums up where I am right now."

"I have run two complete medical scans on you," the alien growled. "The damage to your hands when you fell in the woods was superficial. I have already treated those scrapes. The furred creature did not injure you. *I* did not injure you. I found no other illness or physical damage." His frown deepened. "You should not be in pain. There is nothing to be afraid of here. No reason for you to be unhappy."

"No reason to be unhappy?" she exclaimed, a hot burst of anger giving her the strength to push herself off the table to stand. "How about almost being attacked by a wild animal, then shot and kidnapped by an alien, then knocked out *again* by that alien, *then* finding myself strapped down and a fucking chip in my brain? Any of *those* reasons going to work for you?"

"But your eyes were watering—you were *crying*—in the forest, before the animal attacked, before you had even seen me. Why were you crying then?"

Hope's breath caught. With all that had happened she'd forgotten about Brian's desertion, about him and Megan screwing for months behind her back, how with a couple texts the beautiful future she'd dreamed of had been smashed into a million tiny humiliating pieces.

She found herself twisting the engagement ring on her finger. "Someone—hurt me. He hurt me very badly."

"The human male whose scent lingers on that jewel? He hurt you?"

"Lingers on—? Wait, you can *smell* Brian? On my *ring*? But I haven't even seen him since Wednesday night and—I mean, I've showered, washed my hands dozens of times—"

The alien caught her hand gently in his and brought her palm to his face, her ring just under his nose. He sniffed. "The scent is faint, but detectable."

"Then your sense of smell is . . ." She could hardly think of a word. "Amazing."

"How?" he rumbled, looking down at her, her hand cradled in his. "How did he hurt you, little one?"

Hope ducked her head. Little one? At five-eleven she hadn't been *little* to anyone since kindergarten.

"We were going to get married but now we're not going to, 'cause . . . he was unfaithful."

"Un*faith*ful?"

Hope shut her eyes for a moment. "He's with someone else."

He looked blank. "With?"

"Yeah, you're right, why mince words? He's been fucking another woman. For all I know he's fucking Megan right now. She's—*was* one of my best friends actually."

"But *why?*"

"I guess—" A lump formed in her throat. "I guess because he likes her better than he liked me. Because she's sexier, prettier, than I am."

The alien's fingers went under her chin to gently tilt her face up. He studied her for a few moments, her face, her body.

"I do not believe that is possible," he said finally.

He sounded completely serious and tears stung her eyes again.

"Thank you," she said thickly. "That was . . . that was really nice of you."

"I am not being 'nice.' I evaluated a number of human females for capture in the time I spent on your world. I cannot imagine a female more desirable than you are."

Hope dropped her gaze and withdrew her fingers from his hold. "Yeah, well, thanks . . ." she mumbled.

"You are not looking at me now. You were looking at me before." His brow creased. "I have offended you."

"No." Hope was surprised that after kidnapping her and restraining her *twice* he would even care about that, but he sure sounded like he did. "Of course not."

"It was not my intention to offend."

"You didn't," she insisted. "Really."

He didn't look as if he believed her but apparently decided to let it go. His gaze went to the crown of her head.

"I have never seen hair like this before." He reached out and clasped a curl in front of her eyes between his thumb and forefinger to pull it straight then let it go. "Does it always do that?"

"Whether I want it to or not," she muttered.

The alien pulled then let the curl go, looking delighted at the way it bounced up. "Why would you not want it to? It is a joy."

"Yeah, everyone in my first grade class called me 'Little Orphan Annie' for a solid year but, hey, I'm glad it makes you happy," she grumbled as he pulled the curl and let it go again. "And maybe you could *stop* that now?"

He complied with a nod and it occurred to her that it was the first time he'd done that instead of the chin jerk. He'd mimicked her human mannerism but it was oddly comforting that he had.

His full mouth curved as his fingers lightly brushed her cheek, smoothing away the last of her tears. "I do not even know what you are called, little one."

"You mean my name? It's, uh, Hope."

"Hope," he rumbled from deep in his chest and his glowing green eyes softened. "It is a perfect namesound for you. *Hope*."

The warm way he said her name, the vibration rolling like thunder through her center, the sudden awareness of how amazing he smelled and the remembered feel of his mouth, hot on hers, made her cheeks burn.

She cleared her throat. "What about you? What's your name?"

He put his palm over his heart and bent his head to her as he spoke it.

"Rrr'harrr?" she echoed. It was a pale imitation of the low heavy growl he'd used to utter his name but he looked pleased by her attempt. "Okay, R'har. What are you? I mean, species-wise, since you already know I'm human."

"I am g'hir."

"Grah-here?" she ventured, trying to swallow back the first syllable and roll the r's in the second like he had. She did a lousy job of it too but it was as close as she was likely to come. "That's your species?"

He gave another human-style nod. "And my people. My world is called Hir."

"Nice to know." Hope folded her arms. "So . . . any chance you want to tell me why you've kidnapped me, R'har?"

He grinned, all white teeth, fangs, and glowing eyes. "To prove myself worthy."

"Okay," Hope said after a long moment when he didn't elaborate. "Worthy to who?"

He gave a short, surprised huff. "To you, Hope."

"To *me*?" she echoed. "Okay, again—why?"

"So you would choose me."

"Choose you?" Hope's brow creased. "Choose you for *what*?"

"To mate with."

She blinked up at him.

"You know," Hope finally got out, "you see those tabloid stories about women abducted by aliens for sex but, somehow, you always think it's gonna be the other girl."

"You must not think that now, little one," he assured, his glowing gaze very serious. "There will be no others. Only you."

"I didn't mean—!" Hope passed her hand over her eyes. "Okay, one, I was joking and two, we need to take a step—no, a whole freaking *lot* of steps—back here. Why in hell would you think—" Hope's head came up. "Wait, is that what happened to that other girl, Jenny? Some alien carried her off to be his girlfriend?"

"If you are speaking of Jenna, mate of Ra'kur—yes. I have met her. Jenna is a gracious, well-bred female. She is very happy," he offered, "living at Ra'kur's enclosure."

"And *that's* why you're on Earth?"

"To hunt a mate." He gave a human nod. "Yes."

"Hunt a—? That's what you ali—uh, *g'hir*, do? You came here to hunt women?"

"Not *all* women." His brow creased. "Just one. Just you."

"Look, I hate to point out the obvious but you, well . . . you're not human."

"No," he agreed.

"And I . . . *am*."

He gave a nod. "Yes."

So not getting through here . . .

"I just mean—" Hope shifted her weight. "I don't see how that would work out. With you being g'hir and me being human. You know, for a relationship."

"G'hir and humans are very sexually compatible."

Her glance flicked over him, the broad shoulders and slim hips, the way the leather clung to his muscular thighs, even as she beat back the searing memory of how close she'd been to coming from just that rumble-purr of his—

Hope cleared her throat again. "I probably shouldn't ask you how you know that."

"*I* do not," he growled. "I am only the second warrior to claim a human mate; Ra'kur was the first. I nearly returned home in despair, resigned to live my life out alone. But then the Goddess led me to you." His warm broad hand cupped her cheek. "My mate, my *Hope*."

The thing of it was he looked so damn sincere with those glowing eyes of his and as whacked as it was she really didn't want to hurt him. Luckily she had the ace of all aces right on her ring finger, one that not only allowed her to let a man down super easy in many a Georgetown bar but with the power to win a resigned smile from the drunkest guy—even on Saint Patrick's Day.

"It's not you." She gently took his hand from her cheek and flashed her diamond ring. "I'm engaged to marry someone else."

"No longer." R'har gave the jewelry a dismissive glance. "He is fucking another female now."

Hope shut her eyes briefly. "You know, you could have said *that* a little more tactfully."

"But that is what *you* said! *You* said he is fucking—"

"Yes! I know!" she flared. "Yes, I know *what* he's doing, *who* he's doing it to, and how much the sheets he's doing it *on* cost, *okay*?"

"Yes." He gave a chin jerk, his eyes a little wide from her outburst.

"Good," she gritted out.

"If he had not bonded to another female," R'har offered after a moment, "I would have killed him."

Hope's gaze snapped to him. "What?"

"Killed him," he repeated, then at her stare added helpfully, "To take you from him."

"That's what your—g'hir—do? You kill each other over women?"

"For a warrior to be so determined to take a female from another is a compliment to his mate, a great tribute to her value." He searched her face. "Are you not taking it that way, Hope?"

"Actually right now I would characterize myself as 'creeped out.'"

"I do not think that expression translates well," R'har said slowly. "What I am hearing is 'deeply disturbed by.'"

"Yeah."

R'har's head reared back. "You find me *disturbing*?"

"When you think it's fine and dandy to show up on someone else's planet and just kidnap a woman? Yeah, I'd log that under 'creepy.' I mean, what if it were a g'hir woman we were talking about, instead of a human?"

"A g'hir female longs to be captured by a strong mate, to have the male who takes her be clever, capable, determined," he replied a little sharply. "I am the son of a clanfather. A g'hir female would be *honored* by what I have done, *flattered* by my actions."

Hope put her hands on her hips. "Then it's too bad you didn't get yourself a g'hir woman instead!"

A wounded look flashed in his eyes, and then his expression cooled. "Perhaps you are right."

He turned away and stalked with his catlike movements toward the room's exit.

"Oh, so now you're just going to walk"—the door slid closed behind him—"out?" Hope finished.

With a burst of energy she was across the room, ready to pound on the door, howl curses at him for leaving her locked in *here* of all places, but the door slid open for her too.

Oh sure, now *the fucking thing works!*

She caught sight of R'har at the end of the corridor and plunged into the hallway after him.

"Hey!" she called. "We were in the middle of a conversation back there! Or don't g'hir have any manners?"

He stopped to look round at her, his nostrils flared. "We are a very civilized people!"

"Yeah, I could tell by the handcuffs," Hope snapped as she caught up to him. "I'd like to leave now, if you don't mind. You know, since you're such a *gentleman* alien."

His fangs flashed for an instant, then he bent his head to her. "As you please," he growled, then turned on his heel and headed for the door at the end of the corridor.

"Yeah, well, maybe you could show me the way—"

The door slid shut behind him.

"Damn it!" she gritted out, already following. She waved her hand around at what she thought was the motion detector but, wherever it was, at least this door slid open for her too.

He was halfway to the next one and she jogged to catch up to him.

"I said, I want to leave!"

"I heard you," he snarled, not even pausing in the entryway.

"Well?" she demanded, following him inside. "Are you going to—"

She recognized the equipment here, the four chairs and the control panel, the windows to the outside, but—

"Oh, you have *got* to be kidding me!" Hope gripped the headrest of the nearest chair, taking in blackness out there, the endless star-filled vista visible through the cockpit window. "When the fuck did we leave Earth?"

FOUR

"You are very heated in your speech," R'har grumbled, taking the pilot's seat. "Is this common in human females?"

"Among human females who drive the Capital Beltway? I'd say I'm about average," Hope snapped. "And where the hell *are* we?"

He glanced out the cockpit window at the slowly spinning green planet visible there. "Tenth sector. The Olari system."

Okay, trying not to panic here . . .

She looked at R'har. "We're really in space?"

"Yes."

"We're in space."

"Yes." He frowned. "Your spots have darkened."

Hope used her grip on the seat to stay upright. "I think that's just my face going paler in comparison. And they aren't 'spots,' they're freckles."

His bright glance ran over her. "Why do you not have them everywhere?"

"Well, actually the sun—*Hey!*" she exclaimed, scowling. "How did you know I don't have them everywhere?"

His fangs flashed in a quick smile. "I did not—until now." His bright eyes trailed her form again, slower this time, his growl becoming a little huskier. "What does the skin without the freckles look like?"

Hope's gaze fell on the fullness of his mouth and his glowing gaze met hers. "When—?" she began weakly.

Hope cleared her throat and indicated the stars beyond. "When did we leave Earth, R'har? When did we go into space?"

"While you were sedated."

"Where's Earth?" she asked, proud that question came out almost calmly. "Where's my world?"

He raised an eyebrow. "Likely still in orbit around your sun."

Not panicking, just breathe, absolutely not going to freak out here . . .

"Listen to me carefully, R'har—I really, *really* need to know how far away Earth is right now. Will you tell me that please?"

He tapped a few of the ship's controls. A holographic scrolling alien script appeared over the cockpit window, superimposed over the stars. "Thirty-nine parsecs from our present position."

"Okay." She gave a nod. "Okay, that doesn't sound too far."

He looked back at her.

"Um . . ." She swallowed hard at his raised eyebrows. "How far is that again?"

He thought for a moment. "Twelve hundred and nine trillion kilometers."

"Trillion . . .?" She sank down into the co-pilot's chair. "Just how long was I knocked out for?"

"Three hours." He glanced at the hologram. "Perhaps a little longer."

"Three *hours?* We traveled trillions of kilometers in just *three hours?*"

"Yes."

"Okay . . ." She nodded. "So three hours here, that means three hours back. You can just turn this thing around now and take me back home, right?"

He turned away, his fingers working the controls again and the hologram vanished. In profile his cheekbones were high, his jaw strong, his rippled forehead heavy and profoundly alien.

"Right?" she persisted sharply. "I want to go home, R'har. You *are* going to take me home, aren't you?"

"The ship was badly damaged during the exit jump from your world. *That* is why we are not on Hir. *That* is why we hold position now."

"Damaged?" Hope sent a quick glance around the cockpit. Everything looked fine to her, not that she would know. "What happened?"

"When I generated a wormhole for the jump," he said, his fingers never pausing over the alien equipment, "a feedback loop occurred."

"Okay," she said, nodding. "All right. No idea what you're talking about. How about this—Tell me what you mean by 'badly damaged.'"

"There are numerous critical systems that must be repaired before we can attempt another jump. The directional assembly has been fused. Power to the auxiliary engines is off-line, the secondary couplings are—"

Hope's brow creased as the list went on. "It sounds like we're going to need to be towed in."

"If you mean assistance, we must expect none. I have no way of contacting the homeworld."

"No—? We're on a fucking spaceship!" she burst out with a wave at the control board. "Your people are so advanced you've got brain implants, you can travel across lightyears like it's crossing the street! You can't tell me you haven't got a radio—or whatever you use to growl at the other big scary aliens—on this thing."

He gave an impatient huff. "We are twelve parsecs from Hir and the communication array is damaged. If I send a signal at sublight speed it will not reach Hir until you and I are long dead of old age."

"What about the planet? What did you call it? Olari?" she asked with a glance at the spinning world below. "Can't the people there help us?"

"The Olari colony was abandoned decades ago. Only an automated signaling post remains now."

"You mean we're stuck here with no way to call for help?"

"Yes."

No help on the way, no way to call anyone and on a ship that sounds like it's about to fall apart?

"What aren't telling me? You're hiding something, aren't you?" Hope clasped her now shaking hands together. "Are we—are we going to die up here, R'har?"

His bright gaze met hers and his face softened a little. "No. This is g'hir territory and our borders are well patrolled. I will bring you safely home to my enclosure, little one, you have my vow." He gave a rueful smile. "Although clearly it will take longer than I expected."

"But you're sure you can fix this thing?" she asked. "You can take me home?"

"I possess the skills needed to repair all equipment on this ship," he rumbled. "But I am only one man. Repairs to so many systems will take time."

She frowned. "Wait, just how long are we going to be stuck here together?"

"I do not know. Days. Perhaps several days."

Hope's gaze was drawn back to the cockpit window, to the vastness of space, to the majesty of creation beyond.

"I think I'm gonna be sick," she said.

"That is a common reaction to seeing open space for the first time. It will pass."

"Well . . ." She turned her gaze back to R'har. Even *he* was less terrifying than the frozen, airless vacuum on the other side of that window. "I guess we don't have much choice anyway. At least you know how to fix the ship and we're okay here for now . . . I mean, I lost my job and Brian is—Well, I don't think anyone'll even notice if I'm gone for a few days more—"

He gave a snort. "If that is so, then what reason is there to take you back?"

"I don't have any interest in living on another planet, R'har," she snapped, more than a little unnerved at his casual dismissal of her wishes. "And, flattered as I am that you dig gingers, my life plan doesn't include being your sex slave."

"A pity." His gaze dipped to her mouth. "Your earlier response proves you are ideally suited to the task."

Her face went hot. "If you even think about ever—" Suddenly she broke off, blinking. "You're joking."

R'har laughed, the deep huffing sound filling the cabin.

"Oh, that's just fucking great," she grumbled, her cheeks warmed by embarrassment now rather than outrage. She folded her arms. "I had to get kidnapped by the *funny* alien."

"If you do not wish to be my pleasure slave then I offer myself to be yours."

The smile still tugged a bit at his lips but there was sincerity in those otherworldly eyes and her breath quickened.

"This appeals to you, little one?" he rumbled softly. "To know I will pleasure you at your command?"

Oh, man, if he starts that purring thing again I'm a goner . . .

Hope tossed her head. "Don't you wish?"

"Yes," he growled. "I do."

The feel of his mouth against hers flashed through her mind and Hope blurted, "I don't have casual affairs." She cleared her throat. "And that's all this could be. There's no point in starting anything or anyone getting hur—in us even talking about it."

"I will not hurt you, Hope." His gaze was serious now. "I will never hurt you."

Damn but he looked like he meant that . . .

Her throat tightened. "You won't get a chance to. What Brian did—I'm never going through this again." She lifted her chin. "So the sooner you get me back home, the better."

R'har turned his attention back to the console, checking readouts, making adjustments. "Once the repairs are complete we will jump to Hir."

"Hey, you said Earth was—"

"It is a far closer jump to Hir," he interrupted sharply. "And from this sector it is a much safer journey than to your planet."

"And what about taking me home?" she demanded.

His glowing eyes met and held hers.

"If you do indeed choose not to remain on Hir," he rumbled finally, "I give you my vow, Hope, that I will return you safely to your world."

FIVE

Hope sighed and shifted to a more comfortable position against the wall.

"You do not need to sit here with me," R'har said, not raising his eyes from the component he was working on.

"I don't have anything to do *but* sit here. I'm a gazillion miles from home and even if I had my cell, which I left back at the cabin—a cabin I won't be getting my deposit back for, by the way—I'm pretty sure I'd be paying roaming charges. I don't even have a book to read."

"Rest in the bedroom, then. Or observe the stars from the cockpit."

"Well, the upside to having been knocked out twice since we met is I can probably skip my naptime today and looking at the stars make me nauseous. Besides, you might need my help with something."

In his large hands, R'har rotated the component—about the size of a pencil case—to peer at it from another angle. It was a transducer, he'd explained when he first removed it from behind a panel in the corridor wall—not that she'd know a transducer if she fell over one—a vital but badly damaged part of the directional assembly. And this transducer was a small piece in only one of many systems on the ship that had been fried when he'd opened a wormhole and took them away—or "jumped" as he called it—from Earth.

The panel he'd removed two hours ago leaned against the corridor wall beside her and around them both, neatly organized on the deck, were other pieces of the spaceship that he had methodically disassembled.

He spared her a glance. "I thought you would wish to keep as far from me as possible."

"You're the only other person on this thing. We're going to be stuck together in here for days and my first apartment in Georgetown was bigger—although this place has it beat as far as backyards go. There's no point in trying to avoid you."

"There are entertainments available to you in the common room. There are holodramas and games. You may utilize them to pass the time."

She sighed. "I don't know how to work any of that stuff and this implant apparently doesn't enable me to read your language. I don't want to risk breaking something when you already have so much to do. You'd probably have to come help me every five minutes. That means stopping *this* work, which means drawing out the repair time even longer."

He didn't reply, his focus on his task. He changed his grip on the component and lifted the tool again.

The hardest thing about sitting here was ignoring the amazing warm cinnamon smell of him. Every time his work had him leaning closer to her she had to beat back the impulse to press her cheek to his neck and breathe him in.

She hadn't ever wanted to do that with Brian.

Hope rested the back of her head against the wall and looked up at the corridor's ceiling. "How long have you been on this spaceship anyway?"

The tool made a soft whirring sound as he worked. "I boarded this vessel and departed Hir twelve days ago."

Hope drew her knees up to her chest and wrapped her arms around her legs. "So you don't actually live in space?"

He gave a deep huffing sound—a g'hir chuckle. "I live at my clan's enclosure."

"Okay, 'clan' is making it through the chip—" She rapped her knuckles on her temple meaningfully. "But 'enclosure' isn't. What is that? Is it a house?"

"The word's meaning extends to far more than just a structure now. For our ancestors, 'enclosure' was just the clanhall—a longhouse made of wooden beams with mud walls and a thatch roof, a simple building where those of our blood would gather to shelter from the winter storms. In the spring, our males and their mates and young would depart to live in the forests in portable shelters. Only those with members too elderly to forest—" From the way he said that she realized it was a term encompassing the whole seasonal nomadic life. "—or families with females close to their birthing times would remain to live at the clanhall during the warmer months. Our people would return again to gather as the days grew shorter. In time the building became more advanced, larger, with private rooms, then private quarters and the land surrounding was cultivated and crops grown. Clans made claim to territory to hold against other clans. Now to say 'enclosure' means not only the clanhall and the homes at the center of the territory but the territory itself."

"So for the spring, summer, and fall your people travel around?"

"Not as they once did. Most live nearly year-round at the enclosure's permanent housing but we g'hir have a powerful instinct to explore, to learn, to hunt."

"Hunt women you mean?" she asked sharply.

R'har gave a sigh. "The g'hir hunt beasts of the forest but yes, females too. Unmated males would venture alone to hunt a mate and return with her to his clan's enclosure for the cold season. Marriages are made in the winter at the gathering. It is a time of great joy for the clan."

"So what the hell are you guys doing on Earth anyway? Why not stay at home and get yourself a local girl?"

His shoulders tensed but he didn't raise his eyes from his work.

"R'har?"

"We are a civilized people but at our core we are warriors," he said brittlely. "When we began to expand beyond our homeworld and undertake space travel we made allies, but we made enemies as well. The greatest of these"—his lip curled—"are the Zerar. They are devious creatures, beasts without soul or compassion. Their attacks on our territories were vicious and unwarranted. Our fathers retaliated and were days from victory when—"

She could see his throat working. "When . . . what?"

"The Zerar unleashed the Scourge on us."

Hope's brow creased. "The Scourge? What's that?"

"A plague," he growled. "One that has devastated my kind."

"Wait—there's a *plague* on your planet?" Her gaze went over him quickly, her heart speeding up. "What about you, R'har? Are you all right? I mean—are you sick?"

"Males do not contract the Scourge. It affects . . . it *kills* only females." He raised his bright gaze to meet hers then. "You need not fear, Hope, I gave you the vaccine when I brought you onboard. I will never lose you to the Scourge."

"You just went ahead and—" But the outrage of it paled as the implications of what he'd said came clear. "Wait . . . How many women are we talking about? How many has it killed?"

"The Scourge came through when I was six summers old and it swept through the enclosures like wildfire. The fatality rate was nearly ninety percent."

Hope's mouth parted. "Ninety percent? But that means—"

"Billions of our females died in a matter of weeks. There are very few g'hir females now."

If he was only six . . .

"Your family?" she asked, already knowing what the answer must be.

"I had five sisters, all older. The first case of the Scourge was seen at our enclosure at midday; my sisters—" His face was haunted. "I was the youngest, the baby, and spoiled by them all. But by the following day only I was left to hold my mother's hand when she died."

"I'm sorry." It was so small, so little to offer in the face of all he'd lost that she felt ashamed.

R'har met her gaze then and in those alien eyes she could see the little boy who had sat all alone at his dying mother's side.

"A handful of females in my clan survived. The other enclosures did not fare any better. And our warriors . . . many simply stopped trying to live. My father was one such; he joined my mother and sisters before the next gathering. The younger males, like me, grew into adulthood knowing we would live our lives out alone, that for nearly all of us there would be no mate to protect. We will be the last generation to fully populate our worlds and when we are gone it will take centuries, perhaps millennia, for our species to recover . . . if we ever do. We can hold against the enemy for now but there are not nearly enough young to replace us. Now the Zerar need only wait. In a generation there will be too few of us to mount even a rudimentary defense and the Zerar will sweep through and level our worlds like a storm."

He let his breath out slowly as if reaching for inner control, his shoulders trembling a little with the effort. He lifted the component again.

That's why you couldn't get yourself a local girl. There aren't any to be gotten. Me and my big, stupid mouth . . .

"But," she began awkwardly, "you said you had allies, other species, I'm guessing. I mean, aren't there any females that your people could, uh—?"

He paused in his work, his hand hovering over the component. "None are compatible."

"But human women . . . we are?"

"Yes." His head came up and he met her gaze. "Ra'kur, of the Erah enclosure, ventured far from our space, seeking a mate. He was gone years but he found your world, and his Jenna."

"And that's why you came to Earth. Why you hunted a wo—uh, me."

"I fought in contests, competed in tests of speed and strength for the honor to go. The competition to be selected to travel to your world is fierce. Of those few chosen I was the first." He gave her a faint, bitter smile. "And I will return with a mate who does not want me."

Hope swallowed hard. "It's not you, I—"

"Yes," he growled, turning his attention to his work, his shoulders hunched again, his grip tight on the tool. "You are promised to another. One who now couples with your friend. But *he* is *human*."

"What did you expect?" she demanded. "That you could just show up on another world and steal yourself a woman? That she'd be happy to be yanked right out of her life?"

His head came up, his eyes flashing. "I did not *steal* you!"

"Really? What would you call just grabbing me off my planet?"

R'har's fangs bared. "And I have taken you from so much joy! From a male who promises you himself then bonds with a different female. From a trusted friend who would take your promised for her own!"

Hope folded her arms, glaring at him.

"Well?" he snarled. "You do not deny it is so?"

"Oh, hell, no," she snapped. "I'm just waiting for you to remind me how the company I've worked for since college threw me out on my ass too. I mean, we don't want to leave *that* out, do we?"

He blinked. "Your employers assaulted you?"

"Assaulted—? They didn't *literally* throw me out. It's an expression. They fired me." Seeing the alarmed look in his eyes she quickly amended, "They dismissed me."

"Ah," he said, the tension in his shoulders easing. "Why did they dismiss you?"

"They had enough people who do what I do so they needed one gone. Lucky me as always, I'm the one they picked to go. Guess I'll be blowing the dust off my résumé and finding a new job as soon as I get back." She sighed. "I'm going to move too. I lived in that apartment before I met Brian but—I don't know, maybe Alexandria or downtown. I'll get a new place, a new job, put my life back together and never, *ever*"—she gave a short laugh—"go back to North Carolina again."

He regarded her for a moment, his gaze thoughtful. "What were you employed to do?"

"My job? I was a graphic designer." From the expression on his face it was clear he had no idea what that was. "I did artwork. Commercial art, intended to get people to buy things or purchase another company's services."

He tilted his head. "Were you happy in that task, Hope?"

"Trading virtually all my waking hours to get other people to buy crap they don't really need or want? Yeah, not so much." She gave a short, surprised laugh. "You know, nobody's ever asked me that—if I was happy at my job. Not even Brian. Not even the cheating tool of a boyfriend I had before him, or the one before *him*."

He gave a chin jerk. "You were not happy."

"No, and it's stupid and naïve but . . ." She looked down, plucking at the shoelace of her hiking boots. "I went to art school to be an artist. The commercial stuff just sort of happened." She sighed again. "No, it didn't. I wanted to be an artist but so many artists can't even support themselves. I wasn't brave enough to say 'screw it' and throw myself out there like that so I took a day job thinking that I would work on my art at night. Only a day job isn't forty hours, not really. Between commuting and oh-my-God-we-have-a-deadline hours you wind up with more like seventy hours eaten up and then you're tired . . ." She closed her eyes. "I'm doing it again."

"Doing what?"

"Making excuses. I could have made the time, cut my hours, switched jobs, but I was—*am*—afraid of failing."

"Of course you will fail."

Hope's head came up. "*Excuse* me?"

"You will fail."

"Hey, thanks," she managed. "Wow, this is like talking to the high school guidance counselor again about my dream of being an artist. He suggested I consider medical transcription classes because—and I'm directly quoting Mr. Gernstill here—'nobody ever makes it as an artist.'"

R'har's golden hair caught the light as he shook his head. "I do not mean *you* would be a failure, only that it is to be expected that you will not succeed every time, it is not possible. It is not even *advisable*—for how would you ever learn? It is necessary to fail. You must expect, even joyfully embrace, failing."

Hope blinked. She'd never heard of anyone failing *joyfully*.

"When I was a young male and learning to hunt I often returned to the enclosure empty-handed before I earned my skills. You will fail far more often than you will succeed. As I did."

"Easy for you to say," she grumbled. "My parents were both physicians. They were both still living when I finally decided to suck it up and go into commercial art. Those were two very successful people who absolutely didn't want their only child to be a starving artist. Believe me, they made their thoughts on that subject *very* clear."

"Easy?" R'har gave a short huff. "Do you think an enclosure of hunters—a race of warriors—held their tongues when I returned with an empty pack?"

"Look, we're talking about reputation, respect—the ability to do things like pay the rent and, you know, *eat*."

"For a young male to earn the title of warrior he must eat his own killing for a year. Failure means no meat." He gave a wry look. "*And* hearing every clanbrother's opinion on the source of your ineptness."

"Were you ever afraid?" she blurted then flushed. The guy looked like he could break rocks with his hands, he moved like lightning. What could he possibly be afraid of?

But he gave a nod. "There were many times venturing out into the forests, alone, I was afraid. I feared, too, returning without a kill to face the taunting of my clanbrothers. And many times I did." His mouth curved a little. "But one day I brought down a full-grown ruga by my own hand. I brought the beast back to the enclosure and there was enough meat from my kill that all were able to partake of it at the evening meal."

"That's good," she said. "I mean that you succeeded."

"It is good that I ate my fill that night! It was weeks before I managed to take another animal down."

"Hmm, you know," she said with a small smile, "in the movie version you should just get to the big kill and then end the film."

He gave a shrug. "Life is not a legend or holotale, little one. The day after I brought down the ruga I rode out alone again. And the next season. And the next year. And often I failed." He gave her a sly look. "But by then I had been named a warrior so failure no longer meant an empty belly. I could take my meals in the enclosure's dining hall."

Hope laughed and his fangs flashed in a grin.

He put the component down and stood, offering his hand to her. "All of this talk of meat has wakened my hunger. Come and let me offer you the hospitality my enclosure has prepared for you."

"So what's all this again?" Hope asked, looking over the plate R'har set before her.

"This is braised karlet—a forest beast that populates the mountains of our clan's northern territory. These are greens grown at our enclosure's fields and this is candied cali fruit, a delicacy brought from Be'lyn, Hir's capital city."

"Well, it smells great," Hope said, putting the cloth napkin on her lap and wondering briefly if aliens did that too. Apparently they did, since R'har did the same.

"This ship was stocked by my enclosure's future clanmother. Provisioned well to welcome you to the Yir clan."

"Right," she murmured. Hope picked up the two-pronged fork he'd set beside her plate. It was far too large for her hand, looking more like a serving utensil than an eating one. She hoped she wouldn't make a fool of herself using it.

She managed to spear a piece of meat and get it to her mouth. The seasoning was unfamiliar, of course, as was the meat, but it was delicious. She looked up to see that he was watching her and froze mid-chew.

Had she goofed at g'hir etiquette or something?

"What?" she asked, covering her mouth and talking around a mouthful of braised karlet.

"Jenna, Ra'kur's mate, helped me choose dishes best suited to the human palate. It is my hope you will enjoy what she has chosen."

"Well," she began, then chewed thoughtfully and swallowed. She couldn't imagine it was good manners even on an alien world to talk with her mouth full. "The braised karlet rocks."

He blinked glowing eyes at her. "So . . . it is good then?"

She nodded and speared another piece. "Very good. Actually it reminds me a lot of barbeque. But I guess that makes sense if this Jenna's from North Carolina."

"Because she is a backwoods hick?"

This last was said in growled English and Hope gave a short surprised laugh. "What?"

He paused, his own fork halfway to his mouth. "You said despite the forest I had taken you from you were not a 'backwoods hick,'" he reminded. "Since Jenna's clan makes its home in that territory she must be a backwoods hick."

"Oh!" Hope exclaimed, remembering how she'd insisted he drink from the goblet first, surprised he recalled the English words at all, but the logic of it worked. "I forgot I said that. Well, it was nice of her to help you pick everything out."

"Jenna is lonely for her own kind. I know she wishes that you and she will become friends."

"Her own kind meaning human," Hope said, spearing some of the greens and suddenly more than a little annoyed that this Jenna thought nothing of helping aliens kidnap other women.

What the hell kind of person does something like that?

"I meant female. There are so very few on our world. The son of my father's brother will be clanfather. His mate too, looks forward to your arrival."

"Even though I won't be staying?"

He shrugged but it wasn't an easy or casual movement. "If that is what you decide."

"When I woke up earlier you said that the injury to my palms when I fell in the woods was superficial," she said, holding her water cup between her hands. "You knew I tripped, that I was crying. You were watching me, weren't you?"

"Yes, but I did not anticipate the animal becoming aggressive. Other furred creatures of its kind seemed to take pains to avoid contact. I assumed this one and her offspring would retreat from the area without confrontation. I should have safeguarded you better." He sighed. "You are not looking at me. Are you angry because I did not intervene with the animal sooner?"

He was right; she was having a real hard time meeting his eye.

"R'har, what I am is embarrassed. What you saw—that was a pretty low point in my life, on my hands and knees in the dirt and crying like a baby. It's really not something I would have wanted anyone to see. Honestly, I wish if you were going to kidnap me you would have done it before you saw me fall apart like that."

"I delayed, seeking the right moment to capture you." He looked uncomfortable. "They warned me not to make a mating roar, that it would distress you. But when you looked at me, when your eyes finally met mine I did not think—I *could* not think. I very much wish I had restrained my instincts as it caused you to fear me. And in showing you I was strong enough, fast enough, to be a good protector and a good mate to you, I think I only frightened you further."

"Mating roar? *That's* what that was? Something that was supposed to turn me on and make me want to mate with you?"

He dropped his gaze. "Human males do not do that to attract a mate."

"Nope," Hope agreed. "They sure don't."

It had been one of the most terrifying experiences of her life but now, sitting with R'har at dinner and able to understand these growls of his, it really seemed kind of funny.

Hope gave him a little smile. "Look, it's all right. I understand a lot—jeez, a *whole* lot—more now. And I guess considering that I was almost dinner for a bunch of bears, it's lucky you came along just then."

"You were in no danger, little one," he rumbled. "I had been observing you for nearly nineteen hours by that time and was always close enough to keep you safe."

"Nineteen—?" Hope stared. "But if that's true it means you'd been watching me since . . . Hold on, I picked up the keys before eleven, got groceries in town and made it to the cabin—maybe noon or so? Holy cow, you were watching me the whole flipping time I was at the cabin?"

"*Flipping* time?"

Hope waved her hand impatiently. "Just answer the question. Were you watching me the whole time?"

"I had covered that area days before and found it deserted. I intended to cross that section to continue my hunt when I observed your land vehicle arrive at the shelter. When you exited the transport and I saw you"—his eyes were alight, his mouth curving a bit—"an elegant, fine-boned female, with hair like the fire of a thousand suns . . ."

"Oh," Hope breathed.

His cheeks flushed and he ducked his head.

The redness of his face and his sudden shyness were the absolute best compliments any man had ever given her, maybe *could* ever give her.

"Nineteen hours . . ." She cleared her throat; it had rained all that evening and heavily enough that the ground had been soaked the next day. "You must have been pretty miserable that night."

"No," he growled, sounding surprised. "I found the inside of your shelter quite comfortable. It is a shame it was too dangerous for us to remain there. It was a pleasant enough abode."

"The inside of my shelter?" she repeated, her voice rising toward the end there. "Wait, you mean you were inside the cabin?"

"Of course."

"You were *inside* the cabin with me *all night?*"

"I was mindful at your bedside not to wake you." He paused. "Have I said something to offend you?"

"*Offend* me? You broke into the cabin I was staying in and watched me sleep? No, R'har, 'offended' is definitely not the word I would go with here! Why the hell would you do that anyway?"

"To safeguard you, little one."

The scalding words that were bubbling up, the swift sharp rebuke on the invasion of her privacy, about the utter *wrongness* of what he'd done, caught in her throat at the innocence in his gaze.

His brow creased. "I think your eyes are going to water again."

"It's just nobody's ever—" She gave a short laugh at the tears blurring her vision. "Yeah, I guess so."

"You are sad?" He searched her face. "Are you in pain? Afraid?"

She shook her head. "We humans tear up when something touches us. I guess you just . . . you got me with that one. You're so different. The way you think, just everything."

"There are too many reasons why human eyes water," R'har rumbled, his frown deepening. "How will I ever tell which it is?"

"I don't know," she said honestly. "For humans it's part instinct, part learned. I guess you'd figure it out eventually but if it helps those were the 'that was kinda sweet of you' tears."

He still looked dubious but gave a human-style nod.

"But just so you know," she warned. "The only reason you're getting a pass on this one is because you're an alien.

Clearly g'hir do lots of things differently but if a human guy broke into my place like that I'd get a restraining order."

"I do not know what that is."

"An order by the court to stay far away from me or suffer arrest and criminal charges. I guess the g'hir don't have anything like that to protect women."

"A clan protects a female. Her mate protects her. With so few females among us and each one so precious every one of my clanbrothers would rally with me to your protection." He reached for her, his fingers wrapping around hers. "To die for you, if necessary."

He and his clanbrothers would willingly sacrifice their lives for her because they—and R'har—thought she belonged to him.

But that protection, that devotion, required trust she wasn't sure she could ever bring herself to give to a man again, let alone an alien. If she couldn't make it work with the human men she'd dated—even intended to marry—only disappointment and heartbreak would be waiting for her with R'har.

She dropped her gaze and withdrew her hand from his, covering the action by reaching for her fork. There was no reason to hurt him right now by reminding him those clanbrothers wouldn't have any reason to fight for her. There would be time enough to talk about it again when the ship was fixed and R'har could return her to Earth.

"We better finish up," she said. "You left that transducer in pieces, remember?"

He gave a wry smile. "And many more repairs to complete after that component is reassembled."

Hope speared a bit of the alien greens with the too-large fork as R'har turned his attention to his own meal.

But she couldn't help taking little glances at him. At the light in his eyes, the quiet joy in his bearing, all just because he thought he was going to be taking her home with him.

SIX

R'har worked for another two hours, and while he was happy to explain what he was doing, most of it went right over her head.

"We will be on emergency protocols until the repairs are completed," he said, setting the wall panel into its casing. "And the night power cycle will begin shortly. I will have to continue the work tomorrow."

"You sure know a lot about this stuff," she commented, holding the panel in place for him so he could reattach it to the corridor wall.

"It is part of the reason why I was chosen to travel to your world. I know spacecraft well," he said as he resealed the panel. "My clan conducts a great deal of trade and I have been on many excursions."

Hope climbed to her feet, wiping her hands on her jeans. At least one repair was completed.

"To other planets you mean? How many other planets have you been to?"

R'har gave a shrug. "The g'hir have dozens of allies and many races trade with us. I have not kept count of all the worlds I have visited."

"That's amazing," she said, tilting her face up to meet his eye. He was huge really, tall as basketball player, burly as a linebacker but so very careful with her—as if she were beyond precious, worthy of reverence. "I mean going to new planets, meeting other species."

"Hir is a very beautiful world." His glowing eyes were warm. "It is a great joy to me to be able to share it with you."

An alien planet . . .

In a few days she would actually be standing under an alien sun. A whole new planet to explore, a whole world populated by intelligent beings to talk to and learn from. Part of her could just squeal with excitement at the chance.

But these were also beings who thought nothing of kidnapping her and other human women too.

"Why haven't your people contacted ours, R'har? I don't mean showing up and helping yourself to a woman. I mean officially."

"There are many who argue that is what the g'hir should do," he said reluctantly. "That we should go to your world now in the greatest number possible and take the females we wish by force."

"Oh, you probably wouldn't have to force anybody." She tossed her hair. "If you showed yourselves openly I bet there'd be thousands of women who would go with you willingly."

"Would you be one of them, Hope?"

She brushed her hands briskly against her jeans. "I'm not afraid of you anymore, if that's what you mean. And I bet—if you gave them the chance—other women wouldn't be either. If you showed yourselves openly and gave them a chance to get to know you."

"We cannot," he growled. "As much as we would prefer to. Our nature as warriors is to act with integrity but for our warships to suddenly appear in orbit around your planet would destabilize your world. Politically, economically, socially . . . The repercussions to humans would be devastating."

He was right. Panic would grip the planet, governments would either declare martial law or fall; there would be riots, violence—

"But the g'hir would get what they wanted," she said hoarsely and crossed her arms, leaning back against the corridor wall. "You don't care what the women you take might want. Why should you care what happens to a whole planet of humans?"

His brilliant eyes widened. "You think we do not care? That *I* do not? My people are not brutes; we are not monsters. We know how precious this chance is. If pairings between humans and g'hir are truly viable, then your kind are our hope, our future."

Her face went hot. "That's what you meant. Why you said it was perfect that my name is Hope."

"Yes," he rumbled. "For you are mine."

She glanced away. "What do you mean 'truly viable' anyway? You said you already knew we were compatible."

"Jenna and Ra'kur were able to matebond. She is carrying the first g'hir-human child. We believe other human females are also capable of this but we do not truly know. It is possible that she is unique in this way."

"Hold on!" Hope straightened. "Jenna's pregnant? With a half-g'hir baby?"

"Do you see?" he asked, his tone low, urgent. "That is why we must always act to safeguard your kind, no matter the cost to us. If the All Mother so blesses us, the next generation of g'hir young will be half-human."

"Oh my God . . ." she whispered.

"That is why we cannot simply come to your world in great numbers. The location of your planet is our greatest secret. We must preserve this secrecy or we will be forced to conquer your planet quickly if only to protect it."

"Conquer it to protect it? Oh, come on! That doesn't even make any fucking—" she broke off.

R'har's glowing eyes were grim, his jaw tight.

"Oh, yes it does," she murmured. "If the Zerar would infect your people with a plague that killed billions of women in order to destroy you, what would they do to the species that could save the g'hir? If the Zerar could bring horrors like that to your people when you're so much more advanced than we are, we wouldn't have a chance in hell. But reproducing with humans isn't saving your species," she pointed out. "It's making a new one."

"No, it is not. The g'hir are a hybrid species."

"A hybrid species?" Hope's brow creased. "What does *that* mean?"

"My kind—all of the g'hir—carry human DNA."

"Human—?" She shook her head. "How is that possible?"

"The only explanation is that at some point, long ago, our species—g'hir and human—successfully interbred."

"Wait, so we aren't the first—I mean, Jenna isn't? But if all g'hir carry human DNA that interbreeding would have happened tens of thousands of years ago! Somehow a human and a g'hir—" Hope ran her hands through her hair. "But there wasn't the Scourge back then. Why would they . . .?"

"Perhaps my ancestors felt our kind lacked sufficient stubbornness."

"But if—" She broke off as he gave a g'hir's huffing chuckle. "Oh, funny, R'har. I mean really, just *hilarious*. So you *don't* have human DNA?"

He shrugged, still grinning. "All g'hir have human DNA, to varying degrees. But clearly *I* do not have enough to master your humor."

"Do you know if you personally do or not?"

His smile faded.

"Oh, hell, what am I thinking?" She shook her head. "Of course you do! You said the competition was fierce, that they chose you because you fought well but also"—she indicated the spaceship around them—"because you know this vessel and can fix it if you needed to. But the other reason, maybe the *real* reason, they chose you is because you have more human DNA than the average g'hir." Hope's throat tightened. "And that means you're more likely to make a half-human baby, right?"

"I do wish you to bear my young," he rumbled quietly. "I long for our children as I longed to find you—a mate to protect, a mate to share my life with . . ." His glowing eyes searched her face, his expression guarded. "Are you angry?"

"Disappointed, really. I mean here I thought you wanted me as your own personal sex slave." Hope gave a shrug. "So it's kind of a letdown to know you just want me as breeding stock."

"You are not angry, my Hope." His brow furrowed and his hand came up to cup her cheek. "You are hurt."

"Don't be ridiculous," she snapped, stepping back out of his caress. "None of this matters to me anyway. And I'm not 'your Hope.' You're taking me home, remember?"

He went very still. "I have not forgotten my promise to you."

"Good. 'Cause I'm not gonna forget it either, R'har."

SEVEN

Water was too precious on a spaceship to be used for washing, R'har explained as he showed her what served as the ship's bathing facilities: a "shower" that used a sonic frequency to clean skin and hair. After he'd left her in privacy, Hope stripped down and approached the thing with some trepidation. She tensed as she engaged the cleanse cycle as he'd showed her, praying all those hypersonic waves wouldn't have any unexpected—and unpleasant—effects on human-style cavity fillings.

She's always loved hot showers and wasn't sure she was going to like getting "blasted" clean but the sonic proved remarkably relaxing. Her shoulders relaxed as warm light poured over her body, the sonic shower bathing the room in soothing red and orange tones as it cleaned her. The waves that moved over her body massaged her tired muscles and left her skin tingly clean when the cycle ended.

She had nothing with her except the jeans, T-shirt, sweater, and hiking boots she'd been wearing when R'har kidnapped her—not even her bag. While showing her the bathroom closets, R'har explained that his clan, the Yir, had filled them with g'hir style clothing intended to please his new mate.

As he opened cabinet after cabinet of clothing for her inspection it brought home to Hope that there was a whole family, a whole *clan*, back on Hir right now eagerly anticipating her arrival. And, from the lengths the Yir clan had gone to just clothing-wise, they had some high hopes for their new clansister.

If they even like me . . .

Hope firmly pushed aside both the thought and the butterflies in her stomach. It didn't matter *what* this alien tribe thought, if they liked her or not, if they wanted her there or not. She wasn't staying.

But since his clan obviously had no idea who he'd be bringing back, the dresses—fine, elaborately embroidered things—came in different sizes and the majority of the designs would be suitable to different body types as well. Among the selections there were also a few long tunics, with close-fit trousers meant to be worn beneath. Hope, at five-eleven, discovered that g'hir women too must be tall since all this clothing would be a bit long on her.

Browsing through the selections after her shower, Hope was relieved to find a number of nightgowns included.

She picked the least sexy one.

Which wasn't saying much, since all these had probably been chosen with the g'hir idea of a honeymoon in mind. The fabric was silky, the color a pale blue and the length being too long meant it also plunged too deeply at the bodice. Otherwise it fit fairly well.

The sonic shower left her hair clean and already dry. Checking the mirror, Hope was surprised to discover that, unlike the usual frizzies she was left with after washing her hair, the sonic shower had coaxed her fiery curls into pretty ringlets.

Despite her two "naps" earlier her eyelids were feeling heavy and Hope yawned as she headed into the bedroom.

She stopped short, her fatigue gone in an instant.

R'har stood by the bed, still in his leather warrior's clothing. He looked up when she came in and his eyes widened a bit when he saw her. His glance quickly went over her, taking in her hair, the plunging nightgown, and the abundance of lightly freckled skin she was now showing.

"Hi. I didn't expect—" Her cheeks warm, Hope's hand automatically went to smooth her hair. She caught herself mid-movement, remembering that for once her hair didn't need taming. "You surprised me."

"You are . . ." He cleared his throat. "Did you find everything you needed?"

"Yeah. I even figured out the toothbrush. I think it's intended for fangs so my teeth feel *extra* clean."

"Good," he said, his glance flickering over her again.

Clearly he was too distracted to realize his answer didn't really fit what she'd said at all and she bit the inside of her cheek to hold back a giggle.

He also didn't seem to know what to do with his hands or where to look or what to say.

Hope wasn't a beauty, never had been. Too tall, red-haired, and freckled, she had only been able to stake a claim to "cute" until she'd hit eleven and then somehow managed to stumble right into "awkward" seemingly overnight.

She was the nice one, the smart one, the reliable one. Not the heartbreaker or the pretty one but when she took a step toward R'har she couldn't help but notice that his breath sped up.

And then her ring caught the light, bringing back all the hurt and heartache and that confidence wisped away like mist under strong sunlight.

Her step faltered. "We should probably get some sleep."

"The ship has cycled to night settings," he agreed. "We have seven hours before the day cycle begins."

"Oh." Hope shifted her weight. "Humans sleep for around eight hours," she said, just to fill the awkward silence. "I sleep a little more than that usually. I guess g'hir sleep less?"

"The setting allows the ship to conserve power. You may sleep longer, if you wish. But yes, I—most g'hir—usually sleep about seven hours."

"Well, I'm a fairly heavy sleeper," she said with a wave. "So you sure don't need to worry about waking me if you want to start work early."

He gave a human-style nod and then she remembered how back at the cabin he'd been quiet enough that he hadn't woken her at all, even standing at her bedside.

He took a step toward her. "The g'hir have marriage but we do not have 'engagement'—at least not in the way humans seem to use the word." He indicated her ring. "That jewel clearly has great meaning but I do not understand its purpose in human bonding rituals."

"Oh, uh . . ." she stammered, very aware of him, of how little space lay between them now, the warm, luscious cinnamon scent of him so inviting she found herself instinctively leaning in even closer. "Well, 'engagement' really just means a promise to marry." She held her hand out to show him. "A man gives a woman a ring, like this one, to show he's serious about going through with it. It also lets everyone know that she's taken."

"Is there a ritual for the ring's removal?" He glanced at the diamond. "Now that the marriage will not occur?"

Her throat tightened. "Yeah, with all the wedding traditions and trends and crap, you'd think so, wouldn't you? You know, I have a stack of books at home on weddings—Emily Post, Miss Manners, Martha Stewart, you name it. I mean I read *everything* so this wedding, this marriage, would be perfect. And I—" Hope found herself twisting the ring on her finger. "I just skipped—maybe just ignored really— everything about what to do if the wedding gets called off. Who's supposed to call the caterer, tell the guests . . . me, I guess, but I—I can't remember what I'm supposed to do with the fucking ring. I mean, he ended it, so do I give it back or keep it? Offer to buy it or what? Every time I look at this thing I think of everything I'll never . . ." She swallowed hard. "I'll never have, but I don't know what I'm supposed to *do* with it." She gave a choked laugh. "If this were a country song, I would have already thrown it into a muddy river or my dog would have swallowed it or something but I can't even get myself to take the damned thing *off*."

"Even though the male who gifted this to you has broken his promise to marry?" R'har's glowing eyes met hers. "And bonded with another female?"

Hope looked down at ring, her vision blurring with tears but the diamond sparkled on, optimistic as ever.

"Yeah," she said thickly. "God, I have lousy taste in men. I choose jerks. Liars. *Cheaters*. The Hope MacGowan curse."

"You need fear no longer." R'har's glowing eyes met hers. "For it was I who chose you."

Hope gave a short, humorless laugh. "You mean from all the other women wandering around that mountain?"

"I was on your world for many days. I scouted throughout the settlement seeking a mate. I observed many females but none called to me like you did."

"You went to the town?" Hope exclaimed. "Are you nuts? You could have been seen!"

"I am a g'hir warrior." He gave a careless shrug. "I was armed."

"Armed? Against an entire town of rednecks? You're lucky you didn't get yourself killed!"

He gave a faint smile. "You are outraged, indignant that I could have been harmed."

"Well, of course! But—" Hope broke off, blinking.

Man, he looked sweet, his glowing eyes alight, his mouth curving into a smile. . .

"Look, I'm sorry, R'har. I know why you came to Earth, I even get why you stole me off my planet, and I don't want to hurt you but it's just—" She wet her lips. "I'm done with relationships. I'm better off on my own."

R'har took another step toward her, closing the last bit of distance between them, close enough now that she felt the warmth of his body. He took her hand in his and raised it, moving it this way and that as he studied the ring.

"A fine jewel." In a quick, deft move he slipped it from her finger and held it up to the light to examine it closer. "Very fine."

In the next instant he popped open a storage cubby over the bed and tossed the ring inside.

"Hey!" she cried, yanked out of her shock as he activated the seal on the cubby door. "That's—! What the hell do you think you're doing?"

"It is a handsome bauble." He regarded her mildly. "I have decided to steal it."

Hope shook her head a little. "What?"

"Steal it," he said with a shrug. "I have, as you say, stolen you. I see no reason not to steal that jewel as well."

She glanced at the cubby he'd tossed the ring into. "And what if Brian wants it back? He probably will, you know. Believe me, the man is cheapskate. A lying, cheating, snake of a cheapskate." She closed her eyes briefly. "Boy, can I pick 'em."

"If this male wants back what I have taken—" R'har smiled, his fangs sharp and dangerous in this light. "He is welcome to come ask me for it."

The idea of Brian trying to face down this huge alien warrior for *anything* was so ludicrous that Hope suddenly burst out laughing.

R'har grinned down at her, his glowing eyes warm with humor, his large hand still cradling hers.

Looking at her now bare hand and just having the ring off, not having to see it there, not to have wear that symbol of heartache, to have it just *gone*, was such a blessed relief she felt like she could finally breathe again.

"Thank you, R'har," she said, giving his hand a squeeze. "That was really . . . nice."

"I did not think to impress you by turning thief." His thumb lightly traced the back of her hand. "I have a great deal to learn about human females."

Determined or not, exactly what she could teach him instantly came to mind and she dropped her gaze. Thankfully he didn't seem to notice her warmed cheeks.

He let go of her and turned to hit some keys on a control panel near the door, then sat briefly to pull off his boots.

Or maybe he *had* noticed, because in the next moment he stood, already undoing the fastenings of his shirt.

"Uh, R'har?" Hope cleared her throat. "What are you doing?"

"The night cycle has begun." His shirt slid off his shoulders, to reveal a tan sculpted chest and stomach. "It is time to go to bed."

"Wait . . . You mean both of us . . . in here? Together?"

Tossing his shirt aside he gave a short, huffing g'hir's chuckle, as if her question was silly in the extreme.

"I don't think . . . I mean, since I'm going home and all, that's probably—R'har, would you *please* stop taking your clothes off for a second!"

He paused with raised eyebrows, his hand at the fastening of his half-undone trousers.

"I really—" she began, incredibly proud she managed to keep her gaze at eye-level. "I *really* don't think we should sleep here together."

In response he unfastened his trousers and stepped out of them, leaving him in nothing but dark blue undershorts.

Very form-fitting undershorts . . .

He sat on the bed, stretching out his long, tanned legs, and leaned back on his hands to regard her. "Are we going to fuck now?"

"*What?*" she managed.

"Because if we are going to fuck now then you should get into bed with me," he said reasonably. "But if we are *not* going to fuck now," he continued with a shrug of his huge shoulders, "then there is no reason you should not sleep here beside me."

It was a perfectly logical argument, really . . .

Hope shifted her feet. "I can sleep in the common room."

He gave a g'hir's snort of disbelief. "I do not think you will be comfortable there."

Hope glanced toward the door. The common room couches were almost as wide as a twin bed. "Why not?"

"We are on emergency power protocols. During sleep cycle only three compartments are heated to comfortable temperatures. The cockpit, sickbay, and this room. You could sleep in sickbay," he suggested. "The biobed may be comfortable enough."

She instantly cringed at the idea of spending *any* time in sickbay. "So the rest of the ship isn't heated at all?"

"Without heat the ship would quickly become unlivable. Those rooms are *less* heated, to conserve power."

Hope lifted her chin. "I'll be fine. Just give me an extra blanket."

"Scent matters a great deal in the choosing of a mate. You smell delicious to me," he rumbled, his long fingers spread, lightly moving over the bedclothes as if he were anticipating touching her. "Perhaps my scent is not so appealing to you."

"That's not—" Hope mumbled, her cheeks burning. "You smell . . . amazing really. But you're taking me back to Earth in a couple days, a week at most and—" Hope folded her arms. "I just think it's better if I sleep in the other room."

"I had not kissed before," he said, a little shyly. "The g'hir do not touch mouths as humans do when they mate but it roused me powerfully. I will learn how to kiss to rouse you better—if you will teach me, Hope."

She gave a shocked laugh. "Holy cow, you could have fooled me! You are an incredible—You must be a natural or something at kissing. Really, don't worry about it."

"I give you my word I will not try to couple with you tonight."

That makes one of us!

"This is a comfortable sleeping place," he rumbled and held his hand out to her. "I will keep you warm, tucked safe beside me, little one."

Hope had to clench her fist to keep herself from taking the hand he offered. "I'll sleep in the common room."

His glowing eyes searched her face. "Because I am not human."

Hope looked away. No, he *wasn't* human and it was frightening how little that was starting to matter to her.

"As you like," he said quietly.

R'har stood, unsealed a large compartment near the bed, and handed her a blanket. He gave her a pillow from the bed too.

"Power save protocols have automatically set all doors to manual during sleep hours," he said, touching the panel to open the door to the common room. "If you move about the ship you will have to use the access panels."

Goose bumps rose on her skin as soon as she stepped over the threshold and Hope clutched the blanket closer. It couldn't be more than fifty degrees out here and with the lights powered down to minimum the common room looked about as comfy and appealing as a meat locker.

"I'm not going to be walking around," she assured. "I'm going straight to sleep."

He hesitated a moment, then stepped back into the warmth and light of the bedchamber.

"Sleep well," he growled softly. "My Hope."

"Yeah," she mumbled as the door shut behind her.

The common room's scant lights were blue tinted which—though Hope knew it was impossible—seemed to make the place even *colder*. Shivering, she hurried to the nearest couch to lie down and gritted her teeth at finding that the sofa leather was like ice. The silky nightgown wasn't helping matters but she'd have to go back through the bedroom to get warmer clothing and she'd barely forced herself out of there the first time.

Hope tucked the blanket around her legs and pulled the other end over her head, leaving just her face out so she could breathe. The blanket did help, he'd given her a warm one, but the position she was in—lying on her side and huddled against the seat's back—had the door to the bedroom right in her line of view.

She curled up against the cold and suddenly remembered how she'd cringed away from him when he'd first brought her on board. How he'd knelt to her, trying to soothe her with his soft growls even though she couldn't make any sense of his rumbling; didn't know at first he was even talking.

Tomorrow I should ask him what he was saying . . .

She recalled how he'd sniffed at her ring, the look of dismay on his face. Funny how much lighter her hand felt now with the engagement ring off, lighter than having just the diamond off her finger could justify.

R'har wasn't human, of course, but there was something more about him that set him apart from every other man who'd ever been interested in her. Something about how he met her eye square on, something reliable and trustworthy in that otherworldly gaze . . .

He was probably asleep by now and hell, *she* was the one that insisted on sleeping out here. Changing her mind now and going back in there, and probably waking him up in the process, would be really thoughtless. He was probably exhausted. He'd spent hours working on the ship with no help from her.

And she was going home. He needed to bring back a wife . . . mate, *whatever*. It's not like they could date and see if it worked, for God's sake. His people needed him to have children as much as he wanted to have a family. His whole species depended on R'har finding himself a mate and when he took her back to Earth he'd have to pick another woman to—

Hope sat up, chewing her lip.

He was right; if nothing was going to happen, then nothing was going to happen. There was no reason to freeze her ass off out here.

I'll just go in quietly.

EIGHT

R'har kept still, as motionless as he had learned to be when hunting ruga in the most remote parts of the Atali Mountains as the door to the sleeping chamber slid open. He focused on keeping his breath slow and even to better feign sleep.

She hesitated in the doorway and he could hear her teeth chattering. Icy air from the common room seeped into the bedchamber and for a moment he feared she would retreat, distancing herself from him again.

But the cold proved an even less desirable bedmate than he.

The faint light from the room beyond was shut out as the door slid closed behind her. Her bare feet crossed the space between them quickly, the ships systems already engaging to raise the room's temperature back to optimal.

The bedclothes rustled softly as she felt along the edge, fumbling to find her way. Her flesh was chilled when she climbed into bed with him and he fought the instinct to wrap her in his arms and warm her with his body.

It *hurt* to feel her shivering beside him and do nothing. He struggled to hold his instincts in check now as he should have contained his mating roar back on her world.

Between the room's warmth and the heat from his body warming the bed it was not long before her shivering eased. She turned toward him, adjusting herself to a more comfortable position. He lay still, waiting till her breathing slowed and deepened.

When he knew for certain she slept, he allowed himself the simple joy of looking at her. A cheat really; human eyes did not possess as acute night vision as g'hir's and he had set the night cycle lighting in here so that he could see her easily.

Her eyes were closed but he recalled their color perfectly—crystal blue as a Pundari Mountain lake, shimmering with tiny, ever-changing silver sparkles as they caught the light. Her lips were parted in sleep like a child; her astonishing hair blanched of its fiery color in the dimness. His gaze went over the curves of her face, the fullness of her mouth, the crescent of her red-gold lashes.

His chest ached with wanting, with longing, with guilt.

Lightly he touched one of her curls, tracing its shape with the tip of his finger.

So beautiful. My little one . . .

Time was so precious now, less than a moon's cycle to convince her to choose him, to remain on Hir.

Or he would have to return her to her own world.

I would give all to be a human male, one that you would desire . . .

The letter of Hir law was on his side. He still had time left to convince her to choose him before he had to return her to her world.

But in fairness she had declared her choice already made, many times.

Careful not to wake her, R'har eased closer and gathered her softness against him. He shivered with desire, already hard and aching as her curves settled against him.

His throat tightened.

So little time . . .

He had always known himself to be slow to anger, quick to use humor and considered himself an honest soul, a warrior of integrity and honor.

And the lies he was spinning threatened to crush him.

Someday, I vow, I will tell you the truth.

He had been desperate, seizing on the first thing that came to mind. It had not seemed so terrible a thing to do, a perfect way to gain the opportunity to spend time with her, to learn about her, to let her know him.

And it was only because she did not know this vessel that she believed any repairs needed to be made. Only her innocence, her trust in him, allowed him to pretend a ship in perfect working order urgently needed repairs.

She returned to sleep beside me. She cannot be so afraid now.

He would work on the ship, on his pretend repairs, and he would learn about her. He would learn how to court her as a human male would.

R'har snuggled closer, burying his face in her soft flame-colored curls. He breathed in deeply her tantalizing scent, every nerve alight, contentment blossoming in his chest at her nearness. His hardness aching, already lubricating in eagerness to mate, R'har curled his body around hers, rumble-purring with desire.

Just a little while longer, just until she sees me as a mate and not an alien to be feared.

He would win her to him.

My Hope, my beloved . . .

All he needed was time.

NINE

Warm and safe and content, soothed by rumbling that softened her body, Hope lay lightly between sleep and wakefulness with no wish to leave.

The warmth shifted against her, his arms tightening around her. The tone of the purr changed too, deepening to send tingles up her thighs and tighten her nipples. With a moan, Hope arched back, pressing her buttocks against the hardness there.

Her gown was already bunched high on her legs from sleep but now warm fingers, the skin slightly roughened, slid the silky fabric high, tracing her bare shoulder as the nightdress came over her head to be tossed aside.

Her lips parted as the heat of his mouth touched the spot where her neck and shoulder met, the sweet shock of his bare skin against hers as his fingers skimmed over her hip. With a groan, he slid her panties down and Hope eagerly helped free herself by kicking them off.

His big body curved around her from behind, his fangs ever so slightly nipping at her shoulder as his hand cupped her breast, his roughened fingers teasing the hardened peak there. She could feel him hot and hard against her as his hand slid lower, moving over her belly and lower still to brush the lips there, his touch light as it skimmed her clit.

"God . . ." Hope groaned, her body melting into his as he stroked her to readiness.

Her insides were tight, aching, as she turned toward him. Her hands skimmed his warm skin, his shoulders, the flatness of his belly and hips, the muscles quivering beneath her touch.

Even by this faint light she knew this wasn't Brian, any man she'd ever known or could ever know. This was a lover drawn from her most secret desires, an angel and a beast in one who demanded to be yielded to and she had no desire but to be taken.

The rumbling-purr deepened further, sending insistent waves of heat between her thighs as he brushed his nose to hers, then his mouth covered her own. Hope wound her arms around his neck, her fingers threading in the silkiness of his hair as he deepened the kiss.

He urged her wider and arched over her, his heavy cock resting on her inner thigh. He pressed his nose to the hollow of her throat and a fine tremble ran the length of his body as he breathed her in.

He was fully aroused, her exquisite incubus, beautifully formed, not too different from a man, though his penis had a ruddier color. Moisture glistened at the head and impulsively Hope took his shaft in her hand.

He froze instantly. His mouth parted and the tone of his purr deepened as she stroked him, her thumb running over the slick wetness at the tip. The natural moisture increased, making it easy to slide her hand over his length. Her fingers, wrapped around him, didn't quite touch and instinctively he started to rock against her.

A fine tremble ran the length of his body and his glowing eyes met hers then, wild and a little helpless.

Hope's hand went to his hip to press him forward, shifting beneath him to spread her legs a little wider. He groaned when she brought the head of his cock to her opening.

He was big, bigger than any man she'd ever had before, but he went slowly, almost reverently, the moisture of him with her own wetness spreading her lips easily. His hips drew back and he moved again, plunging his cock a little deeper into her folds each time.

And with every movement, each withdrawal and thrust, his cock slid against her clit. Hope's mouth parted, the waves of aching pleasure through her center carried higher by that rumbling purr of his.

His arms caging her, his body arched over her, he watched transfixed as his cock moved inside her, his fangs bared in pleasure. He rocked against her, his cock growing tauter still as his rhythm increased, and Hope cried out, coming so hard her nails dug into his shoulders.

His thrusts quickened at her release, quickly drumming against her and, stunned, gasping, Hope climaxed again. His rumbling deepened, his whole body trembling, and he thrust once more, pulsing inside her as he came.

His big body still quaking from release, he raised his head to meet her eyes, his gaze bright with that otherworldly glow.

Her mind, so suffused with pleasure, cleared a bit and she knew him then, this angelic beast . . .

"R'har," she murmured.

His full mouth curved into a proud, sexy smile, his fangs gleaming in the faint light.

"Oh, my God," she gasped. "What did we do?"

TEN

He gave a g'hir's huffing chuckle. "We mated, little one."

"We didn't," Hope groaned. "Say we didn't."

"If it pleases you. Then we did not mate," he agreed. "We fucked."

"Yeah, *not* better." Hope passed her hand over her eyes. "Let's stick with 'mated,' okay? And why didn't you *stop*?"

"Why would I?" he rumbled, happily nuzzling the sensitive spot where her neck and shoulder met. He brushed his nose against hers and his eyes shone. "I could not imagine a better mate-bonding. I have never known such pleasure, such a strong release."

"Thanks," she muttered, pushing down an absurd thrill of pride. "I'm glad you liked it."

"Did you not?" He propped himself up on his elbows to search her face. "I felt you contract around me more than once. Your pleasure sounds were loud. Did that not signal your climax?"

"Yes," she mumbled. "Yes, I absolutely—seriously, *no* worries there—what I meant was we shouldn't have done *this*. Uh, mated."

He drew back a little further, regarding her with puzzled alien eyes. "Why not?"

"Because—" Having this discussion while they were still naked, while he was still lying between her legs and—she realized with a surge of wonder and new arousal—hard again, was insane. "Because we shouldn't have! I mean, we met what—yesterday?"

His brow creased. "This time requirement before mating—is it a human rule?"

"No, this is a *Hope* rule. As in, when my life is complete fucking mess, it doesn't improve things any to have sex with an alien."

He froze. "That is all I am to you? Even now, after we have mate-bonded?"

"No, of course not, I just—but come on, R'har, I mean you *aren't* human."

His breath exploded in a snarl and he pushed off the bed. Hope grabbed at the bedclothes to cover herself but apparently g'hir didn't do modesty because he seemed unfazed by the fact that he was completely bare.

"I can *never* be human," he growled. "But I will not let you make me ashamed of what I am!"

Hope blinked. The idea that he should be ashamed never crossed her mind and shock held her speechless while he dressed.

"Hold on, I didn't—! Oh, don't you dare walk—!" But the door was already sliding shut behind him.

"Goddamn it!" she gritted out, yanking the nightgown over her head and scrambling out of the bed. "That's one thing you and human guys have in common—thinking you'll win an argument by walking out in the fucking *middle* of it!"

Hope got to the common room just as R'har was about to head through the opposite door.

"R'har, I didn't mean it that way! I just meant—"

"What?" He rounded on her, his snarl filling the common room. "What did you mean?"

She folded her arms, her feet freezing, ticked both that she had forgotten how freaking cold it was in the common room and that she suddenly felt in the wrong here.

"It isn't going to work between us, R'har. It just *can't*!"

With an angry, impatient gesture he indicated the bedchamber door. "How can you say this when we have already mated?"

"I'm not talking about sex! Even if we forgot about stuff like, oh, I don't know—not living on the same *planet*—you're g'hir, I'm human! We're just—" And for no reason at all her eyes stung with tears. "We're just . . . different, R'har."

"Yes, we are different!" he roared. "Human and g'hir are *different*. My eyes will never water like yours do. You will never truly understand what it means to me to have lifemated to you! I cannot be human for you, but I will give you more of myself than any human male ever could!"

"Lifemated?" she echoed, shaking her head. "What the hell is—"

Hope cried out as the ship's floor tilted violently. The impact of whatever slammed into the ship knocked them off their feet and Hope hit the icy deck hard enough to rattle her teeth. Pain shot through her shoulder and the room plunged into darkness.

She flailed blindly for R'har and for a single terrified instant in the silent blackness she found nothing.

Then his strong warm hand wrapped around hers.

"Hope! Are you injured, little one?"

Her shoulder had been briefly, blessedly numb but now the pain made a grand entrance. It hurt like a bitch but it sure as hell wasn't the highest priority right now.

"I'm fine," she lied. "Are you okay? What's happening?"

"We are under attack! I must—"

Another impact slammed against the hull and cut him off. His grip tightened on her hand as the deck bucked under them.

This time the lights came back on and the blare of alarms with them. The galley beyond looked largely undamaged. Most things on the ship were secured in sealed cabinets and cubbies but those few loose contents of the common room were thrown about and—

"You're hurt!" she cried at seeing R'har's bloodied mouth.

He shook his head sharply. "I have to get to the cockpit! Are you—?"

"I'm fine! Go!" Not true, her shoulder was throbbing, but she was likely no worse off than R'har and he was already pushing to his feet.

Hope made it to standing and into the corridor behind him before another impact rocked the ship. Either this one was a glancing blow or she was getting used to being in a spaceship turned funhouse because she managed to catch herself against the wall and remain upright.

R'har had a g'hir's speed; he was already through the door at the end of the hall.

With hands outstretched to her sides, ready to catch herself in case the ship tilted again, Hope ran after.

R'har sat in the pilot's seat, his fingers flying over the controls, but outside the windows there was nothing but the usual stomach-flipping endlessness of space and the peaceful turning planet, Olari, below.

"What's happening?" Hope slid into the co-pilot's chair beside him but another slam against the hull had her clutching at the armrests to stay there.

"Why are we being fired upon in g'hir space?" he snarled, adjusting the displays. "There should not—" R'har went still and his face blanched. "Goddess, no. It cannot be here . . ."

"What?" Hope demanded. "*What* cannot be here?"

"A Zerar warship."

ELEVEN

"The same people who infected your planet with the plague are trying to blow us to hell?" Hope tightened her hold on the armrests as the ship bucked again. "And hey, have you thought about shooting *back* at them?"

"We *are* shooting back," he growled shortly. "Or we would have already been destroyed by their weapons. The ship's defensive systems and heavy shielding came online at their first volley."

Another blast from the Zerar ship slammed against them.

"We must contact Hir," R'har muttered, his hands moving like lightning over the controls. "We must warn them of this incursion."

"But the communication systems aren't—" Hope bit her lip against a whimper as another blast hit the ship. "And maybe we should think about doing that from someplace else? Like maybe we escape *first* and text *later*?"

His fangs were bared. "They have damaged the directional assembly I repaired yesterday. We cannot jump to Hir."

"Can we, uh . . . 'jump' anywhere?" Hope's stomach clenched as the ship lurched again. "You know, somewhere where we're *not* getting pummeled by these lunatics?"

"We have enough power left for a short jump." R'har shook his head. "It will gain us nothing but a moment's safety and only drain our fighting capabilities further. We have little enough time as it is. It will not be long before our power is drained completely and we are left defenseless."

A burst of foreign lettering filled one of the display screens and although she couldn't read it, Hope recognized that it didn't look like the g'hir language.

R'har gave a deep threatening growl.

"What is it?" she asked. "What are they saying?"

"They demand our surrender."

She wet her lips. "Is that an option?"

"The Zerar have sometimes taken g'hir warriors prisoner. My people know to do anything to avoid capture by these monsters."

"But if we surrender . . . we'll live, right?"

His gaze snapped to hers.

"Right?" she persisted.

"Hope . . ." R'har shook his head again, his face tortured. "You cannot ask me to—I cannot let them take you. I will die first."

"Right. I forgot." Her hands clenched. "The g'hir's big human secret. If the Zerar see me they're going want to know what I am, where I came from. They'll want to know what I'm doing here with you."

"The Zerar will know immediately why you are with me. They will know they have all they need to extract that information from me." His throat worked. "I will not be able to hide being bound to you. They will . . . *hurt* you to force the information they want from me, little one. And then I will tell them everything."

And if the Zerar knew that his people had a chance of survival they would want to destroy that chance as quickly as possible.

Earth . . . Dear God, they would destroy the whole world. And R'har—

Her eyes met his. "Would you consider surrendering if I weren't here?"

His hesitation gave her the answer.

Hope looked across the cockpit at R'har, at his rippled brow, his startling eyes, and remembered the tenderness of his touch on her body. He wouldn't surrender because he was protecting her. Just by being here she was going to get R'har killed.

The hell I will!

"Okay," Hope murmured, scrambling to think. She nodded at the blue-green planet below. "Okay, what about the Olari colony? Can we land?"

"That world has been stripped of its defensive capabilities. The Zerar will only follow us down and destroy us before we can land."

"But you said—a 'jump' opens a wormhole, right? They can't detect us inside a wormhole, can they? You can do a short jump and they won't know where we've gone."

"They will not be able to detect us during the jump but we do not have the power to go far. The instant we emerge in realspace they will detect us."

"Can you jump to Olari? If you could do that—" She gave the abandoned world an anxious glance. "We could hide on the planet, couldn't we?"

R'har's luminous eyes widened. "Make a jump into a planet's atmosphere? That would be insane!"

"Good, maybe the Zerar won't expect us to be as crazy as we really are."

R'har shook his head. "My Hope—"

"They won't know where we've gone! They might just think we scrounged up enough power to get away from them."

The ship bucked underneath them.

"We can't surrender," she reminded. "We can't let them capture us and if we stay here, we're fucking dead anyway. We can't even let them get ahold of us *dead* because that'll start them wondering what I am. I might not agree with the g'hir plan to use human women like this but we just can't—My whole *world* could be destroyed by the Zerar if they find out the g'hir are breeding with humans. So right now, R'har, we're down to two choices to keep them from finding out about me—you destroying this ship with us inside it or," she nodded at Olari below, "jumping to the planet."

"I cannot do this, Hope," he said hoarsely. "I cannot knowingly risk your safety—your life—this way."

"My safety will be a whole lot more than 'risked' if we stay here much longer." She rested her hand lightly on his arm. "You can land this thing, R'har. I know it."

He gave a humorless huffing laugh. "Then you are far more confident than I."

Another burst of alien language scrolled across the screen. Even the Zerar's letters looked menacing.

"Hey, if you've got a better idea—" She wasn't sure what R'har had meant by the Zerar hurting her to get the information out of him but right now her imagination was in overdrive. "Believe me, I am all ears."

"I do not." R'har's jaw worked. "But even if we do survive this jump it will not be . . . pleasant."

"Probably still a hell of a lot more pleasant than being captured by the Zerar."

"Yes." He gave a grim smile. "That at least I can promise you."

She glanced at the controls. "What do you need me to do?"

"Do not die, my Hope," he growled, his glowing eyes serious. "All else I can endure."

She gave a nod. "You got it."

"You might also fasten your safety harness."

"Right," she muttered, even through she had no idea how to do it. Now certainly wasn't the time to ask for directions or help. He was fastening his own so she just copied what he was doing as best she could.

He turned his attention to the controls. "The jump will be short but it is unlikely this ship will withstand the planet's atmospheric pressure upon return to realspace. The controls will likely short out and we are low on power. I cannot be sure of how close to the surface we will emerge. If we are lucky I will have time to land the ship in a controlled crash."

And if we're not lucky? But she nodded anyway. "Okay."

"Are you ready?"

For a moment the cockpit's lights blinked out, leaving them in the utter blackness of space.

R'har's and Hope's eyes met as the lights came back on.

"Whether I am or not," she said, gripping the armrests, "I think we just ran out of time."

TWELVE

"Jump will commence," R'har said, his fingers a blur over the controls as the ship lurched again. "In three . . . two . . . one . . ."

The cockpit view went from blackness and stars and Olari spinning peacefully below to a white that was too bright to look at. In the next instant it was like the whole ship had been dropped into a fiery hurricane.

A scream tore from Hope's throat as the ship bucked like a wild thing, spinning out of control. The safety straps dug into her chest to hold her in her seat, her head pressed to the headrest by the force.

R'har roared, straining against the controls as they hurled toward the ground. The planet's surface tilted at crazy angles through the cockpit windows as the ship spiraled downwards. Time slowed and in the last instant before they hit the ground Hope stretched her hand toward him.

Then the ship bounced upward again, the metal shrieking in protest as it arced, the cockpit windows filled with Olari's cerulean sky for an instant before the ship slammed into the planet's surface hard enough to shatter the cockpit windows.

The hull crumbled on impact; foliage exploded against the broken glass and torn earth splattered the cockpit interior as the ship tumbled over and over.

Slowed in its roll by gravity and the drag of the landscape, the ship teetered for an instant on its side then slammed down to rest—right side up—on the planet's surface.

In the sudden silence Hope's shuddering breath thundered in her ears. Trembling, dizzy and sick from the landing, her arm aching where she'd reached out to R'har only to have the limb slammed down when they hit, Hope blinked rapidly, dazed by the simple fact that she wasn't dead.

Through the ruined cockpit windows she could faintly make out the alarmed cries of birds.

"You did it," she whispered.

The windows were shattered, the port side of the cockpit had been crushed, the ship's controls were dark, and there was no telling what shape the rest of the ship was in—or if the rest of the ship was even still attached to the cockpit.

But they had reached the planet's surface alive so she was going to mark it down as a victory.

"You did it, R'har. You landed the ship." The tremulous smile she threw his way collapsed instantly. "Oh my God!"

He was slumped in the pilot's seat, eyes closed, and the whole left side of his face bloody.

"Hold on!" she cried, her stomach clenching when he showed no sign that he'd heard her. With shaking hands she fumbled at the safety harness. It seemed to take a lifetime to free herself from its entanglement. Her legs were wobbly but she managed the two steps to reach him and caught herself against the pilot's chair.

"R'har!"

He didn't react to his name or her touch and under his lids his eyes didn't move. The bleeding came from an injury to his temple and it looked bad.

She was on an alien world with no knowledge of how or if she could survive here. There were more aliens in orbit above ready to torture her, with the means and will to destroy Earth. But looking at R'har, his slackened jaw and alien forehead bleeding, his glowing eyes shut, Hope knew only one thing mattered right now.

"Don't be dead," she begged, pressing her hand to his chest. "Oh, God, please don't be dead . . ."

Under her palm his heart beat strongly and grateful tears stung her eyes. She reached to release his safety harness, then hesitated. It was likely the harness was all that was holding him upright in the pilot's chair. R'har was a few inches shy of seven feet and solid muscle—there was no way she was going to be able to carry him or even catch him if he fell forward.

She stroked his cheek. "R'har? Can you hear me? Come on, you need to wake up, okay?"

His head was bleeding freely. Using her hands and eyes she did a quick cursory check for other wounds. He wasn't cut anywhere else that she could see but that didn't mean he hadn't suffered internal injuries.

He hadn't even stirred during her exam. Despite being the child of two doctors, she knew next to nothing about giving medical care to a human, let alone a g'hir. She didn't know how to use any of the equipment in sickbay.

"R'har? I really . . ." She swallowed hard and brushed his cheek with trembling fingers. "I need you to be okay."

Think, damn it, think!

"R'har? Can you wake up for me? Please?" She cupped his cheek, warm against her palm. "Please, R'har, wake up. Please wake up . . ."

She knelt beside him, tears wetting her face at the faint but terrifyingly wheeze in his breathing.

"Please, R'har . . ." she whispered. "Please . . ."

His eyelids fluttered a little and his lips drew back in a low, pained groan.

"R'har?"

His eyes opened, unfocused and dazed, to regard her.

"Oh, thank God! I was so afraid—Oh, no, hold on," she said quickly, lightly tapping his cheek when his lids started to droop. "You need to stay awake, okay?"

"Hope?" His bewildered eyes took in the ruined cockpit around them, and he frowned at the green leaves visible through the cracked windows. "What—?"

"We made it. We're on Olari." She gave him a smile, her tears overflowing. "You did it, R'har, you landed the ship."

"Landed—?" Suddenly his breath drew in sharply and his eyes snapped to awareness. "Are you hurt?" His hand came up to clasp her wrist and his worried glance went over her. "You are hurt!"

She looked down and saw the blood on her hands and nightgown. "No, I'm—"

He fumbled to release his safety harness. "I will carry you to the medical bay."

"That's not my blood." She nodded at his temple. "That's yours."

"I am not . . ." He touched his head and looked surprised at the blood on his fingers. "It is nothing."

But his attempt to stand brought another pained groan and he sank down into the pilot's seat.

"Yeah," Hope muttered, helping him ease back against the chair. "I'm not the one who needs carrying to the medical bay right now. But head wounds bleed like crazy so I don't know how bad it really is. Do you hurt anywhere else? Are you dizzy?"

"Hope—"

"I'm fine," she said impatiently. "We're focusing on you right now."

He looked distressed, uneasy, to put himself before her. "My head hurts," he allowed finally. "I am dizzy. My body aches, my right side and shoulder especially."

"I don't know anything about g'hir medicine so you'll have to talk me through it. Is there a medical kit in here? Or one in the medical bay I can go grab?"

R'har glanced at the crumbled port side of the cockpit. "There is a medical kit beneath the environmental controls station. It will contain a portable scanner to determine my injuries. I will—"

She put her hand on his shoulder to hold him down. It didn't take much effort either. "Let me get it."

Picking her way carefully across the cockpit to that station, Hope bent down and felt along the seam of the compartment beneath. The little cubby popped open only partway at her touch, but reaching through the crack, Hope was able—by twisting and pulling—to wiggle the kit out.

She bit the inside of her cheek when she got a good look at it—the kit had been crushed completely on one side. She carried it over to the co-pilot's seat and it took some doing on her part to pull the lid up.

R'har accurately read her dismay when she got a look inside. "The scanner is damaged?"

"More like pulverized."

The cylinder was practically flattened. Quickly she rifled through the case but almost everything in there had been rendered useless. At least there were clean bandages in the kit and she broke the seal on them.

R'har gave a low snarl when she pressed the dressing against his temple.

"Sorry, but I know enough to know we've got to put pressure on it. Can you hold this on?"

His fingers replaced hers but with the way he was bleeding the bandages were going to be soaked through in no time.

"That sure isn't going to cut it," Hope said. "Is there another portable kit in the medical bay I can go get? Or another portable scanner I can grab?"

He began to shake his head and broke the movement short with a stifled groan. "I do not know the condition of the rest of the ship. It is not safe for you to venture through it alone. I will go. This area of the ship appears secure for now. You will stay here and I will return for you as soon as I am able."

She scowled. "Oh, for God's sake, you can't even stand up! Just tell me where the damn kit is."

"My Hope," he growled. "You are not even wearing shoes."

He was right. She was still clad in the silky, sexy nightgown. She'd been in such a rush to go after R'har right before the attack she hadn't even grabbed her underwear.

"I think I have enough brains to watch where I step," she said dryly.

"It is not a question of your intelligence! In a ship this badly damaged, there is no telling what hazards you may face between here and the medical bay." His jaw was set. "As your lifemate I will not allow you to go."

Her eyebrows shot up. *"Allow me?* I hate to point this out, R'har, but I don't think you could take on a kitten right now and I'm pretty mobile for someone you're trying to boss around."

His face was alarmingly pale but a muscle twitched in his cheek. "Where I come from," he growled, "females honor their lifemate's instinct to protect."

"And where *I* come from we don't put the one with the serious head injury in charge." Hope folded her arms. "So you can either tell me where the kit is and I'll go or—if you're really up for a stroll—we can go to sickbay together."

His glowing green eyes narrowed. "Are all human females this stubborn?"

"Yeah," she said, meeting him look for look. "Get used to it."

His huffing laugh was quickly cut short. He winced in pain and blood seeped through his bandage.

"Okay, enough already, let's get you to the medical bay, " Hope said, putting her hand under his elbow. "Try standing up, you can lean on me."

He drew in a deep breath and pushed himself up. Hope hurriedly clasped his wrist to drape his arm over her shoulder as he stood, then slid her arm around his waist to steady him. He took a shuffling half-step, leaning heavily on her, then another.

"Great," she muttered when the cockpit door didn't open at her wave. She didn't know much about g'hir warriors but if R'har was typical of his species there was one thing she could say for sure—they weren't light. "Sometimes they open, sometimes they won't. Do these things just *know* how to piss me off?"

R'har's face was drawn but his growl was patient. "The power outage affects the doors as well, little one."

"Right," she said, her glance darting around the cockpit at the dead controls. "Do you know why the power's out?"

He gave a faint smile. "Certainly not an ill-advised jump into a planetary atmosphere."

"Funny. I meant do you know a way to get the power back on? Or maybe how I can?"

He gave the ruined control room a meaningful glance. "I would judge this ship a total loss and we have not even left the cockpit. Restoring power will not be a simple repair—if it is even possible."

Hope wet her lips. "What about the medical bay?"

If the equipment there didn't function she'd have no way to treat R'har or even know for sure how badly he was hurt.

"The medical bay has extra shielding and a redundant energy system," he said but his deep growl sounded very tired now. "I am hopeful it is still functional."

"It will be." Hope narrowed her gaze at the exit. "We just need to get there."

"There is a manual release for the door behind that lower panel." But when he took a step in that direction he swayed on his feet and she hurriedly leaned him against the cockpit wall, using it—and her own weight—to brace him upright.

"Don't you dare pass out, R'har. All I remember from first aid class is how to apply a tourniquet," she warned. "Probably not the best choice for a head wound."

"But it would stop the bleeding." He managed another faint smile. "And spare you my poor jokes."

"Still, I vote we try for the medical bay first. Here." She moved his hand to one of the rear chair's headrests. "Hold onto this. I'll get the door open."

Hope brushed some of the debris away so she could kneel in front of the compartment. Using the tips of her fingers she managed to pry the panel open. The recessed compartment had a number of controls and a handle.

"What do I do?" she asked, peering into the space.

"Hit the first two controls simultaneously then rotate the handle to the right. The door seal will release and the door will slide open easily."

She hit the two controls but the handle was g'hir sized so she needed to use two hands to clasp it. She pushed hard but the handle seemed welded into place. "Goddamn, sonofabitch—!"

"I will—"

"I've *got* this! Just give me one fucking—!"

With a metallic scraping sound the handle finally budged but it took all of her weight to move it into place. Finally, with a low hiss, the door seal released.

"See?" she said standing, though her hands were hurting from pushing on the handle. "No problem."

She fit her fingertips into the scant space between the door and doorframe then widened her stance, braced herself, and pulled hard.

The door moved a measly inch.

"Oh, you have got to be freaking kidding me!" Gritting her teeth, Hope pulled again and managed to widen the opening another few centimeters. She paused, breathing hard from the effort, and threw R'har an apologetic look. "Might want to go ahead and sit back down. Looks like I'm going to need a minute here."

"Stand aside," he said, straightening. "I will open it."

"No way. You're injured. I'm not. I can do it."

Fitting her fingers into the crack she'd made between the doorway and the door she pulled again.

"Hope—"

"Damn it, R'har, I'm doing this!" she panted, changing her grip. "Just give me a sec here."

Gritting her teeth, working inch by inch, she coaxed the door open.

"Holy cow," she gasped, massaging her sore hands as she peered into the hallway. "How many doors between here and the medical bay again?"

"Three."

"Oh, yippee." Her shoulder felt like fire and pain was running down her right arm.

Suck it up, MacGowan.

The lights in the corridor were out and the light from the cockpit was scant indeed. Hope wrinkled her nose at the charred smell. "Well, something sure got burnt up."

"Systems all over the ship burned out when we jumped into the atmosphere. A number of components likely scorched during the overload."

R'har was so pale she thought he might take a header if he let go of the chair.

"Just let me get the doors between here and the medical bay open," she urged. "I'll make sure the way is clear—or clear it if I have to. I'll come back for you as soon as I can."

"You are my lifemate," he growled. "I will not let you go into danger alone."

Now was not the time to discuss that whole g'hir lifemate thing. Not with him bleeding and the state the ship was in.

And the Zerar still up there.

He probably hadn't forgotten about them any more than she had.

"Any chance there's a flashlight we can take along?"

"There should be a lumina in the compartment next to the door."

This one at least opened without a struggle but it took Hope a moment to figure out how to work the light. Also made for a g'hir's hands, the thing was oversized for hers and awkward to manage.

"Okay," she said, taking up her position at his side and putting her arm around his waist. "Let's go."

They made it down the first corridor without incident. She left R'har leaning heavily against the wall while she worked on getting the next door open. Her fingers were going to be bruised and her hands were already aching.

The sunlight from the cockpit didn't reach this far and this hall was very dark indeed.

"You okay?" she asked worriedly. Standing and walking when he should have been resting had R'har looking far worse. "Do you want to wait here? We're not far now. One more here then the door into the medical bay." She swung the light in that direction. "I'll be right there. You'll be able to see me."

"But not reach you if you had need of me." His jaw hardened. "I am your protector. It shames me that you must struggle to clear the way when I should be doing it for you. That I cannot carry you and you must walk through debris in bare feet. But I *will* be at your side and I will protect you to my last breath."

"There's nothing on this ship you need to protect me from," she pointed out. "I've got a flashlight—lumina—*whatever*. I won't be far away and you look like you just lost a bar fight."

R'har bared his fangs. "I have *never* lost a bar fight." He raised an eyebrow at her short, surprised laugh. "You do not believe me, little one?"

"Oh, I believe you'd win any fight you decided to show up for," she said, taking up position beside him to help him along. If he was going to be this stubborn then the next best option was getting him to the medical bay as soon as she could. "I'm actually torn between wondering who'd be stupid enough to pick one with you and trying to imagine you hanging around in a bar in the first place. You don't strike me as the type."

"What 'type' do I strike you as?"

He was trying not to lean on her, that was obvious, but he couldn't manage without her help.

He was a whole lot more hurt than he was letting on.

"I dunno. The wrestle-an-alien-beast-down-with-your-bare-hands type, I guess."

"I have done that too," he agreed. "But I have fought other males in the taverns as well. There are many warriors with nothing better to do now than drink and pick fights."

"Nothing better to do?" Hope's brow creased. These people had space travel, access to dozens of other alien cultures, incredible technology at their disposal. "What do you mean?"

"G'hir males need . . . *purpose*. Before the plague we had mates to capture, to protect, offspring to safeguard. It was where our energy, our strength, was channeled. This was our sacred calling from the Goddess, the noblest of tasks, the essence of a g'hir warrior's identity. But the Scourge tore that from us too when it killed our females. Many warriors drift now, caught between the space before this life and after with no reason to exist. Many lack direction and struggle for a purpose to their lives. Some have surrendered to drink and foolish scuffles, to the blackness of despair."

"But not you."

"How could I?" Even in this faint light his eyes shone as they met hers. "The Goddess herself gave me hope."

At the warmth in his rumble, the light in his glowing eyes, she ducked her head. "I have to get the door open."

He was silent as she worked. Hope got the panel off, hit the controls, but this time the manual release, still provided with scant power, turned without struggle and this door slid open easily.

"Oh, thank you," she breathed as the lights in the medical bay came up. A quick glance around showed this room had fared pretty well, considering their less than stellar landing. Clearly whatever backup systems were supplying power still worked. She prayed that meant the equipment would be functional as well.

"Come on," she urged as R'har leaned heavily against her. "Just a couple more steps."

He fell onto the exam table, closing his eyes as soon as his head touched the cushioned surface.

"Stay awake, R'har," she pleaded with an anxious glance at the unfamiliar equipment. "You have to talk me through this, remember?"

His eyes opened briefly to meet hers, his gaze a little unfocused. "Commence medical scan."

She was about to remind him that she had no idea how to do that when the exam table rose then snapped into place with a hiss. A horizontal beam of blue-white light, originating from the ceiling above the table, ran the length of him from the top of his head, down over his chest and to the tips of his boots.

Around the room displays came to life to show readings from his scan. Beneath the readings were scrolling words in the g'hir language.

She chewed the inside of her cheek, her glance darting from screen to screen. "You know all this would be really helpful if I could read Hironian."

"Commence audible medical assessment," he murmured.

"Second degree concussion, sub-cranial ridge hematoma . . ." The voice that read out his condition was in the growls and snarls of a g'hir but it was a warm tone, undeniably female, and in Hope's opinion way too chipper sounding for the grim news it was relaying. "Right collarbone, broken at point seven degrees and nineteen degrees. Right shoulder, detached rotator cuff. Right rib cage, fracture of the fifth and seventh ribs. Upper abdominal region, severe trauma to the sorian. Laceration of the liver, internal bleeding . . ."

The medcomp continued its appraisal of his condition. It generated a rotating three-dimensional hologram of a male g'hir form over the exam table, the various areas of injury lighting up in red as they were read off. Just seeing it made Hope swallow hard.

"God," she breathed. "How did you even manage to stand up?"

It took her a moment to realize that while the medical computer was droning on, R'har hadn't answered her.

"R'har?" An alarm buzzed angrily at her when she crossed into the scanner light. Afraid her movement had interfered with the exam she took a quick step back. "R'har?"

He didn't respond. His eyes were closed, the hand that had been holding his bandage on slack beside him.

The medical computer trailed off in its assessment, leaving Hope alone with the rotating figure above R'har's unconscious form detailing injuries she had no idea how to treat.

Thirteen

"R'har?"

She took a tentative step toward him but the medical scanner remained dark and didn't buzz in protest at her approach. Hope laid her hand on his chest. His heart beat under her palm but without the same strength, the same vigor it had before.

He was frighteningly pale now, his vivid eyes closed.

"Please wake up. Please. You have to tell me what to do here, how to help you."

He didn't respond or appear to have even heard her.

I took too long getting him here! I should have moved faster! I should have—

"Stop it," Hope hissed at herself. "You need to think! Just *think* about what you need to do and *do* it."

The three-dimensional figure outlining R'har's many injuries still rotated above the table.

"What do I do?" Hope looked up at the now deactivated medical scanner. "I don't know how to treat him! You have to tell me! *Please!*"

The equipment stayed silent and dark.

"Goddamn it, tell me what to do! How do I treat him?" She threw an impatient gesture at the rotating representation of R'har. "Why show me this if you won't tell me what to do? He needs help *right now!*"

Hope's gaze fell on R'har again, the rippled brow and strong jaw, the full mouth he'd pressed so eagerly to hers.

You're a lot of things, R'har. An alien. A warrior. A pilot. You even think you're my lifemate, whatever that *is.*

Her head came up. "But you never claimed to be a doctor . . ."

Which meant that this equipment was intended for someone with a minimum amount of medical training.

Hope looked back up at the scanner. "Uh, please treat him?"

The equipment didn't respond and her eyes were drawn to R'har again.

"No, that's not what you did," she murmured. "You didn't ask it. You *told* it." Hope raised her voice. "Begin medical treatment!"

Nothing.

"Damn it," she snarled. *But all he did was tell it to start—*

"No!" she cried suddenly. "Not—I mean, *Commence* medical treatment!"

Hope jumped back with a gasp as the scanner above sprang to life, its light already moving over R'har's body. A force field shimmered into place around the table, forcing Hope to retreat further as arms emerged from the table like the legs of a huge metallic spider to hover over him. The medical arms, pinchers, and instruments worked on R'har with cold mechanical efficiency, quickly removing his clothing, even deftly cutting away his boots and discarding the used bandage.

A soft hiss sounded when one of the arms pressed a cylinder to his neck.

New symbols appeared over the rotating figure and Hope gritted her teeth.

As soon as he wakes up he's going to start teaching me to read this stuff!

"Commence, uh . . ." *Damn it, what did he say?* "Commence audible medical assessment!"

"Blood pressure stabilizing," the computer responded in its soothing female g'hir growls. "Blood oxygen levels rising. Beginning vascular repair to sub-cranial ridge trauma . . ."

Hope shifted her feet as the medical equipment worked on him, both relieved to tears that he was finally being treated and wishing she could do more—or at least some of it—herself. The computer voice went on, calmly outlining the different treatments as the arms performed them, giving updates to R'har's vital signs as well.

One by one the red areas highlighted on the rotating hologram went to blue and abruptly the arms retracted back into the table.

The computer's voice came on as the forcefield winked out. "Additional care recommended: Rest. Fluids and light meals to include the following nutrients—" A list she couldn't read appeared and the letters glowed for a moment. "Treatment complete."

The scanner above went dark. The machine had even been thoughtful enough to provide him with a sheet that covered him to the ribs.

She came to the table's edge and leaned over him, her face close to his.

"R'har?" she said softly, her fingers stroking his cheek, tracing the ripples of his forehead. "Can you hear me?"

His eyes opened a little, the glow of his bright green irises just visible under his lids, and he gave her a sleepy smile. "Hope . . ."

His hand came up to cup her cheek and she closed her eyes for a moment, just feeling his skin against hers, the warmth of him.

"You're all right," she whispered. "You're all right."

"My Hope . . ."

His nose brushed hers in a g'hir kiss, then his mouth was hot against hers, and she moaned as his purr started, soft and deep.

His tongue flicked against the inner part of her lip and she breathed in the sweet spice of him, his rumble-purr sending heat curling through her belly as he deepened the kiss. His strong hands went to the curve of her waist and he lifted her easily onto the table to lie beside him.

His lips brushed along her cheek to her throat and he inhaled deeply, a fine tremble running through his body as he breathed in her scent. His hand came up to cup her breast, his thumb tracing her nipple through the thin fabric of the gown, then his fingers were brushing the straps aside and there was a rush of air against her bare skin as the silky fabric fell away.

His fevered gaze fell on her breast, the muscles of his belly bunching as he curled toward her to cover her nipple with the moist heat of his mouth. She bit her lip as his tongue flicked against her and her fingers threaded through his hair as he nuzzled.

But she wasn't content, not at ease yet, even with her center tightening, her mind clouding with pleasure. Hope swung up to sit astride him, tracing the healed hurts with fingers and mouth, assuring herself he was whole again.

Her caresses only drove his need higher. The growling-purring rumble sent tingling fire racing between her legs and then he was spreading her wider, his long fingers at her cleft, stroking her.

"God!" she gasped, pressing harder against him as his fingers quickened, their light strokes against her clit increasing to inhuman speed.

She was teetering just at the peak when R'har caught her waist, lifting his hips to slide easily into her, filling her to the hilt with his slick hot cock. Hope bent her head against the warm smoothness of his neck, holding onto his shoulders as he rocked inside her, his hips picking up speed as she contracted hard around him.

He moved fast and deep then, drumming with a g'hir's speed. He tensed, his big body trembled, his fangs flashing, and then he was pulsing hard inside her.

His breath was still fast, his skin damp with sweat, and she was still shaking from the intensity of her climax when he raised his head to offer her a clumsy nose rub.

R'har gathered her at his side and brushed his lips against her forehead. Hope let her eyes fall shut, her cheek on his chest, feeling how his heart began to slow in his chest as his fingers intertwined with hers. His rumbling fell to a contented purr and he brought her palm to his mouth to kiss.

His purr caught and stopped. "Your hand . . ."

"Hmm . . . what about it?" she mumbled, nestling closer but the sudden tension in his body was jarring.

"There is blood on your hand! Why is there—?" R'har drew back a little to look at her and his brows rushed together. "You are injured!"

She glanced at the black and blue mark already forming on the pale skin of her shoulder. "Yeah that's gonna be an ugly one. Probably happened when the Zerar first attacked."

He shook his head a little. "The Zerar—they . . ."

Suddenly he sat up, dislodging Hope from her comfortable place against him as his glance darted around the room. "We are in the medical bay. How did we come to be in the medical bay?"

"How did we—?" Hope sat up too, frowning at him. "Well, you had a concussion and you were sedated," she said slowly. "Maybe that's why you don't remember."

"I think—" The heel of his hand went to his temple.

"You were cut there," she agreed, tracing the spot and shaking her head in grateful amazement. He didn't even have a scar to show for what he'd suffered. "Pretty badly and you had a whole lot of internal injures too. I can't even believe the technology your people have—the healing it can do."

"The ship spun out of control then we . . ." His eyes widened and his gaze went to her shoulder again. "My injuries were treated but yours were *not*? Goddess, how could I have—?"

In the next instant he was off the table, still naked, his arms sliding underneath her shoulders and knees to move her to the table's center. "Commence medical—"

"*Ohmigod!*" Hope scrambled off the table to escape those dozen mechanical arms before they could close around her. But even in her terror human modesty died hard and she managed to take the sheet with her, wrapping it around her body even as she scrambled away.

R'har rounded the exam table heading for her but she jumped back with a squeak of alarm that stopped him in his tracks.

"You are injured, little one," he said, his growl gentle as a rumble of distant thunder across the sea. "You must lie down." He indicated the exam table. "The medcomp will treat you."

"No—" Hope backpedaled. "—Fucking—" Her back hit the wall. "—*Way!*"

R'har held his palms out to her, his hands spread in what looked like g'hir body language for *I'm not going to hurt you* or maybe *Calm the fuck down.* Either way his soothing pose didn't fool her into thinking he wouldn't try making a grab at her. It was all right for R'har but she wasn't about to let that thing trap *her* with its spider arms, thank you very much.

"You are hurt." He shook his head, bewildered. "You must allow your injuries to be tended."

"No! I'm fine. *Really.*" She wasn't sure how far that thing could reach; for all she knew those arms under the table could grab her from way over there. She sent a wary look its way.

R'har followed her glance. "You were afraid when you first came on board, when I first brought you here," he murmured. His glowing eyes searched her face. "I believed it was I you feared so greatly." His wave indicated the room at large. "It is this *place* that frightens you, little one? The medical bay?"

Hope swallowed hard, still braced for his rush or a mechanical arm's grab. "Yeah, not such a big fan of this stuff. You know, now that you're okay maybe we can get out of here? I mean, seriously, it's a *bruise*, R'har."

"I must—"

He stopped short at her frightened gasp and stared.

"*That* is why would you not sleep in here, although I told you the room would be heated to comfortable levels . . ." He tilted his head, his bright gaze searching hers. "Do you also fear the human medical treatment?"

"Oh, yeah, I'm pretty evolved that way," she said with a nervous wave toward the exam table. "Human medicine, g'hir medicine—I don't discriminate. The sight of anything medical leaves me an irrational whimpering mess."

"You did not flee from me when I was hurt." His brow creased. "You did not abandon me to my injuries. You brought me here. You remained by my side to see to my care."

It was true. Usually she couldn't even walk down the Band-Aid aisle at the drug store without having a panic attack. She could hardly believe a little while ago she'd been eagerly climbing onto the biobed with him. But that rumble-purring of his got her so hot she'd hardly noticed where she was.

Hope shifted her weight. "That was different. I couldn't let myself fall apart then. You needed me."

"Have you always had these fears?"

She gave a meaningful downward glance. "You know, I love that we're having this talk while you're bare-assed naked. I mean, I thought the whole kidnapped-by-an-alien-chip-in-my-head thing was going to make for some interesting talks with a therapist but now, exploring my medical phobia with the naked alien too? This takes crazy to a whole new level. I'm going to wind up putting her kid through *college*."

R'har waited, sinking into that stillness of his again, so silent and steady he could have been carved from marble.

Hope gritted her teeth; the man had patience Gandhi would envy.

"When I was eight I had my tonsils out," she mumbled finally. "I mean, I always *hated* getting shots, my mother said I embarrassed her with how I would scream, but that's when it really got bad."

"You have endured this—alone—for a long time," he said with a slow, human-style nod.

"Yes," she croaked. Brian had been annoyed and embarrassed by her fears. She'd endured lots of ribbing from friends and the impatient frustration of doctors and nurses—and especially her parents—through the years. "Yes, I have."

"I know your fear to be real, little one. I know you feel yourself in danger, even now." He searched her eyes. "But on my word as a warrior of Hir, on my vow as your lifemate, I would never harm you, Hope. I would never allow you to be harmed. I would die first."

"I know," she blurted, surprised by her own admission, at how completely she believed him. She shook her head. "But I'm sorry I just—I can't . . ."

"I ask you to trust me." He offered his hand to her. "Even though your instincts scream at you that you are in danger, that you are not safe. Will you? Will you trust me to care for you? To protect you?"

Her eyes stung and she glanced at the hand he offered. "I'm scared, R'har. I'm so scared."

"I know," he rumbled softly. "But I am here. And I will always stand between you and danger, my Hope."

Looking at this alien warrior standing unabashedly naked, his glowing eyes gentle, his hand held out to her, Hope felt her tears overflow.

"Oh, fucking hell," she muttered thickly and took R'har's hand.

FOURTEEN

Hope recoiled, whimpering.

"The scanner will pass a light over you that penetrates tissue but it will not hurt," R'har rumbled, his growls soft, soothing.

He'd coaxed her back onto the biobed but it took all her will to stay there. Her grip on his hand was so tight her fingernails must be nearly drawing blood by now but he hadn't complained.

"How do you know that this thing can even heal me?" she demanded. "I'm human, not g'hir. Maybe it'll just scramble my organs up."

"I treated you with this equipment once before," he reminded. "It has been calibrated to treat humans."

Of course. The ever-helpful Jenna. Someday she and I are going to have a talk about her handing her own kind over to aliens . . .

"I promise, little one, the medscan is painless."

"Oh, for God's sake, just do it!" Hope tensed as the light ran down her body but he wasn't lying, it didn't hurt. Then something else occurred to her. "But you can't strap me down again! You have to swear you won't!"

"I will not," he assured. "I would never have let you regain consciousness here if I had known this room caused you such terror."

"Yeah, remembering that I was *un*conscious in here is kind of freaking me out," she said, biting back another whimper as the light passed over her again. "Why does it have to keep doing that?"

"It scans at multiple depths to determine the extent of your injuries and evaluate how best to treat them."

"Wonderful. Yay for the scary alien light. Isn't it fucking *done* yet?"

"Pause scan."

The scanner held position and Hope twisted her head around to look up at him. His shirt was a total loss but he'd gotten dressed from the waist down while she kept hold of the sheet for the exam.

"Why'd you stop it?"

"Your breathing is very shallow," he said and rested his warm palm on her lower belly. "Allow yourself to breathe deeper."

"Can't we just get this over with?" she cried. "I just want to get *out* of here!"

"Breathe so that you lift my hand. It will help you feel more comfortable here."

Fucking *nothing* was going to make her comfortable here but R'har was already doing that still-and-silent-as-a-Zen-garden thing again, patient as time itself.

"Fine," she grumbled and sucked in hard.

"Pause there," he said when she'd filled her lungs.

"I'm not a computer!"

"You must pause in your breathing," he said, unperturbed by her snappy tone. "Then let it out slowly."

She didn't see as she had much choice with his hand on her stomach like this. He wasn't about to let her leave with even the littlest mark on her and the sooner he got the scanner back on the sooner she could get out of here.

"I'm dizzy," she complained after several breaths.

"You are over-breathing. Pause longer between the inhale and exhale."

"You know, it really is only a bruise. Maybe we should worry about something more important right now? Like the Zerar maybe?"

"We are safe for the present and nothing is more important than you are," he rumbled. "You require medical treatment and you will have the healing you need. Breathe."

She tried again, slowing her breathing even more, but it wasn't helping much.

"Is there a place where you know yourself protected?" he asked.

She gave a short laugh. "Go to my 'safe place,' you mean?" At the puzzled look he gave her, she waved her hand. "Never mind." Looking up at the scanner, deactivated but hovering ominously above, was making her hands clench. She shut her eyes briefly so she could think clearly enough to answer him and only one place came to mind. "I guess I always felt safe in my room growing up."

"I have not asked you where you spent your childhood." He gave her a faint smile. "It was not the wilderness in which I found you, I know that much."

"Yeah, *no*. I'm definitely a city girl, born and bred. My mom had a place in Takoma Park. A big, old house with about a million plumbing problems. That area was kinda run down then, lots of hippies, but it was nice too, especially in the summer 'cause Rock Creek Park isn't far away. When I was thirteen my mom managed a couple weeks off from the hospital so we painted my room. We tried to wallpaper it first." She smiled, remembering. "But we were terrible at it and a day in we decided to start over with paint. We did the room a real pale violet color and we found some embroidered curtains at a resale shop in Alexandria. We painted the furniture white and did a darn good job too. We didn't get along too well, my mom and me, but that time . . . that was fun." She shook her head a little. "I can't believe I'm saying this but this is actually helping."

"Are you ready for the scan to continue?" He must have felt her tense up again because he added, "We can talk while the scan is performed. It will not affect the results."

"What about your hand?" she asked, glancing at her stomach where his palm still rested lightly. "Don't you have to move it?"

"I can instruct the computer to ignore it if you like."

"Yeah, do that," she said, her throat suddenly tight. "It . . . makes me feel safer."

She didn't miss how his eyes lit up at that. The scanner came back online but she knew what to expect this time and while it wasn't any day at the beach, she managed to unclench her hands at least.

A blue three-dimensional holographic figure—female this time—appeared over the table. Unlike when R'har had been injured, only a few places appeared in red but the diagnosis wasn't any more reassuring.

"Contusions, trauma to the intervertebral discs of the lumbosacral spine . . ." the computer's female g'hir voice droned. "Non-displaced sub cortical fracture . . ."

Hope swallowed hard. "Fracture?"

R'har was frowning at the readout. "You have badly bruised your shoulder bone. This is a painful injury; you should have told me."

She was starting to hyperventilate again. "Aren't all injuries painful?"

"Yours is far worse than I believed. You should have told me you were in such pain."

"I can handle it."

"I think you would not have told me even if the pain were unbearable," he grumbled. "Because I would have insisted you be treated."

"What's the point? Getting treated hurts just as bad or more."

His huffed his breath through his nostrils in g'hir frustration. His attention returned to the readout and his frown deepened. "Your genetic makeup shows marked differences from that of Ra'kur's mate."

"Well, sure. We're different people."

"But you are both human females."

"Yeah, okay, clearly missing something here." Hope shook her head a little. "What are you talking about? What's so different?"

"You have a unique mutation." He pointed at the display. "See here . . ." He pointed again. "And here."

"Uh, quick reminder—the chip you put in my brain doesn't let me read your language. And even if it did I'm not a biologist, I'm an artist."

He was troubled enough by what he was looking at that he gave an absentminded g'hir nod. "Your genetic makeup requires that you receive significantly more pain medication to feel the same relief."

Hope frowned. "Wait—are you saying pain medication doesn't work on me?"

"Not nearly as well as the same dose would on Jenna. And this same mutation makes you more sensitive to pain as well. You require a thirty-five percent higher dose to alleviate your pain than would another human female of your weight and build."

"You mean . . . it's not all in my head?" she asked tightly. "I'm not making it all up?"

"Your fears are not irrational or unfounded, little one. I do not think those who treated you understood the suffering they were inflicting upon you." His vivid gaze reflected sympathy. "If my pain were so poorly controlled I, too, would greatly fear any treatment."

"Oh," Hope murmured. All those impatient doctors and dentists, all those unsympathetic nurses, her parents too, how Brian could shrug off a shot when she hyperventilated through every agonizing millimeter of needle. "That's really . . . I mean knowing that maybe it's not my fault—"

"Is it the pain?" His brow furrowed. "Is that why your eyes water now?"

"Sorry, I'm having kind of an up and down week," she said, laughing a little. *It's not my fault! I have a genetic mutation and it's not my fault!* "But it's okay, really. Happy tears."

R'har was still frowning. "I promise your pain medication will be adjusted to the needed dose." His long fingers brushed at the wetness on her cheek. "I give you my word you will never suffer as you have in the past."

"Okay," she said but couldn't help bracing herself.

"I will begin now." He hesitated, his gaze searching. "If you will trust me?"

"Yeah," Hope said, letting her eyes close again briefly, letting her hands unclench. "I do."

FIFTEEN

Hope fought the urge to rub her newly healed shoulder. The medcomp's treatment had been a cakewalk, not just pain free—for once!—but with R'har's soothing growls and explanation of what was going to happen before the med comp did it, almost anxiety free.

Her shoulder didn't hurt now exactly; it just felt sore, as if she'd spent the day at the gym doing side raises or something. Still, massaging it might help . . .

She glanced at R'har. One tiny indication that everything wasn't sunshine and rainbows and he'd have her right back in that thing. And she had gotten to know g'hir facial expressions a whole lot better since he'd captured her

"So how long?" she asked.

His bright gaze, puzzled now, met hers. "How long for what, little one?"

"Till that Zerar warship figures out they should be looking on Olari for us."

His shoulders fell. "I thought—"

"What? That I'd forgotten about them? That maybe *they* forgot about *us*?"

"That perhaps I could shield you," he said with a sigh.

Hope folded her arms. "From what? Reality?"

"From . . ." He gave a frustrated huff. "You should even now be safely within the borders of the Yir enclosure—not here on this abandoned colony with a warship lurking above! It is my task, my *duty*, to keep you safe and I—"

"You didn't put me in danger. They—the Zerar—did. That's why we're here."

R'har's hands clenched. "You should not *be* here," he growled quietly.

Hope indicated the sleeping quarters with a glance. "What now? Are we going to stay here till we're rescued?"

His gaze met hers and she had her answer.

"No," she said for him, and passed her hand over her eyes. "Because if the Zerar *do* look for us, staying with the ship is the best way to get caught."

"We must gather supplies from the ship and forest," he rumbled. "It is the safest way."

"Forest—as in wander from place to place and sleep in a tent?"

"G'hir have an instinct to travel," he said, sounding a bit surprised that she wasn't jumping at the chance. "We find it very pleasant."

"Yeah," she muttered. "You know what humans enjoy? *Houses*. With hot running water. And *beds*. You know why I booked that three-bedroom-with-Jacuzzi-and-gourmet-kitchen cabin, R'har? Because I hate camping. I also happen to suck at it."

"I will make a sleeping place for us under the stars and though I am new to mating I promise I will do all I can"— R'har gave a slow smile that made her center tighten—"to see you enjoy it."

Then, suddenly, she caught what he'd said.

"Wait—What do you mean you're *new* at it? You don't mean *new* new?"

His glowing eyes blinked.

"As in—" Hope got out. "This morning with me . . . that was your first time? Ever?"

His cheeks flushed. "I have brought myself to release."

"No not—I mean, with a woman—I'm your first?"

"Of course," he said, surprised.

Because most of the g'hir women are dead!

"I, uh—" Hope swallowed hard. "I guess I just wasn't thinking."

"They told me it was likely you would have had other lovers before me," he growled quietly.

It troubled him, she could see that, and in a heartrending flash she wished he'd been her first too.

"I promise to improve my skills," he assured, his brow knitted. "I can scent your heat, detect the changes in your breathing when you are highly aroused. With practice I will learn to please you better."

"Is that what you're—?" Hope gave a short disbelieving laugh. "Oh, believe me. You have nothing to worry about on that account. R'har, you are the absolute best I've ever had."

His face lit up then, his fangs flashing in a proud grin that just had her heart melting.

"And not that you need it but I sure don't mind," she continued, sliding her arms around his waist, "letting you get in some extra practice . . ."

His gaze heated then he gave a rueful smile. "When we are safely forested," he promised, brushing his nose against hers in a light g'hir's kiss, "I will make good on my promise to pleasure you greatly."

"Holy cow," Hope breathed when she got her first full look at the destruction the crash had wrought from the outside.

"It was a good landing," R'har rumbled, looking down from their hillside perch at the wreck below.

"A good landing?" she echoed. Half the ship was crushed and the path of destruction they'd left on the landscape during the crash could have taken out two city blocks.

"The ship did not explode on entry," he offered. "I have never heard of a ship that attempted to jump into an atmosphere that did not. But better to die quickly than let us be taken by the Zerar. The suffering they would have inflicted on you—" He swallowed. "But the All Mother smiled on us."

Hope scanned the peaceful blue sky, fingering the straps of her backpack nervously. Hers was light. He'd packed it with things that she'd need for her comfort, things to keep her alive on the off chance they were separated, but R'har carried the bulk of their supplies. Most of the clothes provided by the Yir were pretty girly so Hope donned her jeans and hiking boots again. Her pack also contained changes of clothes chosen from the most practical of the Yir selections. "Do you think they'll come after us?"

"The Zerar are in our territory and this area of space is patrolled. It would be foolish to stay here endlessly searching for one small ship."

He was trying to reassure her, reassure himself too, probably.

"The communications array was damaged." Hope bit her lip. "Do you think you got a message out to your people? I mean, someone's going to come for us, aren't they?"

"I pray that the Goddess bid it so," he said tightly. "But I do not know. The Zerar were jamming our communications."

Hope regarded the smashed wreck. It looked like some native birds were already planning on using it as a nesting site. "I know it's a real mess but . . . if we can wait the Zerar out and come back can you—I mean do you think you could fix the ship up enough to get us to Hir?"

He shook his head. "I must destroy it."

"Destroy—? You know, it's not like there's a metro station a couple blocks away, R'har! If no one comes for us we don't have another way out of here. You can't just maroon us here." Hope shook her head. "You can't!"

"The Zerar are still in orbit," he growled shortly. "If we are fortunate they will soon cease scanning for our ship spaceside and leave g'hir space." His gaze met hers and his tone softened. "I must choose the path that will see you safe, even if it not comfortable or convenient, little one. The Zerar know they damaged our ship badly. If they scan the surface they *must* find wreckage."

She wrapped her arms around herself. "So even if they find the ship they'll think we're dead."

"There will be nothing left for them to believe we survived." He looked in the direction of the mountains. "We will go to the relay station and contact Hir from there. Until then, the forest will keep us safe." His vivid glance went to the ship. "I will set off the charges I placed. Once the ship is destroyed, we will go."

"But won't the Zerar see that from space?" Hope's brow creased. "An explosion big enough to blow that thing apart is like a bull's-eye showing them exactly where we are."

He shook his head again, his blond hair golden in Olari's afternoon sunlight. "These charges will superheat the ship. They will be hot enough to partially melt the rock beneath but at this distance the sensors of a ship in orbit will dismiss it as an atmospheric fluctuation." R'har glanced skyward, already sliding his pack off his shoulders. "Wait here. I will return shortly."

She took a quick step after him. "You mean you have to set them off from down there? Isn't that, you know, fucking *dangerous*?"

"I will set the charges off from here but I must erase any evidence of our departure. We have left tracks a child could follow."

Hope glanced at the path they'd taken from the ship. The hillside was rocky and *she* sure couldn't see any sign that they'd disturbed things in the valley below.

"Uh, sure," she said, shifting her weight. "Anything you'd like me to do in the meantime?"

"Remain here and do not wander," he warned. "This world has its own dangers."

Hope sent a quick uneasy glance at the woods behind her. "Like what? Space bears?"

"This colony was abandoned many years ago. The settlements are dilapidated, the wildlife unchecked. Most will not recognize bipeds as a danger, only a meal."

"Oh, *grand*. I hope you remembered to put the barbeque sauce in my pack. I'd hate to be thought bland."

"You will be safe here for a few moments," he assured. "I am well armed. I will return swiftly if you have need of me."

"Fine, yes, go on," she said, embarrassed and annoyed at how anxious she was at being separated from him, even for a little while. "I'll stay right here."

He held her eyes for a moment then gave a human-style nod. "I will not be gone from you long."

R'har took off at a jog—a *g'hir's* jog which had him going about twenty-five miles an hour. Hope's mouth parted at his speed, at his *inhuman* speed. He was probably not even trying.

At some point she had started being able to look right past the ridged brow, the glowing eyes, those fangs, and just see *him*, just R'har. His growls even sounded normal now. But when he did things like this, moved like lightning, or fell into that stillness of his, it brought it all back—everything about him, his biology, his culture, his way of thinking was alien.

Hope swallowed hard. Her parents had both been human, both American, both from the DC metro area, both *doctors*, for fuck's sake, and their marriage had been a disaster. And none of those perfect grooms in the bridal magazines sported fangs along with their tuxes.

He was trying to downplay their differences. Trying to nod like a human, rather than a g'hir, trying to mimic human mannerisms, moving far slower than she knew he could. They'd been onboard the ship, confined by its size, so she'd seen him move that fast in the open only once before, back on Earth when he'd cut off her escape, when he'd captured her.

Back on Earth!

Hope's gaze was drawn to the two suns above and the baker's dozen of Olari's moons visible even during daylight. She couldn't see Earth, of course; not even her own world's sun would be visible from here. G'hir ships traveled through space by opening a wormhole between destinations—a "jump" they called it. Earth was trillions of miles away and something about being alone, here on this hillside on a distant abandoned world, brought that home in stomach-clenching knowledge.

"Hope?"

With a gasp, she spun around.

"What is it?" R'har was frowning, his gaze scanning the landscape for any threat. "Did you see something?"

"R'har!" she cried, her hands at her chest. "Jesus! You scared the hell out of me!" She looked back down the hillside they'd traveled up earlier. "Why didn't you come up that way again?"

He blinked. "To better disguise our path." He indicated the drop-off not far from where they stood. "I circled around and climbed."

"You—" Hope took a few steps in that direction. Just peering over the edge made her stomach lurch. "You climbed up *that*? Without any climbing equipment? I didn't even hear you coming up!" Her glance went over him but he didn't look any more taxed than if he'd strolled up the hill. "You didn't even break a sweat!"

He gave a shrug. "It was an easy climb."

"Okay," she said, drawing the word out with another glance over the cliff. "Sure."

R'har smiled and held his hand out to her. "Come, I will set off the charges and we will enjoy our first forest together."

When R'har destroyed the ship it wasn't the tremendous attention-getting *kaboom* that Hope feared. The birds sure took off in a hurry when he set the thing off and even at this great distance she felt a startling wave of heat. For a moment there was nothing then the ship began to melt, collapsing inward on itself as it sunk into the now molten ground.

Her brow creased. "Just how hot did that thing get?"

"Hot enough to incinerate and disguise any organic material among the metal."

A sudden thought stuck her. "Along with my engagement ring?"

"It is possible I forgot to retrieve the jewel before we abandoned the ship," he rumbled.

Hope nipped her lip. "Apparently so did I." She indicated the mass of superheated metal below. "But even if the Zerar do show up they won't be able to tell us from the melted deck plating, right?"

"That was my objective, yes."

R'har led the way, intent on reaching the thickest part of the forest as quickly as possible. The land was gently rolling and a bit hilly in places, the trees hardwoods, the air cool but not chilly. It reminded Hope a bit of the Northeast in early fall, although these trees didn't show any sign of changing colors.

Except, of course, that the grass here wasn't precisely green—more like a dark seaweed color and much softer to the touch. And, while some birds came in plain brown, others glided among the branches in shades of bright scarlet, indigo, fuchsia. Even that might have seemed almost Earth-like—if their eyes didn't glow too.

The forests had their share of furred creatures as well, some in the trees, some on the ground. They didn't come across anything the size of a bear but between the lengthened snouts and unnerving otherworldly eyes of the smaller creatures watching as they passed, she really hoped they wouldn't.

"It's beautiful here." Hope breathed in the sweet, clean air. "Why did the g'hir want leave this place anyway?"

"There was no choice but to leave. The fall in population has forced us inward, closer to the homeworld. We cannot justify the expense of maintaining outpost worlds, we are spread too thinly as it is. The decision was made to abandon many of our colonies so we might better protect Hir."

"There's really no one else on this world but us?"

It was a creepy feeling, knowing that it was just two of them on the planet.

R'har gave the tree cover above them a glance. "I pray so, for then the Zerar have left orbit and are searching for us spaceside."

"If it was one of your colonies, are there still buildings standing? Or cities?"

"They are empty," he reminded. "And unmaintained. Even the largest settlements will have long since been overtaken by plant life and wild animals."

Hope swallowed hard. "We're on a world of nothing but ghost towns?"

He glanced back at her, his expression quizzical as he growled the English word. "'Ghost?'"

"Some humans believe a person's spirit gets—I don't know—*stuck* to a place when they have suffered a traumatic death or a great tragedy. That's a ghost."

"Then the Scourge has left every enclosure with such spirits." He tilted his head. "Do you fear them, then, my Hope? The spirits that humans call ghosts?"

"My parents were doctors, R'har, *scientists*," she sniffed. "They didn't believe in any of that supernatural nonsense."

He waited, his thick eyebrows raised.

"Okay, yes," she mumbled after a long moment, her cheeks warming. "Yes, I think ghosts are real."

"As do I," he rumbled solemnly. "I have sometimes felt the souls of my family around me; my father watching with pride as I hunted, my mother's hand on my cheek in times of despair, my sisters protectively following after me, even I as grew to be older than they ever did."

A lump formed in her throat. "I don't feel my parents. I used to wish that I did." She pushed her hair back behind her ears. "Of course even if they are spirits they wouldn't let me know. That would mean I was right and they were wrong and there's no way they'd admit *that*."

"They were wrong to discourage you from being the artist you longed to be."

Hope blinked. "They were just . . . they wanted me to be practical."

He gave a disapproving huff. "There is nothing practical about a life spent unhappily."

"There's nothing yippee-skippy about not having enough money to eat either, R'har."

"I am your lifemate now. You need never fear hunger again," he growled. "You may pursue any interest you wish."

Hope blinked. "Wait, you mean I'll—I mean, your mate—would be able to work on Hir? What about Jenna? Does she work?"

"I am told Ra'kur's mate intends to sell her confections in Be'lyn City." He frowned at her, looking more than a little affronted. "Did you truly think yourself nothing but breeding stock?"

"I guess I—I just assumed that—"

"There are races among our allies who separate work by gender but the g'hir do not. We do not bar females from any profession. I will always encourage you to undertake any work you wish—if it brings you happiness."

"If women are allowed to do anything—Are there any female warriors? Maybe I could do that."

She had to bite the inside of her cheek to keep from giggling at his startled—and alarmed—expression.

"It is not a common choice for a g'hir female but it is not completely unheard of in our history," he allowed reluctantly. "There are many years of training but if you wish to be a warrior, little one—"

"I'm kidding, R'har," she said, laughing at how his shoulders instantly fell in relief. "Becoming a Hir warrior is *so* not for me. I got lost taking a short walk on my own damn planet, remember? Can you imagine me out spending a year alone in the wilderness hunting? Trust me, I'm much more suited to urban life," she said with a glance at the thick woods around them. "It was *Megan's* idea that we rent a cabin or I never would have been in Brittle Bridge in the first place. Give me crazy drivers and street muggers and I'm fine. You put me in the woods and I see Death lurking behind every tree. Too many teen horror movies, I guess."

"You have nothing to fear." His glowing gaze was serious now. "I am a powerful hunter. I will provide for you. I will protect you. It is my privilege, my honor, to do so."

"Yeah, well—you could probably hike around for weeks in peace. Me? I take a ten-minute walk, get attacked by bears and kidnapped by an alien."

"Two of the creatures were young and helpless. Only the mother showed herself a threat." He gave her a smile. "And I hope the alien is less unwelcome to you than upon your first sighting."

Hope winced, suddenly remembering how she'd knelt on the wet ground, sobbing. "And you got to see me fall apart."

"Do you believe I think less of you?" he asked, surprised. "Your strength through this ordeal has astonished me."

Hope's brow creased. "You're kidding, right?"

"The attack, the crash, my injuries." He gave her a searching look. "I greatly admire how you have endured it all."

Hope gave an embarrassed half-shrug. "Yeah, well, thanks, but I don't think I handled it well at all and that's kind of a thing with me. Keeping a cool head. You know." She tugged on one of her curls meaningfully. "'Cause of the hair."

R'har gave her a puzzled look. "I do not understand."

"Because of my hair," she repeated. "Because it's red."

He looked at her blankly.

"You know—because redheads are supposed to have bad tempers. Because we're supposed to be all fiery and fly off the handle and crap."

R'har's eyebrows rose. "Humans think you ill-tempered because of the pigment in your hair?"

"Why, what do they say about redheads on your planet?"

"No g'hir has hair this color, my Hope." A fond smile touched his mouth and he reached up, his fingers just brushing the nape of her neck as he let the strands run over his fingers. "It is glorious; even now the sight of it in sunlight threatens to hold me spellbound."

She ducked her head, her cheeks hot.

He caught her wrist, his long fingers gentle. "This is a compliment."

"Yeah," she mumbled. "I guess I'm just not used to them."

His smile was a little rueful. "To the g'hir manner of compliments, you mean."

"To any." Hope avoided his bright gaze and turned to continue their walk. "So what's the plan here anyway? Now that our ride has melted into a big lump of metal?"

"The relay station is located at the base of that mountain." He indicated a summit in the distance. "It will be equipped with food, supplies, and medical equipment. From there we will send a signal to Hir and request rescue."

"Hold on, won't sending a signal let the Zerar know that we didn't die in the crash? *And* exactly where we are?"

He shook his head. "With the equipment there I can ascertain if the Zerar have left orbit. I will only send a signal if it is safe to do so."

"What if the Zerar get there first and destroy the place?" she asked, frowning. "I mean, that would keep anyone from knowing they were even here."

"This world is within our territory. If the relay goes dark, a Hironian warship will arrive swiftly to investigate. Our weapons and technology still outpace theirs. They will not risk a confrontation with one of our warships. Not for a small ship that they will think has been destroyed and a crew that has perished."

Hope glanced toward the distant mountain where the station was located. "Still, that's a hell of a hike, it'll take us days to get there. No," she amended. "It'll take *me* days to get there. How long would it take you, R'har?" she asked, curious. "If you were on your own and trying to get there fast?"

He eyed the distance. "The terrain is not challenging and the weather temperate. Six hours, perhaps seven. If not for the packs, I could carry you there easily but I am not willing to abandon our survival gear. The relay station should be intact but I prefer caution to speed." He gave a half-smile. "Besides if the Zerar look for us they would be seeking a crew moving at g'hir speed, not a human pace."

"Jeez." Her brow creased. "It must drive you crazy to have to go so slow-pokey human speed."

"I am honored—*blessed*—to walk beside you through this forest, through my life." His fanged smile was joyful, his eyes soft. "I would have it no other way." His smile faded. "Little one?"

She turned her face away quickly even though she knew he'd already seen her eyes welling up.

"Well," she said, forcing a light tone, "if we're going to have to go at *my* pace, we should get started."

Sixteen

R'har didn't chide her about her speed—or lack thereof—though she tried to keep a brisk pace. He seemed perfectly content to walk beside her, asking questions about Earth. Telling her more about Hir, about life in his clan's enclosure, about the other women who occupied it.

"Wait—" Hope broke into his story of how the next clanmother, Si'hala, had come to the enclosure the previous year. "And with her there's how many women in the Yir clan?"

"Five," he rumbled, his bright eyes warm on her. "Now six."

"But—" Hope began. "I thought you said there were a couple hundred warriors in your clan?"

"Yes, the Yir claim over three hundred."

She stopped, her hiking boots covered with Olari's dust. "There are three hundred warriors in your clan and only *five* women?"

"Six."

"Are all the enclosures like that?"

"Most. Some have more females, as many as twenty. Some as few as one or two."

Hope swallowed hard. "Are they fighting over women? I don't mean contests and challenges over one woman, I mean whole clans fighting."

"The Ruling Council has kept the peace between the enclosures," he said guardedly.

"You mean just barely, right? And human women—how does adding us into the mix change things?"

"You are our salvation," he growled. "And I vow you will be safe on Hir, little one. My clanbrothers will protect you from all threats."

"All?" She searched his face, saw how his mouth settled into a grim line. "There's something else, isn't there?"

"Not every g'hir," he began tightly, "has embraced the idea of our males lifemating with human women. There are among us some who are greatly opposed to the idea. They call themselves 'Purists.'"

Hope put her hands on her hips. "Oh, that's just fucking *grand*. A civil war brewing too? Just the kind of place to raise kids. I can't wait to hear the news about the school district."

"The Purists are a minority," he said, a little sharply. "Fools who cannot see the past will never return. They do not pose a serious threat."

"Right, just a nice, nonhazardous one."

His jaw tightened and he indicated the way ahead. "We have another two hours before evening but I scent a running stream not far from here. We will stop early and make camp."

Sighing, she followed as he made for a nearby clearing and hung back while he assembled their shelter for the night. In a few spare minutes he had the geodesic dome constructed and as soon as he finished the panels shifted in tone, perfectly blending with the landscape around it.

"Nice camouflage," She was going to have be careful not to bump into the shelter even in daylight, it blended so well. "I'm guessing it's waterproof?"

"Yes, and can withstand wind speeds of up to four hundred kilometers per hour. It will hide our thermal signatures as well from even short-range scans." He stood, holding the flap of the shelter open for her to enter.

She slid the pack from her shoulders and ducked inside. Meant to accommodate a g'hir's size, the place was certainly spacious enough. "You spent a year in one of these?"

"This is an emergency shelter," he said, taking her pack and organizing their supplies inside the space with quick efficiency. "It does not contain the comforts we will enjoy when we forest on Hir. That shelter will be larger, there will be multari to ride and to carry supplies for us. I will be able to bring a bed for you as the humans prefer."

He laid out a single sleeping pallet for them, and just watching his broad, rough hands smooth it down for them to share sent a shiver of anticipation through her.

Just then he glanced up and his vivid gaze was hot. "Hungry for pleasure, little one?" His mouth curved a bit. "Or shall I catch us dinner first?"

Her cheeks burned. "Jesus, how do you do that—know when I'm thinking about sex the exact second I do? It's seriously unnerving."

"Your breath quickens, your pupils dilate." His eyes were amused. "Your scent warms . . ."

She cleared her throat. "You must be a good hunter. Clearly I can't hide anything from you."

"I am mate-bound to you. I am greatly attuned to you, to your physical changes." He gave a wolfish grin. "And I am eager not to miss a moment of your heat."

Hope looked down, suddenly and inexplicably shy. After all, he'd seen every part of her, and with his superior senses knew what she liked probably better than she did.

In the next moment he pushed open the tent covering to go outside.

"Come," he said, offering his hand to her. "Tell me what would please you to eat and I will hunt it for you."

Hope put her hand in his and joined him outside. "You don't need to hunt, do you? Don't we have food already in the packs?"

"I cannot prove my prowess to you by unwrapping a meal bar," he said with a g'hir's snort. "What will you have? Beast? Fish? Fowl? Name it."

"I can name it, but I can't cook it," she warned. "I don't even know how to build a fire."

"To have a fire is an integral aspect of foresting." He gave a regretful look. "But tonight we cannot risk a fire attracting our enemies eyes. I will use the portable cooker to prepare our supper."

"If we can't have a fire, that means you probably shouldn't be shooting either," she said with a meaningful look at his blaster. "How are you going to hunt anything?"

His fangs flashed in a grin. "With my own hands."

"You're going to hunt without a weapon?" she asked in disbelief.

In response he pulled a knife from his belt.

"My father's," he said in response to her unspoken question. He offered it to her with obvious pride. "It is the blade of a clanfather. I have been hunting with it since I was a boy."

The blade was very sharp, about eight inches long, the heavily carved handle smooth from use.

"It's beautiful," she said honestly, handing it back.

He took the knife, his expression serious. "I am the son of a clanfather, little one, but I was too young to claim that place when he died. My father's brother assumed the role of the Yir clan's leader. His son has a lifemate, Si'hala, whom I spoke of earlier. She will be clanmother."

"Oh," Hope said, not really following. "Why do I feel like you're apologizing to me about something here?"

"Lihr captured a female before I did, claimed a lifemate first. When my uncle dies and Si'hala's mate becomes leader *she* will be clanmother."

"So if the Scourge hadn't happened or you'd been older when your father died," she said, hoping she was getting it right, "or if you'd found a wife first then you'd be ruling the clan instead of this Lihr guy?"

"Yes." His expression was guarded. "Are you disappointed that you will not have that role as you should, my Hope?"

"No," she said, surprised. "Of course not."

"There were some who protested my entering the competition to journey to your world." The tension in his shoulders didn't ease. "There are many warriors in line to be clanfather . . . who do not yet have mates."

She folded her arms. "I'm not going to throw you over to take a step up on Hironian social ladder, R'har. I'm just fine not being the lady of the castle, thanks."

"Si'hala has not yet borne a child. If she does not before my uncle dies and you do, you will be clanmother." His glowing eyes were worried. "Would being clanmother displease you greatly?"

What am I doing? It's not like I'm really thinking of staying with him.

Right?

"Boy, I just can't win here, can I?" she asked, covering her confusion with a short laugh. "Maybe we should just focus on dinner."

"As you like." He gave a nod. "What you would have me catch for you?"

Just then a flight of birds whizzed over their head, gone in an instant.

"I bet one of *them* would be tough to catch," Hope said. "Human women must be a piece of cake in comparison."

He gave a rueful smile. "It is not enough to capture a female. You must also keep her."

"I meant to ask—the drink you gave me and the cookie-thing . . . was that part of it?"

"When a female takes food and drink from his hand, it symbolizes she acknowledges that warrior's commitment to provide for her."

"Well, that makes sense—now." She considered for a moment. "Truth is I never really liked fish. So either meat or whatever on this planet tastes like chicken, I guess."

His brow furrowed. "Chicken?"

"That's a common Earth fowl. But for tonight I think meat would be great."

He gave a nod and angled his body a little away from her. His bright eyes scanned the woods, and then, sniffing the air, he went very, very still.

Hope was about to ask what he was looking at when, with an explosion of speed, he took off. There was a crash of foliage as he plunged into the woods, the quick startled cry of an animal, and then he was walking back to her, his fangs showing in a grin, the brown furred creature hanging limply in the grip of his broad hand.

"Holy hell!" she gasped, her hand over her pounding heart. "That's un-freaking-believable!"

He glanced at the animal he held. "The fregar is a small creature," he allowed. "But we will not need to bring much meat with us. The planet was stocked with other, larger Hirionian animals when it was colonized but the carcass of a larger beast will attract scavengers."

"R'har, you run like a fucking cheetah!"

His brow creased.

"Fast," she got out before he could ask what a cheetah was. "Really, really—*fast*. I mean, I thought you were moved fast on Earth, but jeez, you're—!"

R'har's glowing eyes blinked.

"Never mind." Hope shook her head. "Okay, so, yeah . . . you know"—she indicated the fregar he held—"good job hunting there."

He gave her the same boyish grin he had on board the ship when she'd asked him if he'd caught her.

"I am glad it pleases you." His eyes shone. "I would bring down any beast you ask, my Hope."

She smiled back, knowing for once this was a g'hir's idea of a compliment and a half, then glanced at the long-snouted creature with a dubious look. "You said you're gonna cook, though, right?"

SEVENTEEN

Thankfully R'har took the creature far from their campsite to butcher it, returning only with strips of meat ready to be cooked.

He brought water from the stream for them to drink and set a light inside the shelter for them to eat by, though they hardly needed it. As soon as the suns set the moons, easily fifteen of them in various phases, shone light down on their little clearing.

"That was delicious," she said, wiping the juices from her fingers on a cloth he had given her for the purpose. "You really are a good hunter. And a good cook too."

"On Hir fathers instruct their sons to hunt and cook, how to forest. I recall fondly the early lessons my father taught me. I often wished I could show my father the hunter I became." He gave her a shy smile. "I am honored to show my mate."

"We have that in common, you know," she said suddenly. "I grew up without a dad too."

R'har's expression became troubled. "I knew your sire had died. I did not realize it was when you were so young."

"Oh, he didn't die when I was a kid." She focused on the hand cloth, rubbing harder to get her nails clean. "He took off."

"Took '*off*'?"

"Yeah, he met some woman, decided he didn't want me and my mom anymore, and walked out."

He shook his head. "I do not understand."

"He walked out," she repeated. "He left us and went to live with another woman."

R'har was still frowning in confusion.

"He, uh, picked another mate."

R'har blinked. "I thought human males were monogamous. Like g'hir."

"Oh, believe me," Hope said with short laugh, "human males are definitely *not* monogamous. And certainly not the ones *I* pick."

"Your sire, he . . . *abandoned* his lifemate?" R'har looked as if it were a struggle just to get the words out. "Deserted his offspring?"

"Yeah. I was eight when he left."

"Human males . . . they do this *'take off'* often?"

"I don't know about often, but it happens, sure."

"But . . ." R'har's frown deepened. "Who hunted for you, little one? For you and your mother?"

"My mom was a physician. She made good money and my dad sent money to support me." Hope shrugged. "We were okay."

"But did he not regret this?" R'har persisted. "Grieve without end for you both?"

"My father?" she scoffed. "I don't think he even missed us. Truth is, I didn't know him that well. I saw him maybe every couple of months, even less after he got remarried. But then they—he and his new wife—got divorced right before I went off to college. I used to think that I'd get to know him when—" She shook her head. "But by the time I had what he called 'a respectable job' he'd gotten sick. He didn't even tell me how serious it was, and the next thing I knew the hospital was calling me as next of kin."

"Do you remember anything of him as a child?" he asked gently. "A memory that brings you comfort?"

She snorted. "He said I was a typical redhead, just like my mom."

"I am sorry he did not protect your home as he should have."

"I don't think I ever really had one—a home, I mean," she said thickly. "I lived with my mom but she was gone so much with work. I sometimes thought she felt like she got stuck behind to raise me. Like she was just going through the motions until I was old enough to go to college so she could go back to her life before she got married, before things went wrong. That's what I was"—she looked away—"what I was *supposed* to have with Brian. A home, a real home, with kids' parties and the house all done up for holidays and flowers planted in the spring and a bench I painted sitting on the porch and—and—"

"I will give you all that." R'har caught her hands in his, his glowing gaze intent. "All that you ever wished for."

Abruptly she pulled her hands away and pushed herself up. She shoved the shelter flap away, scarcely aware of Olari's cool air, the grass under her boots as she plunged into the night.

She was walking fast, almost running. The light breeze of this alien world was chill against her cheeks, her arms folded against the tightness in her chest.

She was well away from the campsite now but Hope heard him behind her and spoke sharply over her shoulder. "I need a few minutes alone, okay?"

"No," he growled. "It is not. I will not leave you unprotected."

"Damn it, I'm talking about five minutes here!"

"You are my responsibility. Mine to keep safe."

She rounded on him. "No, damn it, I'm not, R'har! You keep going on and on about this lifemated stuff like I ever said yes!"

He stopped where he was. "Why can you not envision my home as your own? With me as your mate?"

"Look, I have done some *stupid* things in my life but this—us—is never going to work! It *can't*!"

"How can you say this?" he growled, angry now. "We speak always as friends. We eagerly take pleasure in each other. I have bound myself to you. Why do you refuse me as lifemate?"

"You fucking *kidnapped* me! You shot me and took me off my planet! I'm sorry, R'har, but there's something about that just screams 'relationship red flag' to me! Don't you understand? I didn't choose this! I didn't choose you!"

"*You* choose only worthless males so it will not matter if you lose them!" His fangs flashed in the moonlight and his voice rose to a roar. "You are afraid to choose me because in your heart you know *I* am not worthless!"

The words hung in the air and Hope's mouth parted, her hands pressing hard to her stomach.

All of them, Brian, John, even her first boyfriend Claude, all cheaters, all liars, but she knew—every time she *knew* in her gut—that there was something wrong. The little lies she caught them in that hid even bigger ones. She ignored her own intuition even when it was screaming at her. Even her so-called friends, like Megan, like Keri—she *knew* she couldn't trust them, that they wouldn't be there for her. That was how she kept anyone from getting close; she knew deep down she could never really trust any—

"He did not leave because your hair is red," R'har growled.

"What?" Her head came up. "What did you say?"

"Your father. He did not leave because your hair is red."

What he was saying didn't make any sense. She shook her head but tears still blurred her vision.

"In your heart you believe that his leaving was your fault somehow," he rumbled softly. "But it is not."

The whole idea that she, as a small child—that her fucking hair color—could have had anything to do with her parents splitting up or their unhappiness was just *ludicrous* but R'har kept looking at her with those eerie glowing eyes that saw way too much.

Hope sat down hard in the dirt of an alien world.

"Yeah," she murmured. "I *do*. Deep down I guess I always have." She looked up at R'har in bewilderment. "But how could you know that? G'hir aren't"—her brow creased—"mindreaders, are they?"

"Do you think I—a warrior of Hir—do not understand grief? That I was not tempted to hide myself away so that I need never know it again?" He sat beside her. "I felt the same guilt, the same responsibility, when my mother and sisters died."

"But they were killed by the Scourge, by a plague that killed billions!" She shook her head again. "My father—I went to his office after school and I found him with someone else. He lied, right to my face, saying I'd gotten it wrong, that they were only friends."

"Did you tell your mother what you witnessed?" he asked quietly.

Hope felt her throat closing. "I didn't know what to do, what to think. Jesus, I was only eight! I acted like everything was okay but I knew he was lying to Mom, pretending that when he got a phone call it wasn't his girlfriend on the other end. And it just got worse, no matter how I tried to make it okay, how good I tried to be. One day he just announced at dinner he didn't want to do 'this family thing' any more. He got up, packed some stuff, and left. You know what he meant by 'family thing'? He meant *me*. You lost your mother, R'har, and your sisters but at least you know they didn't *want* to leave you. How could you ever think you were responsible?"

"Whenever we lose someone important to us we look to ourselves to cast the blame. I could not bring my father back from despair. He sat beside my mother's grave until he was so weak he was forced to lie upon the ground. One morning I went to bring him tea and found him there. In his face I saw peace but I stood beside him keening. I thought, if I'd only come sooner, if I'd made the warriors carry him inside whether he wanted to go or not . . ."

"You weren't responsible, you couldn't—I mean, you were just a little boy—"

His hand, solid, strong, and warm, enveloped hers. "For my sake you see a child for whom the burden of adult problems proved too heavy. In yourself, you see only fault."

He was right. She could see in him still the little boy whose world was shattered by war and disease. How could she, as an eight-year-old girl, have fixed anything between her parents? Or been the cause of their unhappiness?

Suddenly as if the light of Olari's moons brightened her inner vision, she saw that it hadn't been about her at all. She could bet that even if she had never been born, her parents, brilliant though they were, would have wound up unhappy anyway.

She'd been carrying that, the guilt, the feeling of not being good enough, not important enough even to her own parents, for such a very long time. She'd based her whole self-image on it—on trying not to be the girl her dad left, the child her mom got stuck raising. On taking so much less than she deserved just so she could be loved, even if that meant giving up the art she loved, even if it meant not being herself at all.

Like I've been looking at myself in some twisted and warped mirror . . .

"I was so mad at them," she said hoarsely. "I never even realized how mad until now. Mad at my dad 'cause he left; mad at my mom too, even though I know it wasn't her fault. Mad 'cause neither one of them really accepted me for who I was. Were you angry with your father when he died?" she asked. "Because he just gave up and left you?"

R'har looked out over the moonlit land. "No and I understand even better now why he had to follow my mother." His fingers brushed her cheek, his glowing eyes soft on her. "When a g'hir male takes a lifemate, he loves very deeply."

Tears blurred her vision. "R'har . . ."

"I know." His mouth curved but it was the saddest smile she'd ever seen. "I am not human so you can never love me. But I am a g'hir warrior, my Hope, and you are my lifemate. I will love you for always."

"Damn it." Her tears overflowed then. "Oh, Goddamn it. . ."

He sighed. "Do your eyes water in pity for me, little one? Because I cannot be human for you as I long to be?"

"No," she said roughly. "Because it doesn't fucking matter anymore."

His brow creased as she took a deep breath and intertwined her fingers with his. She'd spent almost a lifetime trying to set things up so she wouldn't get hurt and yet she still always did. But this was harder than anything she'd ever done before, so hard to let him in and let herself risk her whole heart because—

"I love you too, R'har."

Eighteen

His eyes went wide. "You—?"

"I love you."

"I thought you could never . . ." R'har shook his head looking dazed then as if he were afraid to even ask, "Do you . . . mean this?"

"Oh, God, yes. I love you." She gave a half-laugh, half-sob. "I'll say it all night if you need me to."

Suddenly, as if her words had finally filtered through his shock, he caught her face between his hands.

"My little one." He touched his forehead to hers. "My Hope . . ."

And then his mouth was on hers, his rumble-purr drawing a moan of pleasure from her. She breathed in the spicy scent of him as he lowered her to the downy soft, cool grass.

She was eager, impatient to feel him inside her, but he was tantalizingly slow this time, brushing his nose to hers, kissing her until she was breathless. His fingers trailed the length of her throat to cup her breast through the fabric of her shirt and he caught her hand before she could undo the buttons.

"No," he murmured. "Allow me."

One by one he undid them, leisurely undressing her. She shivered as the last of her clothing came away and he freed himself quickly of his own.

He paused over her. "I want to look at you," he rumbled. "Just for a moment."

His face was shadowed above, his eyes with their green glow piercing, and she gave a breathless laugh. "You can barely see me."

"I can see you perfectly." He bent his head to her breast then his warmth was on her, his heat blocking the chill of the night air, his bare flesh smooth against hers. "And you are exquisite.

"Your fine bones, your breasts, your spo—" His fangs flashed in a hot smile. "*Freckles.* How they dapple your skin here—" His lips brushed her breast bone. "Then you fade to white . . . then pink," he purred, his breath hot against her skin for an instant before the moist heat of his mouth covered her nipple.

Hope gasped, her hands coming up to thread through his hair, but he drew away, his thumb tracing the other peak, watching her reaction, his rumbling-purr sending her arousal soaring. She hooked her leg around his hip, the insistent heat between her legs urging her on, moving against him as his sound thrummed through her.

"R'har, you're making me crazy!"

"Good," he rumbled.

"Please . . ."

"Hmm, I like this, little one." His voice grew huskier as his fingers slid to her cleft. "To hear you begging me for your pleasure . . ."

The smart retort that flashed through her mind vanished as he found her clit and Hope's mouth parted as he stroked her. Her center was so tight now; she was only a moment from coming.

"So ready . . ." he groaned.

His green eyes glowed eerily under Olari's many moons, his blond hair robbed of its golden hue by the cool light as he positioned his cock at her opening, holding her gaze as he entered her.

He bent forward to gently brush his nose against hers. Caught between the hardness of his body and the softness of the grass beneath, she parted her mouth in pleasure as he slid inside her, his rumble-purr vibrating through her clit with every stroke.

Wild with it, his gaze burned into hers and he bared his fangs as he plunged deeply within her, claiming her as his own with each stroke. Hope cried out as she came, his rumbling carrying her along, deepening and extending her climax even as he rode her, roaring, to his own pulsing release.

He bent his head, his cheek to hers, his breath ragged, his body still trembling as he settled beside her to gather her into his arms.

Hope lay in R'har's embrace looking up at the moons, at the mind-bending number of stars above, the soft grass of an alien world under her, nestled close enough to feel his strong heartbeat against her cheek.

"I could fall asleep right here," she murmured.

He purred, cradling her closer. "And I feel great contentment in watching you sleep."

"Like you did back on Earth, at the cabin?" she asked. "I know g'hir ways are different but I guess—I guess I just don't understand, really understand, *why* you did that. Stood at my bedside all night, I mean."

He gave a huff of surprise. "To offer myself to you, little one. To stand guard over you so that you might rest easy in the night. To place my strength between you and the dangers of your world. I kept my senses sharp, alert to any threat to you. I gave this of myself, willingly. I would give more," he rumbled, his luminous gaze serious. "I would give my last breath to protect you . . ."

Hope tightened her arms around him. "I love you, R'har."

"And I you." His lips brushed her temple. "My Hope."

She closed her eyes, letting herself relax against him, the sound of his heartbeat soothing her. She had searched her whole life for this, for someone she could let her guard down with, let into her heart . . .

He stroked her back. "Are you warm enough?"

She smiled against his shoulder. "Except my feet. Maybe next time I'll leave my hiking boots on. The extra traction might be fun too."

She thought he would chuckle at that but instantly he was sitting up, gathering her things.

"We should return to the campsite," he rumbled. "I have kept you out in the night air too long. Your physiology makes you more susceptible to this chill than I am."

"I'm fine," she protested, though without his heat next to her in the grass it was pretty freaking cold on the ground. "Just lie down."

"You are shivering." R'har already had her things assembled and his growl brooked no argument. "Here, I will help you to dress quickly."

She sighed. "Okay, but just to be clear for future reference—this is *not* a satisfactory amount of cuddling."

She stood, placing her hands on his shoulders for balance as he knelt before her, the grass chilly beneath her feet. He held her underwear for her to step into and slid the panties up to her hips, his fingers tracing the sides of her legs. His hands brushed her breasts as he helped her into her bra, lingering for an instant over her nipples. He helped her into her jeans and she trembled a little as he pulled the tee shirt over her head, his hands smoothing the fabric to her hips, then fastened the buttoned shirt over it.

He knelt again, naked in the moonlight, to slide her feet into her boots, quickly tying the laces and looked up at her breathless laugh.

"I'm sorry," she said. "I never thought it would be so hot to have someone put my clothes *on*."

His fangs flashed in a grin and R'har got to his feet, his cock again at full stand. He pulled her against him and lowered his mouth to hers, the sweet cinnamon taste of him and rumbling purr bringing her right back to readiness.

"I must stop," he murmured against her mouth, his rumble-purr lowering in volume as if he were willing himself to it. "Or I will have you here beneath me again, despite the chill."

"I don't mind."

"I do."

"Then let's get back to camp quick, okay?" she suggested as he reluctantly let her go.

He gave a soft huffing chuckle as he bent to retrieve his clothes. "I will carry you back and you will see just how fast I truly can run."

Nineteen

Hope stirred and reached for R'har only to find his place beside her on the sleeping pallet empty.

Off hunting again probably.

She smiled sleepily and arched her back in a stretch, still amazed at how comfortable this sleeping pallet was. She hadn't been kidding when she said she hated camping but two days out and she could understand why the g'hir loved "foresting."

This wasn't camping. This was marvelous.

Then again, she was with R'har, and he could make anything fun.

He was eager, proud, to prove his skills as a hunter, a provider, a protector. Each morning he prepared her breakfast, some of it from the supplies he carried, some from fruit he'd picked or an animal he'd hunted.

R'har would pack up while she ate and by the time they headed on toward the relay station there wasn't a trace of their campsite left. They would break at midday and rest a few times in between. Before sunset he would have their new camp made and the evenings were spent in talk and lovemaking.

She almost didn't want to be rescued—

Hope sat up as R'har came into the tent, smiling and bringing a plate and the mouthwatering smell of breakfast with him.

She smiled back. "What's this? More repari?"

"Because it pleases you so," he agreed.

He'd included some grains from the packs that reminded her a bit of grits but she quickly dug in to the meat, closing her eyes in pleasure at the first succulent taste.

"I will hunt more for you tonight," he growled in amusement. "You do not need to lick your fingers raw."

"R'har," she said around a mouthful of repari and pointing at her plate, "this stuff is like the best maple-bacon-baby-back-rib *yum* ever. Seriously, you could put a steakhouse out of business with it."

"I am very glad this animal is plentiful on Yir lands." He gave a huffing chuckle as he packed up around her. "Or I would be forced to encroach on another enclosure's land to hunt it for you."

Hope ducked her head over her breakfast. It was crazy to think that she trusted someone so completely who wasn't even human, that she could open herself up to an alien she hadn't even known for an entire week. That she could know herself truly safe with him when her own kind had lied to her, deceived her, used her. But with every passing hour the idea—once so absolutely *absurd*—of giving up returning to Earth to live on an alien world instead, even actually having a half-alien baby seemed, well . . .

Not absurd at all.

And R'har would make a great dad, not like hers had been—

"We are but a day's walk at most from the relay." His words jarred her out of imagining a little one with R'har's luminescent green eyes. "We will almost certainly reach it by late afternoon tomorrow. There will be a real bed for you within its walls."

"I don't mind." She grinned. "I'm kinda liking roughing it."

She sought to draw him down beside her on the pallet and while he kissed her with equal heat, he gave a low groan of protest and caught her hand when she stroked his shaft, already at full stand, through his clothes.

"The sun will be high before we leave if we linger any longer," he reminded, his voice hoarse. "If we delay we will not likely reach the relay by tomorrow at all."

His molten green gaze was conflicted, his cock rock hard against her hand. One more light stroke would have him throwing his good intentions away and forgetting all about the relay.

He was inexperienced enough that he probably didn't even know if it was okay to ask her to wait and he also took his role as her protector very seriously.

She just wasn't playing fair here.

"All right." She let him go but she gave a smirk. "You're off the hook. For now."

His glance went to her breasts and she saw him swallow.

"I guess you should go break camp while I get dressed," she said with a shrug.

"Yes, the camp . . ." he mumbled and Hope, never the beauty or the heartbreaker, allowed herself a grin as R'har, flushed and utterly distracted, pushed his way out of the shelter.

They made camp just at the edge of the forest late that afternoon. There was a stream nearby and R'har, smiling, took her hand and led her there.

She watched from the shore as he waded in.

"You just want me here so you can show off, don't you?" she called, smiling.

Over his shoulder he threw her a half-amused, half-exasperated look. "Yes. Now you must be quiet or you will scare off our supper, little one."

"Oh, right, sorry," she said in a stage whisper.

He threw her a last lighthearted look then turned his attention to the water.

In the fading light of day his big body went very still, the stream moving around his legs. The trees rustled above but R'har didn't even twitch a muscle as time went on.

Hope didn't have half his patience and she was about to call out again, suggest that since it was getting dark they just make do with what they had back at the camp, when his hand shot downward into the water like a striking cobra.

Even partly expecting it, Hope gasped at his speed; he straightened and tossed the fish onto the bank at her feet.

With a yelp Hope scrambled back from the writhing thing.

R'har laughed and joined her on the bank. He bent to scoop up the fish by the tail and held it high for her approval.

"Very—" she said, holding her hands in front of her as the fish made one last squirm and flung droplets of stream water at her. "Nice. I mean, really, wow. I've never seen anyone fish like that."

He dropped a kiss to her mouth and took her hand with his free one. "How do humans fish?"

"Well, I've been fishing exactly *never* but usually humans tie a hook to a string then put something the fish will be interested in eating on the hook. When the fish bites it the hook catches in its mouth and you pull the fish out."

He gave a dismissive *snorf*. "It does not sound very challenging."

"Yeah, well, I'm sure I'm making it sound a hell of a lot easier than it is," she allowed. "And I'm not exactly a fish fan."

"You will like this fish very much." He gave her a confident look. "Once I have prepared it for you. It is the one that tastes most like game."

The sun had set now but there was no chance *he* would get them lost. The forest was bright with moonlight and even if it hadn't been R'har's night vision was tons better than any human's.

"This really is a beautiful place," Hope said as they walked hand in hand, tiny, harmless phosphorescent bugs flittering among the branches above. "The forests, the rivers. And all these moons—it's just amazing!"

"Hir has only three moons, but the environment on this part of the planet is not so different from the Atarra valley, where the Yir lands are located."

"Yeah, but here it's just you and me. I'm kinda liking having this whole world as a playground just for us."

"I too." He gave her hand a gentle squeeze. "But I promise there will be much time for play when you are safely on Hir. The winter gathering is coming. There is so much to see in the cities, our museums have much to offer an artist to enjoy."

"It sounds great," she murmured. "Makes me not want to go home."

R'har stopped short, his wide glowing gaze searching her face. "Hope?"

"I mean it," she said thickly. "I mean it, R'har. I've thought about it. I can't *stop* thinking about it and I-I want to stay with you. On Hir."

He closed his eyes for an instant, his expression almost pained.

Hope shifted her weight, made uneasy by his odd reaction and by his silence. "I thought you would be happy that I want to stay with you."

"I cannot express the joy I feel," he growled roughly. "My heart overflows with it."

"Oh," she said, her brow furrowed. "So, then what was that a second ago? With you shutting your eyes like that?"

"I thanked the All Mother," he rumbled, his hand cupping her cheek. "I lift my heart in thanks to the Goddess for the gift of you, my Hope."

He bent down and lightly brushed her nose with his, the gentlest of g'hir kisses, then covered her mouth with his own in a human kiss.

Hope smiled up at him as he drew away. "Well, it's settled then. Though I wouldn't mind a few more days here." With this much moonlight the mountain with the relay was visible, though she couldn't see the station itself but they would be there tomorrow. "Once we send the message, how long before a ship arrives to take us to Hir?"

"I do not know," he admitted. "Our ships patrol the borders regularly but a warship's arrival will depend on its proximity to Olari, but it will not be long. Though the ship may have to complete its patrol before it can carry us to Hir."

She bit her lip. "I'm nervous about going, you know. I mean, there's no one back home who'll really miss me. Some people might wonder where I've gone off to but they certainly won't tear up the countryside looking. It's just . . . you're the only g'hir I've ever met. And what you told me about the Purists—"

"The great majority of my people are eager for the arrival of human women," he reminded. "Little one, you are a treasure to our enclosure. They will welcome you as their clansister with great joy."

"Still . . ." The campsite was just ahead and it was growing a little chilly. Truth to tell she was looking forward to ducking into the warm shelter. "I've got so much to learn about your people."

"I will teach you," he promised. "It will be my joy to teach you. To show you all that my world has to offer."

"You're going to teach me to read Hironian, right?" she asked dryly. "'Cause not being able to read your language is really annoying."

"I do not understand why your chip is not allowing visual translation as well." He looked troubled now. "I can read English. This has not been an issue with other races."

"Guess humans are special," she said with a laugh, already around the shelter, her hand reaching for the flap to enter. "But you probably already—"

Hope broke off, her breath rushing out of her lungs as two beings emerged from the tree line. Physically they were humanoid, nearly as tall as R'har but bulkier, clumsier and hairless, their small-eyed faces vicious even in the twilight. They wore no clothes—she couldn't honestly guess if they were male or female—but straps around their bodies held both equipment and weapons in addition to the blasters in their meaty grips.

Those black eyes fixed on her and as one their mouths opened. Her eyes widened as their jaws fell to an unbelievable width, wide as snakes consuming prey, their teeth as long and thick as a man's thumb, their tongues long and pointed. Hope made a choking sound of horror as secondary mouths on their bare chests also opened, revealing equally sharp teeth.

These creatures were nightmares, the very image of demons.

R'har's growl rose to a hate-filled snarl and Hope knew those *things* were Zerar.

TWENTY

With unholy shrieks the Zerar raised their weapons and, roaring, R'har threw himself at them. The blue light of weapons' fire blinded her and Hope's hands instinctively came up to protect her face.

There was the awful sound of crunching bones and tearing sinew, a body hitting the ground hard.

In the next instant something hit her square in the belly, knocking the breath out of her lungs and lifting her right off her feet.

Then she was hanging forward, the blur of moonlit ground speeding by under her. Dazed, it took her an instant to realize R'har had swung her over his shoulder, his arm around her knees to keep firm hold of her as he ran full out.

Hope gripped the leather of his jacket to steady herself, trying not to be sick. He plunged into the forest, zigzagging as he ran, and with every change of direction her hip hit painfully against the bone of his shoulder.

"R'har, I—"

"Quiet!" he hissed without breaking his pace.

Hope pressed her lips together and kept her jaw clenched to keep silent against the bruising blows to her hip. For a long time there was nothing but the ground blurring by, the sound of his footfalls, the crush of leaves and twigs beneath.

Hope gasped as icy water splashed her face. He'd plunged into a stream, running still, then they were out of the water and back into the woods, but the branches above must be far denser, enough so that they blocked the moons' light because she couldn't see the ground at all now.

R'har stumbled a bit in the darkness and instinctively her hold on his jacket tightened. He trotted a few more paces then stopped. Even he, g'hir that he was, was breathing hard and ragged after *that* run. Blades of soft grass suddenly came into her view again, lit by Olari's strong moonlight as he stopped just at the edge of a clearing.

He paused and she knew he was listening for sounds of pursuit. Motion sick from the upside down journey, Hope had to focus her full attention on just keeping the roasted fregar from lunch from making an appearance.

R'har bent to set her on her feet but she couldn't stay there. Her head still spinning, Hope landed hard on her butt in the dirt.

"Are you hurt?" R'har rasped, squatting down to peer at her. "Little one, are you hurt?"

"Oh man," she groaned. She pressed her palms down into the ground at her sides, trying to fight off the nausea. "No, but my stomach sure isn't happy right now . . ." She grimaced. "And in the *dark*. Jeez, let's not do that again, okay?"

He pushed himself up to stand, facing back the way they'd come.

"I do not hear them on foot. I do not hear a scout ship." His breath was still coming hard but he sniffed deeply, then again. "I do not scent their stench on the breeze at all. We have eluded them—for now."

"Those were Zerar?" Hope shuddered. "Ugly fucks, aren't they?"

"Yes," he spat. "With souls as hideous and twisted as their forms."

Hope shook her head. "I thought—I mean, it's been days! I really thought they'd given up on us."

"They should have long since left this system." His hands clenched into fists. "They should not have such interest in one small ship!"

"R'har, they saw me," Hope whispered, ice running through her veins. "Those two back there. They saw me. They know I'm not g'hir."

"It does not matter. They are dead."

"But my world, Earth . . ." It had happened so fast she hadn't even seen most of it and was really glad too. "Are you *sure*? That you killed them, I mean? You have to be sure."

"I killed them."

R'har snarl was so fierce she lifted her head to look up at him. "Are you okay?"

"They threatened you." His fists were still clenched, his body so tense it was trembling, his fangs white in the moonlight. "That filth raised their weapons against *you*!"

"I'm okay," she assured. "Really."

"I broke their necks but they did not deserve such quick deaths." His lips were drawn back, his face savage, alien. "I should have made them suffer!"

Hope wet her lips. "R'har, you're scaring me."

His glowing eyes blinked, his brow furrowed. "You need never fear me."

"I don't mean—I know you'd never hurt *me*. I just—you kinda look like you wish you'd torn their heads off or something."

For an instant his expression said that he would have preferred that exactly but then his face softened.

"You are my lifemate, my little one, my Hope," he growled with warm overtones of that rumble-purr of his. "I cannot bear the idea of a threat to you. You are everything to me."

"I'm fine." Hope pushed herself up to stand and spread her arms to show him. "See?"

"Hope—"

"I'm fine," she repeated.

His knees buckled.

"R'har!" She tried to catch him but all she managed to do was fall with him.

He gave a low moan, his body curling in toward his left side.

"What is it?" she cried. "I can't see!"

She fumbled around at his pockets and found the mini-lumina there.

"No! The Zerar will—"

"Fuck the Zerar!" She got the lumina working and shone the light on his side. Her eyes widened at the wounds, at the blood he was losing. "You were shot?" she gasped. "They *shot* you? Damn it, R'har! Why didn't you tell me?"

"You are safe." He shook his head. "You are all that matters."

"The medical kit," she muttered, pushing to stand. "There's a medical kit back at the camp—"

He caught her before she could gain her feet, his eyes wild. "No."

"Let go!" she cried, struggling against his hold. "They're dead, you said so yourself! Let go! I have to go back for the fucking—"

"No!" His grip tightened. "They will not have sent only two soldiers, there will be more. More on this world now, hunting us. You cannot return to the campsite."

"Then tell me what to do here!" He didn't reply and she pushed her hair out of her face. "We should—I'll tear my shirt, yours too, we'll bind it and then—"

"Little one—" He gave her wrist a tug to get her attention, his breath coming in wheezes now. "The relay station. Hide yourself from them . . . find it . . ."

"I am *not* leaving you." Hope's nostrils flared. "I won't ever leave you."

He gave a choked sound. "And I would give anything—not to leave you . . ."

"There'll be medical supplies at the relay station, R'har. We just have to get there, okay? We've just got to figure out how to stop the bleeding long enough to—"

"Zerar weapons prevent the blood from clotting, there is no stopping it now. My beloved . . ." He cupped her cheek in his warm palm and his growl was forced now. "I am dying."

"No." Hope shook her head, her vision blurring. "No!"

"Do not make tears. I will not have you blame yourself . . . and I will not have you grieve for me. I do not deserve it." His face was ragged as his hand slipped from her cheek. "It is my fault you are here . . . that you are—in danger—the ship—"

"This is *not* your fault, R'har." She pressed harder, but his blood continued to flow between her fingers. "You were working as fast as you could!"

"No, it was—my doing—"

"No, R'har." Was he in shock or something? "Don't you remember? The ship was damaged when we jumped away from Earth. You were making repairs—"

"I vowed to you." He caught her wrist again but his grip was weak now, his gaze desperate, startlingly bright in the moonlight. "Promised—to tell you. The ship . . . was not damaged."

"But you said—I mean the repairs you were—"

Hope searched his eyes, his wretched, raw expression.

"You lied," she breathed. "You lied to me."

His eyes shut briefly. "Yes," he croaked.

"The communications array . . ." she remembered. "You said—you said it was too damaged to call for help but then during the attack you used it. I *knew* and I just—just like always I—" She shook her head again. The hurt of it, the betrayal, was like a knife twisting in her gut. "But . . . why, R'har? Why tell me that we were stranded? Why pretend that the ship needed repairs?"

"I thought . . . if you came to love me . . ." His fingers intertwined with hers. "You would not wish to return to your world."

"Fucking hell!" Hope yanked her hand away. "How could you do that to me?" she cried. "Manipulate me like that? How could you *lie* like that? You're just like my—I trusted you! You were the only one I actually opened—" She clenched her fists. "I fucking *trusted* you!"

"I believed us safe in g'hir space. I promised—tell you . . ." He closed his eyes and his voice became a murmur. "I have failed you . . . I die shamed that I leave you unprotected, my lifemate . . ." His head fell back. "My Hope . . ."

"Oh, no, you fucking *don't*!" She shook her head violently. "You are not going to smash my heart into a million pieces and then leave me alone on this godforsaken rock! You promised if I wanted to go home you'd take me, and you are going to fucking *keep* that promise, R'har!"

He didn't answer and she shook him hard. "R'har! Don't you leave me!"

He was limp, his head lolling.

"No . . ." she whispered.

There was a sound then, the crunch of leaves and twigs beneath a heavy footfall, and then more, headed this way, closing in.

Hope scrambled for R'har's weapon and twisted, raising the blaster to face the Zerar.

Come on, you ugly fuckers.

Their shadowy forms were visible now, advancing toward her through the woods. Hope's grip tightened on the weapon. There were easily a dozen of them, maybe more.

Her hand rested on R'har's chest, his heart stuttering under her palm. They stepped into the clearing then, their huge forms visible now by the moons' light.

Hope let out a strangled sob as their alien eyes fixed on her.

They were g'hir warriors.

TWENTY-ONE

"How is he?"

It was the same question Hope had asked for the past twelve hours but the doctor—a g'hir too—showed no impatience with her. Doctor Ki'san was about R'har's age, one of the younger males on board the Hironian warship but a skilled and compassionate healer. His hair was dark, almost black, his glowing eyes amber in color.

Those amber eyes regarded the scrolling readouts over the biobed where R'har lay. "His condition is unchanged."

As soon as the medical staff cleared her Hope had taken up vigil at his bedside. R'har, the sole patient in the warship's sickbay, lay with his face obscured by a breathing mask, constantly monitored by the medical team. The complexity of this equipment made what he'd had aboard his ship look like a first aid kit. According to Doctor Ki'san, R'har's new internal organs—cloned and grown here to replace the ones so badly damaged by the Zerar's weapons—showed every sign of functioning properly.

She watched the Hironian symbols scroll by. She still couldn't read them but she'd been looking at them so long now that some were starting to look familiar. The three-dimensional holo image representing R'har's health status still remained a reassuring blue.

By the time the search party got them back to the shuttle and into the care of the medic onboard, R'har had weakened to the point of needing total life support. She sat at his side, murmuring to him, encouraging him to fight, to live, as the shuttle made the painfully slow trip to the orbiting warship.

R'har had been hemorrhaging internally even as he raced through the forests of Olari with her swung over his shoulder. Doctor Ki'san was astonished that, with his injuries, R'har survived long enough to make it onboard the warship.

And he hadn't regained consciousness.

From the shuttle crew's talk Hope knew the Zerar, confronted with the g'hir warship's superior firepower, had swiftly retreated from Hironian space.

The men onboard the Hironian warship were every bit as huge as R'har and some stood even taller than he. In their midst even Hope felt positively petite but it was their attitude toward her that was really jolting.

One of the youngest warriors in the rescue party had stopped short, transfixed, upon seeing her when she turned to face him. His commander's barked order had him ducking his head but even as he passed the spot where she knelt at R'har's side he snuck little glances at her.

Every last one of them did.

Whether it was because she was female or human or—seeing the way even the commander's eyes lingered on her curls—the color of her hair, she couldn't help but feel their intense awareness of her.

It wasn't as if they were rude, everyone made a great show of respect, careful to call her "Mata"—the g'hir term for an honored female. But when their eyes fell on R'har, it was plain these warriors were trying to judge his likelyhood of survival, subtly eyeing each other, each weighing his own chances of winning her, should R'har die.

"You have been here for nearly thirteen hours," Doctor Ki'san growled quietly as he came to stand beside her. "The captain has vacated his quarters. He offers them for your use for the remainder of our journey to Hir." He indicated the medical suite's exit. "There is an honor guard to escort you there and a hot meal awaits you. Go and rest, Mata. I will contact you if there is any change in his condition."

Hope glanced that way and one of the medics by the door dropped his gaze to pretend he hadn't been staring at her.

"Once I'm sure R'har will be all right. Once I know that . . ." Hope shook her head. "Right now, Doctor, you just worry about him."

Ki'san raised his eyebrows. "Your health is my responsibility as well."

"Right, I forgot. Human females are valuable breeding stock."

"Hope—*Mata*," he corrected, "my interest in you is for your own sake, not what value you might have as a mate."

"Jesus." Hope shut her eyes briefly. "Not you too."

"I am sorry." Doctor Ki'san's rippled brow creased. "I do not understand."

"Listen, I'm not looking for someone to take R'har's place." She sent a meaningful glance at another medic who was trying hard to look suddenly absorbed in the medical equipment in front of him, at the guards who continuously glanced her way. "Everyone seems to be waiting around, just in case R'har doesn't make it. They want to be first in line when I start taking applications for a new . . ." She pushed her hair back. "*Companion.*"

"I would not presume, Mata," Doctor Ki'san said, straightening. "If it came to that, I am sure Hir's mightiest warriors would be invited to battle for the privilege of courting you. I am merely a physician."

Hope blinked. "What—you mean you don't even get to try for a wife?"

"Warriors are of a higher social status and there are so few females now—if one chose me for herself that would be—" He looked away. "But that will never happen."

"I thought—" Hope frowned. "I thought among the g'hir the males picked the mates. That they captured women to prove themselves or something."

'Course what the hell did she know? That could have been just another of R'har's lies.

Her face got hot just thinking about sitting beside him as he worked, following him around the ship like a fucking puppy. Thinking that somehow she was helping him had made her feel good, remembering how much she'd enjoyed their talks . . .

When it was all just R'har's unbelievably calculated manipulation.

She knew better now, knew that he'd been hiding more from her than just the phony repairs. R'har had "captured" her but she got the final say-so about whether or not she stayed with him. His claim on her would end in thirteen days. Then Hir law said they had to let her return to Earth if that's what she chose.

Ki'san gave a g'hir nod. "Our traditions hold that if he can prove himself worthy after capturing her, she may choose a male as her own. But since the Scourge a female can choose for herself as well—any male would welcome a mate now. Females, even those from what were once considered less influential enclosures, now choose only the best and take only warriors as mates."

"If that's the case, why didn't you become a warrior then? You look like you could do it."

He hesitated. "I considered my path carefully. I trained, as all g'hir males do, to be a warrior until I reached seventeen summers. But while I was capable of a warrior's tasks, my heart belonged to medicine." The glance he sent her was rueful. "I do not regret my choice. I love my work. I am grateful to be able to do it but still . . ."

Ki'san was gorgeous and brilliant. He might not be a warrior—at least as the g'hir thought of them—but at nearly seven feet tall he was every bit as burly as one.

"Well, just get yourself on the next ship to Earth," she said. "Women would fight over someone like you."

"I am a physician," he repeated. "Not the son of a clanfather, not even a warrior. I would not be a choice mate."

"Hey, doctors are very highly regarded in human culture. Plenty of human women *dream* of marrying a doctor; they'd pick a doctor over a warrior any day of the week. The power to heal is considered very sexy."

It was really sweet how Ki'san's whole face lit up. Then his brow creased. "But only warriors are allowed to visit your world."

"You're pretty smart," she pointed out. "I'm sure you can figure out a way—if you really want to."

His eyes met hers and in those glowing amber depths she saw excitement, doubt, expectancy.

"Mata, would you—" He swallowed. "Would you tell me more of your world? Your culture?"

I'm as bad as that Jenna chick. Sending another one of these g'hir to kidnap some poor woman . . .

And what really sucked was that she could see Ki'san's side too. He was a beautiful, intelligent young man who wanted nothing more than to share his life with someone.

Hope passed her hand over her eyes.

Fuck, whose side am I on here?

"Mata, are you all right?" he asked, instantly concerned, his hand gently cupping her elbow. "Are you dizzy or in pain?"

"No." Hope rubbed her eyes. "I'm just tired."

"If you would consent to rest—" At her headshake he offered: "Are you hungry? I can have food brought."

"No. I'm good, thanks."

"Water perhaps? I do not think you are properly hydrated."

Before he'd cleared her Ki'san had insisted she take fluids intravenously to hydrate and balance her electrolytes and while she hadn't panicked—for the first time she could remember—she wasn't in a hurry for any more medical treatment either. "Water I'll take."

She followed one of the medics down the hall to a small galley. Apparently meant as a break area for the medical staff, it was empty, she was glad to see. She stood with the cup in her hand, her gaze fixed on the galley's windows, at the stars beyond, and she found herself surprised that it didn't make her sick anymore.

Guess I'm getting used to it. Like the g'hir.

Less than a week ago she would have—did—run screaming at the sight of one of them but now the medic who'd accompanied her seemed not just harmless, but damn near bashful.

"May I bring you more to drink?" he asked, his vivid blue eyes eager, his cheeks flushed. "Or a meal, perhaps? You have not eaten."

Probably not an accident that sounds just like the g'hir mating ritual . . .

"No," she said, handing over the now empty cup. "Thanks, I'm good."

He led the way back and she could hardly miss how every pair of glowing eyes followed her.

I'm a woman and most of them rarely even get to talk to one. I bet that none of these guys have even seen a human woman before.

And she saw it in their faces, the eagerness, the interest, the heated looks they were struggling to curtail lest they offend her and ruin their chances completely.

Each of them had an electric, sexual male beauty to him and they looked at her as if she were some sort of goddess. If R'har weren't in there, unconscious still, with a breathing mask on, if dozens of sensors weren't monitoring him to make sure whole organs didn't shut down, she'd really be enjoying this.

If he hadn't shattered her heart.

Ki'san hurried to meet her at the medcenter entrance. "R'har has regained consciousness," he said as soon as she was through the door, his hand already at her arm to lead her forward.

Hope stopped, resisting the doctor's pull, her gaze going to the observation window and the flurry of activity around R'har. "He's awake?"

"He is groggy but that is to be expected," Doctor Ki'san said. "But my readings show full brain function." He offered a smile, but it was a little pained. "I am sure with time he will make a full recovery."

Hope gave a nod. "Thank you."

She pulled her arm from his grasp and turned away.

"Mata!" Ki'san caught up to her outside the sickbay doors, his brow furrowed. "Where are you going?"

"To the quarters they're giving me."

"But—you may go inside. You may be with R'har."

"No."

"But—do you not wish to speak to him? You have been waiting—"

"No." She gave Ki'san a level look. "You're his doctor. You say he's okay and I believe you. That's all I needed."

The doctor shook his head. "I do not understand. Do you not wish to see your lifemate?"

"He's not my lifemate!" she flared. "He is not my *anything*, okay?"

Ki'san blinked down at her and she felt immediately chagrined. He had been nothing but kind, nothing but polite to her.

"I'm sorry, I shouldn't be snapping at you. But I just—" Hope let her breath out slowly. "Look, he's okay." She straightened. "And that means I'm done here."

Ki'san shook his head a little and glanced back toward the room where R'har lay. "He will want you. He will ask for you. What . . . What do you wish me to tell him?"

She couldn't go back in there.

He was a liar. Just like Brian and the others.

Just like her dad.

If she went back in there now, if she gave him even the slightest opportunity to speak to her, she knew, lovesick idiot that she was, she'd probably wind up believing anything he said, accepting any excuse he had that would make everything okay again.

She wanted him to make it okay, so very badly, even if it meant closing her eyes to everything, just like she always did . . .

"Tell R'har—" Hope wet her lips. "Tell him whatever was between us is finished now. Tell him—I never want to see him again."

TWENTY-TWO

R'har cracked his eyes open. His body felt heavy, battered, and sore, and his vision swam as he tried to focus. He squinted against the brightness, the irritation making his eyes water like hers sometimes did.

He heard the reassuring growls of the Hironian language, the smell of his own kind, and the soft, sweet promise of—

"Hope . . ."

His voice sounded weak and muffled to his own ears. His vision was blurred and his glance darted about, seeking her with all his senses, but whatever covered his face also interfered with his sense of smell.

His arm felt leaden as he raised his hand to free himself of the thing over his nose and mouth. Suddenly they were crowding around him—other g'hir males—the scent of metal and laboratory and *her* filled his nostrils for the brief moment he was able to lift the thing off.

A strong grip pulled his hand away clamped it back on.

"Check the reaction rate in the corpus callosum." The order was rapid but had the steady evenness of a professional well used to crisis. "Check for damage in the higher reasoning functions."

A healer.

The room, with its medical systems, some familiar, some not, swam over his head. R'har fell back, sinking into the warm darkness as g'hir moved around him, snapping off readings to each other.

A healer . . .

"*Hope!*" he roared, his eyes flying open.

He fought the strong hands that moved swiftly to hold him down. Her scent was here but faint enough to flood his body with adrenaline. He flailed for her, every cell in his body demanding he protect—

"Hold him!"

"Hope!" He had gotten the mask off in the struggle to call her name but could not see her through the press of their bodies.

A medical bay! He could scent her, but not nearby. Where was she? Was she hurt? The dark forest on Olari flashed through his mind, the chill of the ground beneath and her tearstained face above him, the Zerar hunting them—

"Stop this immediately or I will have you sedated!"

R'har bared his fangs. The man's face looming over him was flushed and angry. He wore the blue garb of a healer and for an instant the doctor's own fangs flashed.

Then the man's face relaxed into a more professional, detached expression. "I am Doctor Ki'san. You are onboard the Hironian cruiser *Tribute*. You are being treated for injuries sustained from a Zerar's weapon. You are not in danger but you must lie still. Do you understand me?"

R'har's challenge snarl showed an invitation to fight greatly out of place when addressing one's own healer, but with her so nearby, her well-being in question, he could not contain himself, no matter how rude it was. "Hope—my lifemate—"

"She is aboard," the physician assured, his gaze now on the display above R'har's head.

"Is she here?" R'har twisted, trying to see the rest of the medical bay. "Please—is she hurt?"

"She was treated for minor injuries and I cleared her for release from the medical bay hours ago," the doctor said curtly. "Get the backup systems online," he said to one of the medics and his voice fell to a grumble. "He has damaged half the sensors on this side of the biobed."

"I cannot *see* her! Let me see her and I—"

"Our scout team picked you up nearly fourteen hours ago," the doctor interrupted, his gaze on the display. "The Mata has been given the captain's quarters for her own. She left the medical bay only a short time ago."

He could not detect any signs of deception in the healer's tone or expression and a glance at the others did not reveal any clue that the man was lying.

"But she is . . ." R'har wet his lips. "She is safe? She is well, my Hope?"

The doctor was not looking at him, but in the man's face R'har detected the tiniest of flinches.

"Yes," Ki'san said. "She has been provided an honor guard and the captain himself has pledged himself to her protection. If necessary he will sacrifice the ship for her safety."

R'har breathed in deeply, and his shoulders relaxed, positive now that he detected no scent of human blood. She had not been wounded. She was safe.

"The Yir clan are in your debt." He sought the healer's gaze. "*I* am in your debt."

"This is my calling," the doctor said shortly. "To heal all those who have need of it. You owe me no debt, warrior."

"Still," R'har said. "I undertake the obligation gratefully."

He breathed in again and his brow creased at the lingering tang of her anxiety. He should have been awake, been at her side to soothe her fears when they did their exam. Finding Hope had once been his purpose; now serving her, safeguarding her and their offspring, was the sacred task the Goddess had entrusted to him.

The medics' press on him was unrelenting and R'har forced himself to relax. The sooner the medical officer released him from sickbay, the sooner he would be with her. After a moment the men, seeing his cooperation, let go. He tried to be still, to let the healers attend to their task, but it was not easy.

It had been explained to him, when he was selected to journey to Earth, that human males did not bond to their females like this, that his new mate would not understand at first. Ra'kur had told him, privately, that his own lifemate, Jenna, struggled to comprehend the depth of that bond even now.

He had long dreamed of a lifemate of his own and now he had bonded to Hope he was ill at ease at being separated from her, as if part of him were missing when she was not with him. He felt agitated when he could not scent her, when he could not see her, truly content now only when she was nearby.

She was safe here, somewhere on the ship. That was something at least, but it did not compare to seeing her with his own eyes, breathing in her scent, feeling her warmth for himself.

R'har shifted, impatient to be with her again.

"Your annoyance will not affect the speed of the exam," the doctor said, his eyes on the datapad in his hand.

"I feel strong enough to leave the medical bay now," R'har offered, hoping he could manage to walk out unassisted. "I will return if I feel unwell."

"Your injuries were severe." The doctor continued his scans, unperturbed. "And you were too long unconscious. I have a number of tests I must perform before I can release you." Ki'san glanced up at the display over the biobed then at R'har. "You might as well resign yourself to it and use the time as an opportunity to rest."

"I will rest easier if I know Hope is well and cared for," R'har growled. "Allow me to see her and assure myself of her safety and comfort then I will return here. You may do any exam or test you like then."

"You will not depart my medical bay until I am certain you are recovered enough to do so." The doctor's hand rested on R'har's shoulder to halt his attempt to sit up, his hold steady and unyielding. "I would prefer not to have you restrained."

Ki'san's coloring placed him as clanbrother at any number of enclosures but R'har detected a crispness to the man's words, often the hallmark of one of the northern mountainous regions of Hir. The mountain clans' fighting style was slower, relying more on blunt force than speed—

"This is a warship," the doctor reminded calmly, clearly not having missed R'har's quick estimation of his potential fighting skills. "I am as trained as any warrior here." Ki'san's eyebrows rose. "But more importantly, I outrank many of those warriors. I can—and will—order them to strap you down if you force me to it."

R'har bared his fangs fully but the doctor's gaze was unwavering and the medics too tensed.

Finally R'har blew out his breath and lay back on the biobed.

"Your cooperation is appreciated," the doctor said dryly.

R'har glanced toward the medcenter's doors. "If you will not let me go to her, will you do me the simple courtesy of letting her come to me?"

"After many hours in the medcenter she has just been escorted to her quarters to rest," the doctor returned. "At my recommendation."

"But—is she sleeping, do you think?" R'har's brow creased. "I long for her but I will not have you disturb her, if she is resting."

"I am—if you have not noticed—currently occupied in treating a patient," Ki'san said without looking up from his datapad. "That is my priority now."

R'har felt his nostrils flare. "You do this because you not have a lifemate of your own. You would not deny me her presence if you did!"

The doctor's face tightened ever so slightly. "I am well versed in the biology of a male's bond to his lifemate."

"That is not the same as having it!" R'har snarled. "*You* will never understand what it means to be separated from the female you are bonded to!"

Ki'san dropped his gaze to his datapad. "I am sure that is true."

The doctor remained focused on his task and R'har felt his face flush, ashamed at having exposed the agony of a solitary life, a deep hurt he himself knew too well.

Before he had found Hope.

"What of the Zerar?" R'har asked at last. "Was the confrontation a lengthy one?"

"I am not versed in the specifics of the *Tribute's* military engagements," Ki'san replied. "But I can tell you that the Zerar warship retreated quickly. From the sole report I was privy to, the enemy has left our territory."

For now.

The words were unspoken but the Zerar were growing bolder, testing the Hironian borders to see where they might breech and claim territory. Those like this physician and himself, the youngest generation of the g'hir, were adults now and in desperate need of offspring to replace their numbers, mates to give their lives purpose.

She had been here for hours . . .

R'har did not miss the looks the warriors sent his way, looks of envy, weighing his fighting skills, some no doubt wondering how his clanbrothers might retaliate if one of the Yir females was stolen.

Finally Ki'san gave a nod.

"Your vitals are good. There does not appear to be any residual neural or nerve damage. I am releasing you from the medical center," the doctor said, tapping the order into his datapad. "But I am ordering rest and I want to see you again in twelve hours."

R'har let his breath out in relief. "I thank you."

"At the first sign of dizziness, headache, or any other new symptom, no matter how mild, you are to return here immediately."

"I will," R'har promised, already pushing off the biobed to stand.

But he had taken only a step toward the medcenter doors when the doctor put his hand out to stop him.

Ki'san addressed the medical staff. "Clear the room. I need a moment to consult privately with my patient."

"What is—?" he began as the men left, then his heart sped up. "Is Hope all right? Was there something you did not tell me?"

"She left here sound in body," Ki'san assured quickly. "This is a personal, not medical, matter. Hope—the Mata—has asked me to deliver a message to you."

"A message?" R'har's brow furrowed. "Why would she ask you to give a message to me? I will see her in a few moments."

Ki'san shifted his weight slightly, glancing away, and R'har's stomach clenched.

"Well, what is it then, physician?" he demanded. "What is this message my lifemate would entrust to one not even of her own enclosure?"

"She asked me to relay to you . . ." Ki'san met his gaze. "She does not ever wish to see you again."

R'har blinked and the simple absurdity of the words made his mind go white.

Then he brushed away the doctor's hand with a dismissive huff. "Get out of my way, healer!"

In a quick move Ki'san blocked his exit. "This is the message she asked me to deliver to you."

R'har stared, caught between outrage and disbelief. "Whatever it is you are attempting to—"

"I do not enjoy being the bearer of these words!" the doctor interrupted sharply. "I do *not* relish this task. But she has given it to me and I gave my word I would deliver this message to you."

"Who are *you* that she should give any task to?" R'har roared, his face going hot, his fangs bared. "*I* am her lifemate! You are *nothing*!"

Ki'san's face tightened. "What I am is immaterial. These are her words. She does not wish to see you again. She made me promise I would—"

"These are lies!" But the healer did not look malicious, he looked grieved. Nostrils flared, R'har pushed past him. "I must see her—"

"The captain has already issued orders in accordance with her wishes!" the doctor warned. "The guards will not permit you near her."

R'har shook his head again. "But—why?" he rasped. "Why would she do this?"

But he knew.

"She did not confide that in me." Ki'san passed his hand over his eyes. "But others heard her words. She made the declaration publicly."

"No." R'har staggered back. "No . . ."

"I am sorry, R'har," Ki'san said quietly, and his gaze reflected sympathy. "She has abjured you."

TWENTY-THREE

Holy crap.

Hope stood at the top of the shuttle's ramp and swallowed hard. The chill air of Hir's autumn stung her cheeks as she regarded the scores of Yir warriors in the courtyard below, all assembled expressly to welcome her to their enclosure.

She hadn't wanted to come here, to R'har's home in the Atarra valley, but being human meant she didn't have an enclosure of her own to return to. She might have ended things with R'har but the Yir—in fact the g'hir as a people—weren't about to make it easy for a fertile human female go home. R'har had captured her, and by their law he had an entire moon cycle to convince her to stay.

Unless she wanted to choose another mate.

She wasn't about to pick another g'hir male but by her own declaration wasn't R'har's mate either, even though he still had a claim to her. The whole thing left her in a kind of legal limbo she scarcely understood, and offers to pay formal court to her poured in within an hour of her arrival on Hir.

The Ruling Council, aware of the danger of having a human female up for grabs in their custody, argued hotly amongst themselves. Fearful of an attack on the Council building itself, the majority voted to acknowledge the claim of R'har's clan and declared she be sent to the Yir enclosure for their clanbrother's remaining choosing time. She was placed her under the protection of his clan and spirited out of the capital.

Hope didn't want to be here at all and she sure hadn't expected this kind of turnout for her arrival.

Arrayed in the courtyard below stood rows and rows of Yir clanbrothers in respectful anticipation. The hundreds of glowing eyes fixed on her had Hope gripping the doorway and fighting the urge to retreat back into the warm shuttle's cabin to hide.

"Mata?"

Hope glanced over her shoulder and *up* at Ha'kin, one of the eight warriors who had raced to the capital to claim her for the Yir. These warriors, all Yir clanbrothers, had surrounded her the instant the Ruling Counsel acknowledged their claim to her. From their narrowed eyes, the way their hands hovered near their blasters and how their fangs showed in warning as they eyed other g'hir males in the capital, it was clear they were prepared to defend that claim with violence.

The whole idea of being something—a *commodity*—that these people willingly would shed blood over churned her stomach.

Ha'kin hadn't left her side since that moment and she appreciated his protection even if she didn't take the same comfort in his presence as she had R'har's. A g'hir warrior, Ha'kin was nearly seven feet tall and powerfully built. He was blond, an apparently common trait for the Yir, his hair a darker shade than R'har's but lightened here and there by Hir's suns.

His startling teal-colored eyes regarded her now with concern. "Are you all right?"

Hope looked back at the hundreds of men awaiting her in the courtyard. "I, uh, I just didn't expect such a turnout."

Her gaze took in banners and streamers that must have been hung for her arrival. "This is a little much."

"I will send them away," he offered swiftly. "I will tell them they have made you uneasy, that they must disperse immediately."

Hope shifted her weight. Ha'kin struck her as a truly nice guy, the kind who would probably stand up for her even if she weren't up for grabs. But he—and the other clanbrothers who had escorted her here—would probably do cartwheels for her if it meant getting her attention and furthering their chances of being chosen as her new mate.

Her attention was drawn back to the warriors below and her gaze darted about, seeking him among the men assembled. She'd felt R'har's absence from the moment the medical doors slid shut behind her, almost as if she'd lost a part of herself. She'd never felt anything like it; not even losing her "perfect" fiancé had compared. And now, arriving at R'har's enclosure and seeing the scores of alien strangers awaiting her, she felt such a wave of longing for him, such a need just to know him nearby no matter how mad she was, that it was painful.

But R'har was not numbered here among the many warriors or part of the pair who came forward to greet her at the bottom of the ramp. One was another g'hir warrior but the other, decked out like a queen, was clearly the Yir's future clanmother.

Hope's gaze met the g'hir female's and even from here she could see that the woman's rippled brow creased at how Hope lingered in the doorway and delayed her descent from the shuttle.

It hadn't really struck home how little Hope knew about the g'hir people, about their culture and etiquette, till she'd broken it off with R'har and had to deal with the captain and crew of the warship on her own. Either because he'd spent time on Earth or because he'd been prepared as one selected to travel there or simply because he'd spent time with her and been a quick study, it seemed R'har had gone out of his way to act human.

But the g'hir she'd met since she'd walked out of the medical center *didn't*. They certainly weren't out to offend her but these were aliens, with their own rules of society including their own manners and expectations—nearly all of which she was completely ignorant.

And from the look the woman standing at the bottom of the ramp was giving her, clearly lingering here was *not* what she was supposed to be doing.

"No," Hope said quietly. "I'm going to have to meet them sooner or later anyway."

But it wasn't easy to walk down there, with all the expectations they had of her, with all those gazes watching her every move, so many of them hoping she would choose him as a mate instead.

The outfit she was wearing didn't help either. The men had brought with them clothing for her that consisted of soft boots and a dress embroidered in silver thread. Over it she wore a sweeping floor-length coat in matching ivory, trimmed at the hood, wrists, and hem with some kind of fluffy, soft white fur. The whole ensemble looked like something a medieval Russian princess might have worn.

She wasn't used to the length but at least the boots were flats and easy to walk in. At her height she'd always felt self-conscious about wearing heels but here, at least, she wouldn't have to worry about that. When she stepped from the ramp onto the courtyard Hope, so tall for a human, found herself having the unusual experience of looking up at another woman.

The g'hir female was easily over six feet tall in flats. She was lovely too, her ridges and the bones of her face far more delicate than the males', and she certainly took pains to show off her good looks. Her eyes, bright green and a bit upturned at the corners, were highlighted with shimmery, sparkly shadow, her full mouth bright with a red lip shade. Jeweled earrings, a darker green than her eyes, dangled and swayed as the woman stepped forward, her pretty fangs flashing in a smile.

"Mata, I am Si'hala," she said, her growl softer, higher in pitch than that of the males. She indicated the man at her side. "My mate, Lihr."

The man bent his head to her. "Mata."

"Hi," Hope said, giving him a nod. She immediately realized it was a human mannerism and wondered if she should do the g'hir chin thing instead, but then Si'hala was talking again.

"On behalf of the whole Yir enclosure, Mata," Si'hala continued, indicating the rows of warriors behind her, "I welcome you home."

"I appreciate your kindness, Si'hala, and theirs," Hope began guardedly. "But I'm not staying. I'm just here until I can return to Earth."

"If that is what you decide," Si'hala agreed, her growl warm, friendly, and too quick to be really sincere. "But for now, the Yir enclosure is your home."

"This isn't an 'if,'" Hope began, her face flushing with annoyance. The wind had picked up, the fur trim of the hood tickling her eyes, and she pushed the thing back. "I *am* going back to—"

A ripple of shock ran through the assembled g'hir, and the warriors, who had been so silent and still, shifted, trying to get a better look at her, murmuring.

Si'hala's mouth dropped open and she too was staring.

"What?" Hope exclaimed, alarmed. "What's wrong?"

"Your hair . . ."

"What about it?" Hope sent a questioning look at Ha'kin. The clanbrothers who had escorted her here had stared at her, sure, being human and female and all but they hadn't made a big deal about her hair in particular.

"It is . . . *fire*," one of the warriors who stood behind Lihr murmured.

"Oh," Hope said, her hand going to her curls, trying to tame them against the blowing wind. "Yes, it is."

Si'hala's eyebrows shot up. "'Oh, yes, it is'?" She looked pointedly at Hope's red hair and shook her head in wonderment. "Hair like that and *she* says . . ."

Suddenly Si'hala sent a quick darting glance at the warriors around them, at how the men were breaking lines, pressing forward to get a better look, and quickly clasped Hope's upper arm.

"But I must not keep you here shivering in the cold!" she said a little too loudly, already urging Hope through the staring crowd and toward the largest building in the courtyard. "Come indoors where it is warm."

Si'hala hurried her along inside and Hope drew in her breath, taking in the soaring entry hall with wide eyes. The place was huge; a wide staircase that wound upwards to floors above and rooms lined either side of this center area. Tiles of blue shimmered beneath her feet and the whole space had an ancient organic feel and an astonishing majestic grandeur.

"*This* is a clan hall?" she asked. "It looks like a palace!"

It gave her a funny feeling to be in the place where R'har been a carefree child before the Scourge, then a grieving boy and an orphan in its wake. To stand here, on the stones he'd walked across as a young man, proud to have earned the title of "warrior" among his people, sent an shock of awareness through her.

She wet her lips and glanced about but R'har didn't await her inside the hall either.

So where the hell is he?

She'd made a mistake by having the doctor tell him for her. She should have broken it off in person. Since then she caught herself rehearsing in her mind what she'd say to him, just how she'd really let him have it for all the bullshit he'd pulled.

But now, knowing she'd see him any moment, all those angry words and clever cuts vanished from her mind. She had not a single idea what she'd say to him.

This was his home and he'd never spoken of his enclosure without pride. He was here somewhere and sooner or later she'd have to deal with him.

She just hoped when they did meet up she held it together.

"I forgot that you have never been inside one," Si'hala said.

"No, I haven't," Hope murmured. "I mean, I only got to Hir this morning."

The rest of the clan, warriors mostly, although Hope did spy a handful of women among them, had followed them inside and were filling the hall.

All those bright, glowing eyes still on her.

Here and there she could see the warriors jostling each other to get nearer, to get even a half step closer to her. Ha'kin and her original honor guard had quietly imposed themselves between her and them.

Si'hala indicated a large archway and the room beyond furnished with long tables, the space beribboned with colorful streamers. "Your welcome banquet has been prepared."

"Banquet?" Hope stopped short, her darting glance now seeking some route of escape. The last thing she wanted to do was eat with so many people watching her. "Oh, no, I don't think—"

"Of *course* you will want to refresh your appearance before we go in." Si'hala addressed her mate as she urged Hope toward the stairs. "Lihr, we will join you and the others shortly but do not feel you need wait to begin the feast." She sent a warm smile at Hope. "We are all family, after all."

"Of course." He turned with good humor toward his clanbrothers. "Come, we must feast well for we have much to thank the All Mother for." Lihr clapped one warrior on the shoulder. "And I for one am famished."

Hope followed Si'hala up the stairs to the third level but she couldn't miss how some of the men lingered below to watch her till the very last second.

"Are you all right?" Si'hala asked quietly. "Your face shows much distress."

"Just a bit shaken up," Hope admitted. "God, I thought they were going to start fighting down there."

"We were fortunate they did not," Si'hala said, with a glance back the way they had come. "The whole clan is gathered here to welcome you. We will have our hands full keeping the peace among them as they compete for your favor."

"It's a problem, isn't it?" Hope asked. "Me being here."

Si'hala blinked and her pretty, feminine fangs flashed as she burst out laughing. "A problem? *You* are the best thing to come to the Yir enclosure since . . ." She gave a smirk. "Since me."

The g'hir woman opened one of a set of double doors and shut it behind Hope as soon as they were both inside.

The ceilings of these apartment were high, white, and domed, the walls a soft cream, the green tile floor covered in places by bright luxurious rugs. The furniture here, larger and meant to accommodate g'hir bodies, seemed fussier than what she'd seen before, almost rococo in style. She hadn't spent much time with Si'hala but the place, with its spacious five bedrooms and large-scale artwork, seemed to suit her girly style perfectly.

I wonder how Lihr stands it.

Si'hala grandly led her to the largest of the bedrooms. The huge carved bed was piled high with pillows and dark blue velvety bedclothes.

"What do you think?" Si'hala asked with a gesture at the bed. "Is it not fit for a clanmother?"

All it's missing is a couple cupids on the bedposts and it would be fit for Marie Antoinette.

"It's great," Hope said aloud. "I've . . . never even imagined having a bed like that."

Si'hala gave a pleased nod and threw the doors open to an adjoining room. "*Here* is where the clothes and jewels are kept." Si'hala urged her into the sumptuous dressing room. "These are for the current season," she continued, bounding ahead to indicate the clothes hanging nearest to them. "*Those* are for winter . . . formal things for the gathering . . . garb suitable for riding . . ."

Hope nodded at the right times as Si'hala went on extolling the virtues of the various accessories and footwear.

Guess she doesn't have any girlfriends to show it off to.

Finally Si'hala seemed to wind down and turned to regard her, her glowing eyes expectant.

"This is lovely," Hope said truthfully, fingering the skirt of one of the closest dresses. It was a gorgeous icy blue, heavy and a lot like silk duchesse. The dressing room was filled with clothes of similar quality; she'd been in wedding boutiques that didn't have fabric this luscious. "I mean, well, jeez, these are *all* just beautiful."

Si'hala flashed a fanged smile. "I spent months choosing designs and the last few days supervising their construction. I wanted everything to be perfect."

Months? What, does she do this every year or something?

"Well, your hard work certainly shows," Hope assured. "You did a great job."

"Here!" Si'hala cried, catching Hope's hand to pull her deeper into the dressing room. "Let me show you the jewels!"

Hope sighed inwardly as the g'hir woman threw open the center cabinet, pulling one drawer after another to reveal sparkling collections of earrings, bracelets, rings.

"I have grouped them by color and stone. I thought to divide them by season too but," she laughed lightly, "do gems truly *have* a season?"

"How could they?" Hope murmured. There was something about all this that was a little sad. Sure, Si'hala's closet looked like a boutique where they only stocked one of anything and every neatly handwritten price tag had four digits, but Hope couldn't imagine the warriors cared much for this stuff. Si'hala must be incredibly lonely.

"Well, you did a great job," Hope said again. "Everything is gorgeous and really, uh . . ." Her gaze ran along the well-stocked shelves. ". . . well organized."

"What would you like to wear for the feast?" Si'hala asked, indicating the closet's contents. "Choose whatever you please!"

"Oh," Hope demurred. "I'm fine. I mean, I've only been wearing this"—she indicated the dress, more elaborate than the wedding gown she had hanging in the closet at home—"for a couple hours."

"Everything will fit you," Si'hala assured. "I had them send me your measurements from the warship."

Hope blinked. "The warship? How did the people on the warship get my measurements?"

"The medical scans," Si'hala said with a shrug. "They made a record of your height, weight, body mass—"

"Wait, so the medical scans recorded my measurements and you got them from the warship?"

"Of course."

Hope stared. "Why the hell would—I mean, isn't that private information? *My* private information?"

"The Yir are your clan now and in any case"—Si'hala gave a careless wave—"there is nothing *I* cannot get if I have set my mind to have it."

"Uh-huh," Hope murmured, shifting her weight. "Well, anyway, thanks but I think I'll just stick with what I'm wearing."

Si'hala looked utterly crestfallen, then brightened. "But you will need to get dressed tomorrow! I will come back in the morning as soon as you are awake to help you."

"Come back? Wait, isn't this *your* place?"

"No, Mata, these are your quarters." The g'hir woman indicated the dressing room around them. "These are your clothes."

For a moment all Hope could do was stare at Si'hala. "You're kidding."

"You do not care for these quarters? There are others in the clanhall that you may find—"

"There are *five* bedrooms!" Hope burst out. "I don't need this much room, not for just me."

"The other rooms are for the offspring you will bear."

Hope shook her head a little, not even wanting to touch that one. "Look, and all these clothes—!"

Si'hala's lip trembled a little. "You do not like them?"

"Well, of course I like them! I mean, holy cow, they're gorgeous! But I don't need—You shouldn't have gone to all this trouble for me!"

"But you are my clansister!" Si'hala caught Hope's hands in hers. "The only other female of my age here. It was my joy to make your quarters pleasant, Mata, and welcome my new friend home!"

There are moments in life when someone has given so much more than you could possibly expect; called you beautiful when that's the last thing you're feeling, gone further than needed simply from the goodness of their heart, when the gift is too big or expensive but so lovingly and sincerely given that anything less than genuine gratitude is just plain wrong.

And this was one of them.

"Thank you, Si'hala," Hope said. "What you did—everything you've done—to make me feel welcome is amazing." She smiled a little. "And no matter how long I live, I promise you this—I'll never ever forget it."

Si'hala beamed. "I am so glad. We wish for you to be happy here, Mata." The g'hir woman ducked her head a bit. "And I wish for us to be friends."

"We *are* friends, Si'hala," she assured, thinking that it would never occur to Keri—never mind Megan—to do anything so thoughtful. "So you should probably stop calling me 'Mata.' Just 'Hope' is fine."

"Hope." Si'hala smiled and gave a g'hir nod. "It is a perfect namesound for you."

Hope abruptly turned away.

"I have said something wrong?" Si'hala asked worriedly, following Hope out to the balcony.

"No," she said thickly. "It's just—that's what R'har said."

Hope looked out over the valley, deep in autumn now the leaves were golden, orange and pink.

It's funny. I didn't stop to think about stuff like the leaves changing.

It made her wonder what it was like in the spring.

Hope swallowed hard. *Not that I'll be here to find out.*

"You said the whole clan is gathered here. Is . . . is *he* here?"

"R'har is on our lands but he will not cross your sight," Si'hala promised. "He is forbidden to enter the clanhall again."

"Wait—" Hope turned back, wide-eyed. "You mean R'har can't come home because *I'm* here? What about—" She wasn't planning to be here that long, not at all but— "What about the Gathering? You won't let him come to that either? It's so important to him."

He was the same as all the others, the same lying, cheating jerk she always wound up with. But she didn't mean to cost him his home.

"He is one warrior among hundreds," Si'hala said with a careless wave. "*You* are the only unmated female in ten thousand hectares."

God, she had to leave. She had to go back to Earth as soon as she could so he could come home.

"Now, we must go down to the welcoming feast." Si'hala hooked her arm in Hope's to lead her along. "Choose any Yir clanbrother you please to be your new mate. There are dozens in the hall below who long to make a mating roar to you tonight."

Hope's eyes shut briefly remembering how R'har's roar had left her ears ringing. "Not all at once, though, right?"

TWENTY-FOUR

R'har tried to calm his breath. The clanhall was visible from his place here in the orchard, an imposing structure that bespoke of the enclosure's influence and wealth.

The recent arrival of a new Mata seemed to have transformed these lands from the tragic echo of the Scourge to a glow of happy optimism. The promise of a rich and bright future filled with new hope for the g'hir of this lucky clan . . .

R'har closed his eyes briefly in prayer to the All Mother. He had made an offering of his blood to the Goddess before venturing to these lands, humbly beseeching Her to grant him Her blessing in his mission.

He had been forbidden the clanhall of the Yir enclosure. He would be allowed to live on Yir land but he was directed never again to cause her to set her eyes upon him.

The loss of his home was nothing compared to the loss of his lifemate. Her absence was like a wound, a dull pain that had settled in his chest and never left him, even in the deepest sleep.

He dreamed of her every night—his little one, his Hope—reaching for her only to have her recede from his grasp. He would awaken, gasping, his heart thudding in his chest. He would leave the shelter and run the land of the Yir then slow to silently edge forward when the clanhall came into view. R'har would wait there, in the darkness, looking toward the rooms where she slept, lingering until the last moments when dawn forced his retreat.

He was lifemated to her and he could not be with her.

But he would never be without her . . .

Now there was only one living being who could help him, one whom he must somehow convince to intervene on his behalf—

Footfalls along the path, coming in his direction, made R'har hurriedly finish his plea to the Goddess.

"R'har," Jenna called out in warm greeting as she and her mate, Ra'kur, headed his way. Her rounded belly was not yet slowing her steps and she smiled widely at him, her delicate human face aglow with the beauty of motherhood. "I'm real glad to see you!"

He gave a nod, momentarily robbed of words by the fear that he should blurt out his desperate plea and destroy this one last chance.

"R'har of the Yir clan," Ra'kur began formally but his smile was warm. "Welcome to the Erah enclosure."

He was no orator, like Council Member Mirak, no poet or bard, and his words tumbled out before he could stop them. "Mata, I need your help!"

Jenna's brow knitted, her human features making her almost supernaturally lovely but nothing like—

"Okay," she said, exchanging a look with her mate. "What's the matter?" Her frown deepened. "Did something go wrong on Earth?"

"Did you not find a lifemate, my friend?" Ra'kur asked, looking grieved.

"Yes, I found a lifemate. *Hope*." Just to say it brought joy . . . and pain. "Her namesound is Hope."

"Okay," Jenna said again. "So, what's wrong?"

R'har closed his eyes briefly. "I have lost her."

"*Lost* her?" Jenna exclaimed. "What do you mean you 'lost her'?"

"She has abjured me."

Ra'kur made a sound of shock and sympathy but Jenna shook her head.

"I thought—you just said you were lifemated—"

"She has forsworn me," R'har said, lowering his gaze. "She has formally rejected my claim to her."

Jenna's face fell. "Oh, R'har! I'm so sorry."

He could not make tears as humans did but his throat closed against the keening of g'hir grief. He swallowed hard.

"Look," Jenna began gently. "If there is something I can do—"

"She has publicly declared she will not see me again."

"Oh, boy," Jenna murmured. "I can see where this is headed."

"Please . . ." He raised his eyes. "Please, I beg of you, Mata, will you speak to her on my behalf?"

Jenna shifted her weight. "You know, in my experience, it's always better if you deal with these things yourself. You're the one who needs to talk to her, R'har."

"I have been forbidden the clanhouse. By clan directive I must not offend her sight."

Ra'kur's eyes widened and Jenna's lovely face was deeply troubled.

"What about a letter?" she asked. "Wouldn't you be allowed to write to your own—uh, Hope?"

"No." He wet his lips. "And none of the Yir enclosure will speak on my behalf. There is no one to help me now but—"

"Me," Jenna finished.

She searched his face, looking thoughtful, and R'har held his breath. He had heard Si'hala once say that the human woman considered her eyes plain, a simple brown color, but to g'hir her eyes were a glorious russet with flecks of gold and green throughout.

He hoped the Goddess would let this woman read his heart in his gaze, that she would be moved enough to help . . .

She sighed. "So, what'd you do anyway? To lose her?"

"I . . ." His voice fell to a shamed whisper. "I deceived her."

The human woman's eyes narrowed. "About what, exactly?"

"My Hope, she . . . did not wish to be my mate. I thought I could win her if I had more time so I . . ."

"You what?" Jenna prompted.

R'har forced himself to meet Jenna's gaze. "I told her our ship required repairs. That we could not continue to Hir, that I could not return her to Earth," he admitted, wretched, and spread his hands. "But this . . . was not true."

Ra'kur scowled in disapproval but Jenna burst out laughing.

"Billy Harding did that once, said he just clean forgot to fill the tank. 'Course he didn't know I could see the red gas can from right where I was sittin' in the cab."

Ra'kur's fangs flashed. "Biiilleeeharrrding?"

"Don't worry, it didn't work." Jenna smirked. "Much." She looked back at R'har. "Maybe you should start at the beginning, catch me up a bit? And just call me 'Jenna,' okay?"

His heart surged at her kind attention and he relayed how he had captured Hope for his own, how she had softened toward him during their time on the ship, the Zerar attack and his ultimate confession, the agony of the voyage on the warship knowing he had lost her—

Jenna laid her hand on his arm gently. "I'm sorry."

"You are the only one who can help me, Jenna." R'har swallowed hard. "Only you can carry my heart to her. Will you—will you help me?"

Jenna's eyes shone as Hope's did when her eyes were about to water. Then she nodded as the humans did. "Okay, R'har. I'll do what I can."

He closed his eyes for an instant in silent thanks.

"I suppose I could just drop in and say hi to Si'hala," Jenna mused. "I'll just hang around until I can get a word in with Hope, private-like. Hope . . ." Her brow creased thoughtfully. "I don't know any girl in Brittle Bridge by that name. Is she from around there?"

"I captured her in the same area where you resided, although, unlike you, she is not a backwoods hick."

"*What?*" Jenna gasped. "What did you just call me?"

R'har exchanged looks with her mate but clearly the other warrior, too, was bewildered by her reaction.

"A backwoods hick," R'har repeated, speaking the English words more carefully, in case it was the pronunciation that he had gotten incorrect.

Jenna took a step forward, her hands on her hips and her unusual eyes narrowed dangerously. "I don't know where you picked that up, R'har, but that's quite an insult you just delivered."

R'har blinked. "My apologies, I did not know this phrase to be offensive! It has no translation in Hironian."

Jenna glanced at her mate, who silently shook his head. After a moment she looked back R'har. "I take it that charming phrase is from your new mate? She say anything else?"

R'har glanced at her throat, though he could see no difference in the skin shade there so Jenna was not likely to take offense at this term. "Only that people of your territory have necks that are reddened."

"Rednecks." Jenna fairly spat the English word.

His stomach sank. Without this human female's help he could lose his Hope forever. "Please, I meant no offense—"

Jenna waved her hand. "No, I know you didn't but *jeez*." She shook her head. "Are you sure you want her back? I mean, if you can get Ra'kur to take me along to Earth I could find you a sweet little *backwoods hick* girl who actually *deserves* a g'hir warrior."

"I want Hope." R'har's face heated at the aching longing in his own voice. "I will want for no other my whole life."

"Yeah, I figured you'd say something like that." Jenna sighed again. "You g'hir warriors. You love too much."

Ra'kur raised his eyebrow. "Do you mean that, little bird?"

Her mouth curved a bit. "No, I surely don't." Jenna looked at R'har. "All right, I'll do what I can." She folded her arms. "But if you want my opinion, that girl needs some sense knocked into her."

TWENTY-FIVE

Hope kept her eyes forward as she descended the stairs of the clanhall, determined to get outside alone—for once. In the past week she'd been overwhelmed with clanbrothers seeking to attract her attention. They lingered in the hall outside her quarters, pretending to be on one errand or another, they hovered about the dining hall when she came down for meals—late to avoid the majority of them—eager to ask after her health, to inquire how the night's rest was, to comment on the fine weather or the coming Gathering.

She didn't want to be rude, she really didn't. But even the smallest smile or casual answer was proving too much encouragement. Hope was so focused now on not making eye contact she didn't notice the older, elegantly garbed man until she reached the bottom of the staircase and he, a younger warrior, and Lihr literally blocked her way.

"Mata," Lihr began, looking uncomfortable. "May I present Council Member Mirak of the Betari enclosure?"

"We met before—" the silver-haired g'hir began smoothly.

"Yeah," Hope interrupted. "I remember you. You were at the meeting of the Ruling Council when I arrived at Be'lyn City." She glanced at Lihr. The future clanfather's face was tense; likely he too was remembering how Mirak had tried to dismiss the Yir's claim at that meeting so she'd be up for grabs. "But the Yir enclosure is pretty far from the capital so I'm sure you aren't dropping in to say hi. What are you doing here?"

"I have come to see how you are faring, Mata," Mirak said, sounding surprised. "We have had no news of you."

Hope glanced at the young man with Mirak and who, with the same amber glowing eyes, strongly resembled the Council member.

"My son, Ar'ar." Mirak put a hand at the young man's shoulder and urged him forward. He was gorgeous and tall—of course—with dark hair and bright yellow eyes.

Ar'ar bent his head to her, his gaze holding hers. "Mata."

It didn't take a genius to figure out why Mirak had brought his son along for her to take a look at.

Hope used to envy great beauties. At first all the attention here had been really ego boosting. Now being a piece of meat was just getting . . . depressing.

"Nice to meet you," Hope muttered. "But now's not a good time. I was just on my way out to—"

"It is," Mirak broke in, "rather important that I speak to you, Mata."

Hope felt her blood pressure rising. All she wanted to do was get away from this for a little while. "About what?"

"The Day of Choosing is nearly upon us," Mirak reminded. "As the designated representative in this matter, it is my responsibility to discuss your wishes and convey them back to the Ruling Council."

No wonder Lihr looks so upset.

The warriors here all hoped to be chosen as her new mate and Lihr had made it clear that the Yir as a clan wanted her to stay. He wanted her to pick one—any one—of his clanbrothers rather than return to Earth.

If she hadn't met R'har first, she might have actually considered it but now all she wanted to do was to go home.

"The Yir have prepared a room where we can speak in private," Mirak said, indicating the many warriors who lingered here in the grand hall. "You will be able to speak freely of your decision."

Hope blew her breath out. "Okay, fine. Let's just do this."

She followed the Council member to a quiet room off the main hall. She preceded him into the comfortably furnished sunlit room. Ar'ar took up position outside but Lihr was about to follow them in when Mirak stopped him at the door.

"We must speak in private," Mirak said firmly.

Lihr glanced at her, his rippled brow creased. "Mata?"

"Don't worry," Hope said and narrowed her gaze at Mirak. "I can handle it."

Reluctantly Lihr left, closing the door behind him.

Mirak turned to her with a smile. "How are you enjoying your time on Hir?"

"Not enough to *stay* on Hir," Hope said, folding her arms. "I'm going back to Earth, Council Member."

"Are the Yir treating you well?" Mirak asked. "Other arrangements can be made for your remaining time on our world if they have not."

"Like spending it at your enclosure with the Betari clan?" Hope asked. "Yeah, as I recall you were really vocal about me not coming to the Yir enclosure."

"You have abjured their clanbrother R'har." Mirak spread his hands. "What is the use of forcing you to uphold some ancient tradition when you clearly do not wish to be among the Yir at all?"

"The Yir," she began heatedly, "are wonderful people. They've been nothing but kind to me."

"I am also deeply . . . *troubled* that you might be influenced to accept a situation so far below your obvious worth."

"You know, the red hair must really be catching up with me," Hope said. "'Cause I'm a little short on patience these days. Why don't you just cut the crap and get to the point?"

"Very well. The Betari are a stronger clan than the Yir," Mirak said bluntly. "We have more wealth, more influence, more power. If—the All Mother forbid—the Zerar do invade Hir we are prepared to protect our own. Choose Ar'ar as your mate and *you* will be the next clanmother of the Betari. Your child would rule our clan and my son, Ar'ar—"

"Is. Smoking. Hot. But still, no thanks."

"Please, Mata," Mirak urged, his face serious. "Come and evaluate my clan for yourself before you decide. Reside with the Betari for a few days. Let us welcome you properly. Let us show you what your life could be like as our clanmother. You have nothing to tie you to the Yir. No reason to remain among them now that the warrior R'har is shamed and cast out. Why will you not consider the Betari instead of the Yir?"

"Maybe because the Yir don't annoy the fuck out of me," Hope snapped and headed for the door. "I'm going home, Mirak. Back to Earth, get it? All *you* have to do is deliver that simple message to the Ruling Council—so make sure you get it right."

Mirak's expression cooled but he clearly wasn't one to give up easily. "Their clanbrother's humiliation at losing a lifemate stains all the Yir. You are welcome among the Betari, Mata, anytime you wish to join us."

"Have a nice trip back to the capital, Council Member," Hope said and threw the door open.

Lihr hurried after her as she stomped through the grand hall. "Is everything all right, clansister?"

"Just dandy," Hope snapped. "You know, you've got some really nice breakables in here. Better let me go out for that ride before I decide to stay here and start smashing things."

Lihr took the hint and fell back. Hope stalked through the courtyard and headed toward the outlying buildings where the multari—beasts that the g'hir rode—were stabled. She was a lousy rider and they wouldn't have let her ride out alone even if she could have won prizes, but at least it would be harder for anyone to hit on her when they were all trotting.

"Hope!" Si'hala called.

Fucking hell, what now?

Hope turned and went stock-still at the sight of the two women headed her way. At Si'hala's side, dressed in Hironian clothes, pink-cheeked and round bellied, was a human woman.

Hope stared; she just couldn't help it. She'd spent so much time looking at g'hir lately that this woman, even clearly pregnant, with her smooth human features and smaller, slighter frame, seemed as light and delicate as a fey.

I wonder if that's why he used to call me "little one" . .
.

"Hope," Si'hala said, smiling widely. "Allow me to present the future clanmother of the Erah enclosure and the mate of Ra—"

"The famous Jenna," Hope finished, folding her arms.

The woman was startled but recovered quickly to offer a smile. "Pleased to meet you."

She had a southerner's drawl, pure North Carolina and soft on the ear. She was pretty too, with warm, chocolate brown eyes and hair just a shade darker than that. She was shorter than Hope, her gaze friendly and intelligent. If she'd met this woman under any other circumstance she would have liked her right off.

But this was the woman who had helped the g'hir by giving them information about Earth, about human women, who was directly responsible for her own kidnapping and the kidnapping of God knew how many women to come.

Hell, this woman was the reason Hope was even here. If it weren't for *Jenna* she'd never even have heard of the g'hir.

Or R'har.

"Nice town you got," Hope said, then at Jenna's blank look added, "Brittle Bridge. You know, on Earth, where you come from? The townsfolk think you're dead, by the way. Murdered by that raving sheriff and buried out in the woods somewhere."

"Raving sheriff? What raving—?" Jenna's eyes widened. "Bill Riley? They think Bill Riley *killed* me?"

"Well, they sure 'nough don't believe you was kidnapped by aliens, sugar," Hope said, aping Jenna's drawl.

Jenna's face tightened. "But—Bill? I mean, he's not in jail or anything, is he?"

"No, on Earth we still have that 'habeas corpus' thing going on," Hope said. "They can't convict him of murder without a body."

"But that's what everybody thinks, though," Jenna murmured and shut her eyes briefly. "Oh, poor Bill."

"Wow, you seem genuinely somewhat distressed for him."

Jenna's brown eyes flashed fire. "I've known Bill my whole life, the man's practically family!"

"Perhaps," Si'hala interjected, her tone bright although she was wringing her hands, "I should have refreshments brought to the atrium for our guest—"

"*Your* guest," Hope snapped, her temper threatening to burn out of control. "Not mine. I live on Earth where humans *belong* and right now I'm going riding."

Hope turned on her heel and, breathing hard with the effort of keeping her anger in check, headed for the outbuildings.

She made it as far as the field that lay between the clanhall and the stables before the southern girl caught up to her.

"You know what, Miss Hope? You are really fucking rude!"

"Rude?" Hope exclaimed, turning to face Jenna. "You have the nerve to call me rude? After what *you* did?"

"We've just met," Jenna reminded sharply, a little out of breath from hurrying with that big belly. "What the hell could I possibly have done to you?"

"What did you—?" Hope's hands clenched into fists. "It's your goddamn fault I got kidnapped in the first place. You *helped* them! You told them all about us—about humans. You made it easy for them to just show up and hunt women down like prey!"

Jenna's face flushed. "The g'hir were going to Earth no matter what I said or did. And yes, I did give them information that I thought could help, that I thought could save both g'hir *and* human lives! And—just so you know—

I'm the one who made it possible for you to go home at all!"

"*You?* The Ruling Council are the ones who are sending me home!"

"Because I only agreed to help them if the women they brought here had a choice about staying!" Jenna snapped. "You can go home because I made sure that you could! But let me tell you something, *sugar*," Jenna gritted out. "As far as I'm concerned R'har should have his head examined for even sending me to talk to you!"

"R'har?" Hope's blinked. "He sent you? You've . . . seen him?"

"So you do remember the man you had banished from his own home?"

"I didn't know they were going to do that," Hope said thickly. "I said I didn't want to see him again, but I—I never meant that they should keep him from his home."

Jenna shook her head. "Do you have any idea how much he's suffering right now? Do you even care? Do you know what it means to have you send him away like that?"

"Look, when I'm gone, he can come back." Hope swallowed hard. "He'll be able to go back to the clanhall by the next Gathering."

Jenna took a few steps closer, shaking her head. "I'm not talking about the clanhall. I'm talking about you. He loves you."

"He lied to me! Or didn't he tell you that? He *lied* to me!"

"He—" Jenna offered a half-shrug. "*Fibbed* . . . a bit."

"Fibbed," Hope repeated flatly. "That's what you'd call it? He kidnapped me—"

Jenna quickly held up her index finger. "Captured!"

"—and he told me that we couldn't go anywhere because the—*perfectly functioning*—ship we were on was too damaged to move!"

Jenna gave a short laugh. "Didn't you ever have a boy pretend to run out of gas so the two of you could get stuck someplace private together?"

"No," Hope said coolly. "But then again, none of my boyfriends drove me home in a pickup truck though the Appalachian backwoods."

Jenna's eyes narrowed. "Smoky Mountains. The Appalachians are farther north."

"Point is," Hope continued, "he lied."

"The *point* is," Jenna returned sharply, "he's crazy about you." Her eyes flickered over Hope. "Though I guess there's no accounting for taste."

"You know," Hope said, stepping back, "this has been really great—catching up with a fellow human and all—but I think I'm all 'girlfriended' out for now."

"Maybe he should have been honest with you!" Jenna called, doggedly following. "But I'm willing to bet you made it plain that this playing for time stunt might be the only chance he had with you!"

Hope turned to stare. "So this *my* fault? He barefaced lies to me and it's *my* fault?"

"He made a mistake. He's paid for it. From what I understand the Zerar almost killed him."

"You don't have to remind me," Hope said roughly. "I was there."

Jenna took a step closer and softened her voice. "Do you know what it must have been like for him to wake up out of that and find that he'd lost you, his lifemate? He says you won't even speak to him."

Hope felt her nostrils flare. "I don't have anything to say to him."

"Oh, it strikes me that you got yourself *tons* to say to him. R'har loves you, Hope. And I'd bet the necklace my Pap gave me," she said, touching the tiny gold bird charm around her neck, "that you aren't even really mad at me at all—or him even really. I think you're mad cause you love him too and it scares the hell out of you."

"You know, I really don't think I need to psychoanalyzed by someone personally acquainted with mountain men," Hope sneered and turned away.

"Did it work?"

Hope threw an annoyed look back. "Did *what* work?"

"That whole pretending to run outta gas so the two of you could spend some time together. Did it work?" Jenna raised her eyebrows. "Did you start to see him as a man, not an alien? As not just a man but a damn good one?"

"What he did—kidnapping . . . *capturing* me." Hope shook her head. "What he did was *wrong*."

"Wrong for humans maybe. Right for g'hir. And he's g'hir."

He'd saved her from the bear, thrown himself between her and danger without hesitation. He'd saved her life on Olari and nearly died doing it. He'd been gentle, polite—*alien* polite, anyway—kind but . . .

"Yeah, well, however he intended it," Hope said, her throat tight, "that's *not* how a man treats a woman he cares about."

Jenna sighed. "He's a warrior of Hir. R'har hasn't had an opportunity to find out the rights and wrongs of courting a girl—human or otherwise. You and me, Hope, we grew up way different but not that far from each other—in the scheme of things. What I think is okay and what you do might never match up . . . and we're both human. You might want to give R'har a bit of slack on account of him, you know, being from an entirely different *planet*." Jenna gave her a searching look. "How well would you say you've treated him—from a g'hir point of view?"

"Goddamn it!" Hope burst out. "I'm *human*, Jenna, just like you! Are you even thinking about whose side you really should be on here?"

"You mean between an honorable g'hir warrior who loves you with his whole fool heart and some stuck-up city bitch?" Jenna pursed her lips for a moment then gave a firm nod. "Yeah, g'hir warrior. All the way."

Hope's hands balled into fists. "Don't you get it? I *trusted* R'har! I never really trusted *anyone* after my dad!" Hope's eyes stung. "And I thought . . . R'har was different."

"He is."

"Yeah," Hope choked, wiping her nose with the back of her hand. "He's not human."

"That's part of it," Jenna agreed. "He's not a human man and he's not going to act like one or think like one. And he feels things a whole lot deeper than you can probably imagine. He loves you a whole lot more than you'd believe." Jenna gave a sad, fond smile. "That's how they are with a lifemate. But Hope, the real question is—Do you love him?"

She looked away. "You don't understand, I mean. . .what if this lie—this *fib*—is just the start? What if he's like . . . my father? And my ex-fiancé, and the others?" Hope asked, her voice very low. "What if he cheats on me too? I just . . . I can't handle that, not from him. I just—I'm sorry, I *can't*. Look, once I'm home—I mean, he can just find someone else that could—"

The expression on Jenna's face made her break off.

"What?" Hope's brow creased. "What did I say?"

"Uh . . . did R'har explain the 'lifemate' thing to you?"

"Well, yeah." Hope's frown deepened. "It's like being married, right?"

"No . . . I mean a man and his lifemate marry but that's later, at the winter Gathering." Jenna scrubbed her face. "Jeez, R'har really should have explained this to you."

"Explained *what* to me?"

"Okay." Jenna regarded Hope for a moment. "Okay . . . Wait, I know—How much do you know about ducklings?"

Hope blinked. "Excuse me?"

"Baby ducks."

"I *know* what ducklings are! I *meant*—what the hell are you talking about?"

"Have you ever seen how baby ducks imprint on their mothers?"

Hope threw her hands out in frustration. "Again—what the hell are we talking about?"

"*Have* you?" Jenna persisted.

"I guess so. Yeah, I saw a video of it in psych class—attachment theory or something."

"Right, ducklings imprint on their mother. It's just a natural, biological force."

"And, still, *really* not seeing how any of this is relevant."

"Well, lifemating has a lot in common with imprinting." Jenna bit her lip, looking a little sympathetic now. "R'har has lifemated to you—imprinted on you, Hope, if that makes it easier to understand. There isn't going to *be* anyone else for him."

The breath rushed out of Hope's lungs. "He's *what*?"

"That's what male g'hir do—when they mate with a female, they bind to them. Imprint on them. For life."

"Wait, what about the women?"

Jenna shook her head. "Nope, just the men. So if you're leaving because you're scared he's gonna run around on you, because you're scared he's going to leave you? Well, girl," Jenna sighed, "you're leaving for the wrong damn reasons."

Hope turned her face away, suddenly remembering what he'd said just before the Zerar attack—

You will never truly understand what it means to me to have lifemated to you!

R'har waited for Jenna, his heart thudding with slow, heavy beats, offering a prayer to the Goddess with every breath.

He did not have to wait long. It was only midmorning when he saw the Erah clan's shuttle approaching his campsite.

He hurried forward to meet the shuttle as soon as it landed. R'har shifted his weight restlessly as the shuttle door opened and the ramp extended. He was waiting at the bottom as soon as the ramp touched the ground.

Jenna came to the shuttle doorway and R'har's heart dropped.

There was no reason to ask Hope's answer to his plea; the look on Jenna's face said it all . . .

The future clanmother of the Erah descended and placed her delicate hand on his arm. "I'm sorry, R'har. I tried."

He nodded, his throat too tight for words.

"If it makes any difference, I think she's making a mistake. And I think, deep down, she knows it too."

There was, around Ra'kur's mate, just the smallest scent of *her* and he shut his eyes to breathe it in deeply, to take that much of her into himself.

A drop against an ocean of need . . .

"Please, Mata, is she—is she well?" He hated this, having to ask another about her well-being when every fiber of his body demanded he be there, safeguarding her. "Is she . . . happy?"

Jenna sighed. "I'd say she's hale 'n' hearty, all right, but happy? No."

"But my clan—They treat her well? They are kindly to her?"

Jenna hesitated, her lovely eyes pitying.

"Ah," he murmured and his stomach churned. "They are competing for her, my clanbrothers. Vying against each other in hopes she will choose one of them as mate."

"Yeah," Jenna admitted reluctantly. "Nobody said anything, but you'd have to be blind not to see them tripping over themselves to impress her."

Which would condemn me to a greater hell? To have her leave Hir—and me—forever? Or have her choose another among my brethren and end my banishment so I could gaze upon her all my days, but only as mate to another?

"Does she . . ." He had to force the words out. "Is there one among the warriors she favors?"

"No there isn't," Jenna said quietly. "And I'm sorry, R'har, Hope has made up her mind. She's going back to Earth."

TWENTY-SIX

With the last day of R'har's claim on her ending tomorrow Hope felt positively claustrophobic at the Yir clanhouse. The Council allowed each warrior thirty days from the time he landed on Earth to find a human woman willing to bond with him—dawn would bring an end to Ra'kur's time. They called it the Day of Choosing and tomorrow Council Member Mirak would be on hand to make the announcement and to escort her to the vessel that would return her to Earth.

The Yir warriors, even Ha'kin, who'd escorted her from the capital city, saw this time as their last chance to present themselves as suitors before she returned to Earth.

Unable to take it another minute, Hope headed for the only place that she could be sure no warrior would be, where none would follow her and certainly none would think to court her—the Remembrance Stones.

Dressed in feminine g'hir clothing of tunic, trousers, and soft boots, her clothes—thanks to Si'hala's taste—were a little too fancy but still suitable for the walk. Every warrior she encountered on the way offered to escort her on her stroll—until she named her destination.

Situated a good hour's—for her anyway—walk from the Yir's clanhall the memorial was accessible by a quiet road surrounded by forest. A prayer gate marked the entrance to the lush, walled-off garden and paved paths within led through the flowers and fruit trees to the center of the space, where jewels had been placed in an outward swirling pattern, like the arms of a spinning galaxy—the g'hir symbol for eternity.

The flowers and plants surrounding the space were lovingly tended but visitors here were rare. The entire clan came once a year on the anniversary of the day the Scourge came to their enclosure to honor their fallen but none needed a stone to remember the lost. Now, at midmorning, the place was deserted.

Hope let her breath out as soon as she was through the prayer gate, relieved simply to have escaped the warriors and their hopeful eyes, glad to have a moment's peace since Si'hala, so eager for the company of another woman her age, thought nothing of dropping by Hope's quarters day and night.

She paused on the path to lift her face to the suns and breathed in the sweet air of the gardens around her and the forest beyond. Listening to the birdcalls of this alien world, she tried to let the tension ease from her shoulders but the thought that plagued her since her talk with Jenna wouldn't let her be.

Because if what Jenna said was true—
It still didn't stop him from lying to me!

Hope folded her arms, her shoulders hunched as she followed the winding path through the gardens to the center of the memorial.

Open to the sky and set alight by Hir's suns, the Remembrance Stones were a breathtaking outdoor sculpture. Nearly fourteen feet across, it would have been a beautiful piece of artwork—except that each of these rainbow-hued stones represented a woman, girl, or baby the Yir clan had lost to the Scourge.

The precious jewels, varying in size, represented an astonishing investment, a treasure equal to hundreds of the finest diamonds on Earth.

Hope stood at their center, taking in their beauty, imagining what this world would have been without the Scourge. The g'hir would be a thriving race, instead of a dying one. There would be matings and weddings at the winter Gatherings, glowing-eyed children aplenty playing in the clanhalls, and women filling this world instead of millions of warriors doomed to watch their kind end.

If it weren't for the Scourge these people would have no interest in humans at all.

And R'har would never have come to Earth.

Hope thought too about the g'hir women, how their lives and dreams and futures had been stolen from them by the Zerar's horrific weapon.

"I'm sorry," she said softly to the stones, to the women and girls and babies they represented. "I'm so sorry."

The suns were warm on her but a chill suddenly raised goose bumps on her arms. As if all those women were suddenly surrounding her, scowling, angry that their lives had been torn from them and that *she*, who could offer a chance for their people to survive, was turning her back on them, making a mockery of their suffering—

Hope took a step back, her gaze darting around the quiet, empty space.

Man, I'm losing it.

Still, getting the hell out of here and back to the clanhall seemed like a freaking great idea. Hope backed away from the stones as if those spirits would appear in truth if she dared look away. She stumbled in her hurry and had just made it to the path that led to the prayer gate, to the road beyond that would take her to the clanhall, only to stop short.

The man blocking her way was a g'hir warrior but not one that she recognized. He wore the usual leather clothing of a warrior but his hair was darker than the Yir usually had, a warm brown in color, his eyes a startling lavender.

"Oh," Hope blurted. "Hi. I didn't see you there."

"I have come to honor the dead," he said gravely.

His serious manner was appropriate for a memorial to genocide but Hope had a sudden impulse to retreat back into the Remembrance Stones and take the other way out.

You're being ridiculous! Of course he's not all smiles. He's grieving—probably the loss of his whole family!

"Of course," Hope mumbled, stepping to the side to go around him. "I was just leav—"

He moved quickly, blocking her way, but his gaze was over her shoulder. "You are alone here."

Hope's mouth went dry.

He's the only g'hir who hasn't called me "Mata" . . .

"Oh," she said, her voice high and tight, and sent an airy wavy in the direction of the clanhall. "They're right behind me. Should be here any second. In fact, there they—"

His eerie eyes focused on her. "I am g'hir."

"Yeah, I know that," she stammered, taking a half-step back.

"This world is ours," he said, his advance forcing her to retreat further. "Given to the g'hir by the All Mother. We will not let the Zerar defeat us. We will not let our own fears defeat us. We are g'hir. We will die g'hir." His fangs bared. "Your presence here dishonors our dead. Your very presence on our world offends them, *human*."

Hope felt herself blanch. "You're a Purist . . ."

The fact that he'd gotten onto the Yir enclosure, that he'd managed to elude hundreds of warriors to get to her, paled beside the horrifying realization that she was utterly alone with him in a place no other would accidently venture.

He came closer, looming over her. "It is better that we all return to Goddess pure than offend Her by sullying our blood with your kind."

"Hey, you don't have to worry about anybody sullying anything with me," Hope offered as she retreated. "I'm going back to Earth. Tomorrow."

"They will just bring more in your stead to pollute our world," he snarled, his alien visage hideous with hatred. "More like *you* to whelp their half-breeds."

"Please . . ." she whispered as he closed the distance between them. "The Yir—"

"*You* will be our message to the Yir, human," he spat, his hand rising to her throat. "Your torn bloodied corpse staining the stones of the dead will be our message to every enclosure. The All Mother will not tolerate this sacrilege."

He had a g'hir speed, a g'hir's strength. Hope drew a breath, already knowing she wouldn't have time to scream—

TWENTY-SEVEN

Hope hit the ground hard, her chest aching from the blow, her palms stinging from scraping along the path's rough stones. Gasping and dazed from the hit, it took her a moment to realize the thunderous sound in her ears was roaring.

R'har!

His fangs were fully bared, his face more terrifying than she had ever seen him, his movements a blur as he attacked the Purist. There was the sound of flesh hitting flesh as the men fought, snarling.

The Purist was taller than R'har, with a greater reach, and equally quick. Hope winced as the Purist landed two sharp strikes to R'har's abdomen, blows that should have brought him to his knees, hits that would have broken human bones, but R'har was a force of nature in his fury.

R'har caught the taller man with a strike to the face then kicked out, sweeping the Purist's feet from beneath him. Hope watched as if in slow motion R'har twisted to catch the Purist by the throat. In the next instant the man collapsed to the ground, his neck broken.

R'har stood over the body of the Purist, his chest heaving. His head came up, his lips still drawn back baring his fangs and his wild, glowing eyes locked with hers.

He looked thinner, as if in the short time since she'd last seen him he had forgone sustenance entirely. His face was etched with new lines and there were shadows of care beneath those glowing eyes.

"Are you hurt?" he demanded. Not waiting for her answer, he crossed to her in two strides and crouched beside her to clasp her arms, to check her for himself.

"I don't think so," she got out, rubbing her chest.

"I did not mean to strike you so hard when I knocked you out of the way," he growled. "If I have injured you—"

"No," she said, starting to tremble. "It mean yeah, I'm gonna have a bruise but—He was a Purist, R'har. He was going to kill me!"

R'har bared his fangs at the dead man. "I knew this warrior was not of the Yir. I thought him a guest of our clan but I should never have allowed him to get so close to you!" His gaze darted about. "I detect no others here but I must get you back to the safety of the clanhall immediately. Lihr must have every stone of our enclosure searched for other Purist vermin."

"Yeah," she said and tried to stand but her shaking had just gotten worse and she couldn't. "We . . . should warn—"

In the next instant Hope was in his arms and he was carrying her away with his long strides, past the prayer gate to the cool quiet of the tree-lined road.

R'har was here, cradling her, and she was safe in his arms, the warm cinnamon scent of him bringing back a thousand tender memories, and for a moment he was all that mattered.

"You should not be here alone!" R'har growled. "It is the height of foolishness that you would be."

Hope blinked, her warm fuzzies evaporating at his scold. "Wait—Are you saying this is my fault?"

His jaw tightened. "Did Si'hala give you no guards? No escort? Is *this* how they safeguard my lifemate?"

"I'm not—And I didn't *want* guards! In fact I came here just to be alone for one damn minute," she snapped, stiffening in his embrace. "What are *you* doing here anyway?"

His mouth settled into a tight line, his gaze straight ahead on the road before him. "You are still my responsibility."

"Like hell I am! We're not—*whatever* we were—anymore. And I know they told you I didn't want to see you again!"

"I have kept out of your sight until now," he rumbled, his fangs showing a bit again. "I have not imposed my presence on you."

"Not imposed—?" Hope felt her nostrils flare and she started to struggle in his arms. "Goddamn it, R'har! Put me down! I mean it! Put me down *now*!"

He hesitated for a moment then gently complied.

"You've been watching me, following me whenever I leave the clanhouse, haven't you?" she demanded as soon as she gained her feet.

"Of course."

She stared. "You know, on Earth stalking a woman is creepy. And illegal." She folded her arms. "And *creepy*."

His brow creased a little. "You said 'creepy' twice."

"I didn't want you to miss it," she snapped, pushing past him and heading down the road toward the clanhall.

"I would not have let him hurt you, little one. I would have died first."

Hope stopped. "I know. And I'm—grateful you were there. You saved my life. Again."

"Tomorrow is the last day of the moon cycle," he said hoarsely and the pain in his voice made her wince. "My claim to you ends with the dawn."

Hope swallowed hard. "I know that too. But when I'm gone you can go home, back to the clanhall, where you belong."

She heard him draw closer, could feel the warmth of him at her back.

"I do not care about the clanhall, little one," he said roughly. "Nothing matters but you, and tomorrow . . . I will no longer have any claim to you. The Yir clan will no longer be yours. And you will leave my world, my life, forever." He touched her hair and she closed her eyes at the sweetness of it, this lightest of stokes. "My sweet Hope . . ."

"You shouldn't have—" Tears stung her eyes. "If you just hadn't lied to me . . ."

"I would have revealed the truth to you in time."

"When you felt like it," she said bitterly.

"When I had won your heart."

"I couldn't—" She shut her eyes. "I'm so stupid. I am just so fucking *stupid*. After what Brian did, I promised myself I'd never fall for—And you could have told me at any time, but you didn't. You kept that deception up for days, until I loved you so much I couldn't see straight. And it was all a lie."

"I never meant to hurt you. My regret knows no bounds. I regretted it then but . . ."

At that she turned to spear him with a look. "But what? It was just so much fun you couldn't help yourself?"

His glowing eyes widened. "You think my deception an act of contempt?"

"I think lying to me doesn't show me a whole lot of respect, no."

R'har regarded her silently for a moment.

"The All Mother is right to take you from me," he said finally. "What I did—that the Goddess gifted you to me and

I coveted you so that I resorted to lies to keep you with me—reveals a terrible flaw in my soul that shames me." His face was grave. "Her only mercy now is that you will not recall my deception . . . or me."

Hope gave a snort of disbelief. "A nearly seven-foot-tall alien I had sex with is not someone I'm likely to forget, R'har."

"Yes, little one," he growled and sorrow settled over him. "You will."

"Wait a second, you really mean that." Her brow creased. "There's more, isn't there? Goddamn it, what aren't you telling me? *Why* won't I remember you?"

"Have they not told you?" he asked heavily. "They will wipe your memory before they return you home. Erase all trace of the g'hir people. Of this world." He touched her cheek lightly. "Of me."

"*What?* What the fuck are—" Hope's chest was so tight it was a moment before she could force air into her lungs. "Your people have the technology to do that? They're going to make me forget everything that's happened?"

"From the moment you entered the woods that day. For you, everything from that instant on . . . will never have been." His gaze was dull. "You will return to your world with no memory of this one."

Hope's eyes widened in horror. "But—*why?* Why would they do that to me?"

"It will be this way with every human female who chooses to return home." He dropped his hand. "We cannot have the knowledge of our kind, of our plan for survival, known to the humans, to anyone."

Hope wrapped her arms around herself. "No, there has to be—What if I promised not to say anything? Never tell anyone?"

"I wish—" he began hoarsely then shook his head. "They will not allow it."

"Everything?" she asked, her voice sounding very tiny to her own ears.

R'har searched her face, as if committing every curve and shadow to memory.

And right now she could look all she wanted to at his bright, sad eyes, at his full mouth and ridged brow, but tomorrow all of it, *all of it*—the smiles and laughter and the first kiss and how his eyes looked as they made love under the dozens of moons in an alien sky, the tenderness of his hand in hers as he soothed her fears in the medical bay— would be torn from her.

"But they can't!" she cried. "They can't just take everything away from me!"

"I have broken clan directive in allowing you to see me and I know myself unworthy of you. I should not add to my offenses but I beg you, little one—" He took a step closer. "Please, allow me this . . ."

In the next moment R'har cupped her face in his hands, his nose brushing hers, then his lips were on her own, the slow bittersweetness of this last kiss making her eyes sting.

The sound of riders made her glance that way and she saw a half-dozen Yir warriors coming in their direction. The Yir's mounts tossed their heads as the beasts galloped down the road from the clanhall, headed to where she and R'har stood.

Apparently that Purist hadn't gotten in so quietly after all . . .

R'har saw the approaching warriors too. His face was ragged as his glowing eyes met hers.

"I will remember, my Hope," he promised. R'har touched his lips lightly to her forehead, the utter tenderness of it squeezing her heart. "I will remember enough for both of us."

Then he let her go.

TWENTY-EIGHT

Standing on the balcony of her quarters, Hope rested her hands on the waist-high wall, the surface rough beneath her palms. The third and smallest of Hir's moon—the Little Sister, as the g'hir called it—hovered just above the western horizon.

Behind her Hope heard Si'hala enter her quarters. The soft sound of her slippered feet crossed the living area then stopped at the entrance of the balcony.

Very soon the Little Sister would vanish behind the Atali Mountains, marking the end of R'har's claim to her.

After a long moment Si'hala cleared her throat. "It is nearly time."

"I know," Hope murmured.

"Are you ready?"

Hope rubbed her stinging eyes. Comfortable as that big bed was, she hadn't slept well in it. She'd finally drifted off sometime in the middle of the night only to dream she was back standing among the Remembrance Stones, but this time R'har stood in the center with her. His arms encircled her and she clung to him but then the jewels around them began to vanish, disappearing faster and faster around them. His challenging snarl rose as the emptiness raced toward them, getting closer and closer, and then his roar stopped and there was nothing but silence.

She'd woken up sobbing.

"Do you have any questions about the parting ceremony before we go down?"

Taken

Hope shook her head. "Mirak announces that R'har's claim to me is ended. And then you'll say the Yir release me willingly and then Mirak takes me back to the capital for a big fat dose of amnesia and then . . . I wake up on Earth thinking none of this ever happened."

Si'hala's rippled brow creased. "Are you afraid of the coming procedure? They have perfected this memory wipe," she assured. "It was developed for the treatment of psychological trauma. It is very effective."

"And irreversible." Hope wiped her palms against her jeans. She'd be going back to Earth in the same clothes she'd come in. "The doctor who examined me yesterday afternoon explained that they're going to fix it so I'll just remember wanting time alone to think. I'll have some fuzzy memories of long walks and appreciating nature and crap." She tossed her head with a carelessness she didn't feel. "He said I'd have a strong aversion to thinking too much about it. Apparently my subconscious will provide the answers I need as I need them—like why the hell I didn't call anybody, why I just walked out of the rental and left all my stuff there. I'm kinda curious myself what I'll come up with but of course I won't even realize I'm lying. The doctor said I might dream about being here though, about—" Hope swallowed hard. "Some of you."

Si'hala gave a faint smile. "Happy dreams, I hope."

Who would she think he was, the glowing-eyed creature who would haunt her dreams? Would she know R'har when she slept only to forget again when she awoke?

Hope glanced at the still dark courtyard below. In the dimness she could make out the figures of warriors, land tillers, servants, all those g'hir males gathering for her departure. "Is he here?"

"R'har must attend to formally relinquish his claim, just as I must be present to release you as a clansister of the Yir enclosure." Si'hala hesitated. "The entire Yir enclosure has been searched and no other trespassers found. Lihr has increased the patrols and doubled the guards. The Yir have lodged a formal complaint with the Ruling Council. In the wake of this horrific assault we have demanded the arrest of all Purists." She took a step closer, her glowing eyes solemn. "If you stay, I vow we will never be lax in your protection again."

"I don't blame you for the attack yesterday," Hope said. "And you know the Purists are not the reason I'm leaving."

"There are any number of warriors who still long for your eyes to turn their way in favor, if you—"

"Please, Si'hala," Hope pleaded, passing her hand over her eyes. "I can't take any more. I bet Council Member Mirak already packed my shuttle back to the capital with warriors from his enclosure to pick from since I passed on his son."

"Mirak is supposed to be impartial!" Si'hala's mouth tightened. "His role is to officiate on behalf of the Ruling Council, not use the opportunity to push his clanbrothers at you!"

"Speak of the devil," Hope murmured.

The women watched silently as a dark shape sped toward them, its signaling lights marking it out as a shuttle.

"Let's get down there." Hope straightened and headed inside. "I just want to get this over with."

"Hope—" Si'hala paused at the doorway. "What I said about Mirak—Please do not think I am motivated only by my clan's interests. I have so enjoyed having you among us. I would very much like to keep you as my clansister."

"I like you too, Si'hala but I—I just can't," Hope said, her throat tight. "I'm going home. I have to."

Si'hala gave a nod—a human nod—and while her brilliant eyes couldn't tear up, they were very sad indeed as she turned to lead the way.

The faces of the assembled clan were grave and the courtyard, which had been so brightly decorated for her arrival, was gray under the overcast skies. It was chilly too, at this hour of the morning, as Hope took her place at the clanhall door.

On the opposite side of the door R'har came to stand between Lihr and Si'hala, facing her. Those who had assembled in the courtyard quieted to bear witness.

"The Day of Choosing is here." Mirak raised his voice loud enough to be heard even by those farthest away. "R'har of the Yir enclosure, you captured this female in honor but she has not accepted you as her lifemate."

R'har was pale, his eyes shadowed and his shoulders tight, but he met her gaze.

"I concede my claim is at an end," he growled, low and rough. "I have no further right to the one called Hope. I know myself forbidden to capture her again."

Mirak directed his attention to Si'hala, and the future clanmother inclined her head.

"The Yir clan also yields its claim to this female," Si'hala intoned. "In peace we release this clansister from our enclosure and into the protection of the Ruling Council."

"I accept this responsibility from you," Mirak returned briskly. "Be assured that I hold it as an honor."

The Council Member was already urging her away but Hope paused to address Lihr and Si'hala. "Thank you both, for trying so hard to make me feel welcome here."

Si'hala gave a sad smile in return. "In my heart, Hope, you will always be my clansister."

Hope raised her eyes to meet R'har's but she couldn't speak, not even to say goodbye.

I won't remember! I should be glad I won't remember him!

"Mata?" Mirak indicated that Hope should precede him to the shuttle.

"Right," she murmured, turning that way.

"A moment—" R'har stepped forward quickly. "Please!"

Mirak gave a low snarl of disapproval at this breech of protocol but Hope spoke first.

"R'har?" She searched his raw gaze. "What is it?"

"Hope, I deeply regret my deception," he rumbled softly, words intended for her alone. "And I will forever regret your loss. Soon you will have no memory of me, little one, but for me your light will never dim." A gentle smile curved his mouth, his bright eyes soft on her. "The time we shared has been the greatest joy I could ever know. I pray the All Mother grants you every future happiness, my belov—" He broke off and she could see him swallow, suddenly aware again of the others present. "Mata."

Hope looked up at him for a long moment. "What about today, R'har?"

His brow creased. "Mata?"

"What about today?" she asked again. "Do you think She'd do that for me today? The All Mother? I mean, She hardly knows me."

The g'hir gathered for her departure were shifting in their places, murmuring in confusion.

R'har' shook his head a little. "I do not understand."

Mirak cleared his throat. "Mata, the shuttle—"

"I'm in the middle of something here," Hope said shortly, never taking her eyes off R'har. "So—do you think She would grant me every happiness? Today?"

"I am sure," R'har replied, his bright green eyes bewildered, "that you are worthy of every happiness the All Mother can bestow."

"You know, I'm pretty damn good at screwing things up for myself. So I'm hoping you're right about Her wanting to help me out because I am absolutely sure"—she wet her lips—"that I can't *do* this."

He blinked. "Do what, Hope?"

"This!" she cried, throwing her hands out. "Do this! Get on that shuttle and lose—*everything*!"

His brow furrowed and suddenly her words were tumbling out so quick she was stumbling over them.

"Like how scary you looked but sexy too—'cause you did!—when you saved me from the bear and that cookie-thing you fed me—which was really awesome and I could eat by the truckload—and how you managed to land that ship even though it shouldn't have been possible. And how you held my hand"—Hope reached out and clasped his warm broad, rough hand in hers—"when the medcomp was working on me and for once I wasn't scared. And how you carried me away from the Zerar when they'd just *shot* you. And I don't care that I could get my heart smashed up again—" Tears blurred her vision as she shook her head. "No, that's not true, I do care. And I'm scared out of my mind right now but I can't lose all those moments and smiles and—growls of yours, R'har. I can't lose *you*."

"My Hope . . ." His face worked, his glowing eyes agonized, his fingers gently intertwining with hers. "But I have no claim on you now. I am forbidden to make another."

Hope gave a choked sob and he closed his eyes briefly.

"For you I would—" His hold on her tightened and then, as if forcing himself to do it, he let her go. "But I cannot. By g'hir law my claim is ended now."

"G'hir law." Hope wiped at her face roughly and gave a nod. "Okay, fine, g'hir law it is—I choose you, R'har."

He blinked. "You—?"

They were all staring at her.

"But—" Mirak sputtered. "Dawn has come and—"

"And R'har's claim is over, yeah, everybody's got that, thanks," Hope snapped. "When I was onboard the warship, Doctor Ki'san said that since the Scourge, women could choose a mate for themselves without being captured. That's right, isn't it? I can do that if I want to, right?"

"Yes," Si'hala agreed reluctantly. "But R'har is—"

"Oh, hold up," Hope said, cutting her off. "You said—like a *million* times—that I was welcome to choose any warrior of the Yir enclosure as a mate. *Any* warrior. R'har is a warrior of the Yir enclosure. So I choose R'har." She looked at him. "To be my mate." At his staring silence she cleared her throat. "Okay?"

"Hope," he rumbled finally, his eyes searching hers. "You do not sound certain."

"Oh, I'm certain I love you, R'har and I'm sure I want you. It's just—" She wet her lips. "Look, I really suck at this—you know, picking men? I wasn't kidding when I said I'm cursed. And maybe that Purist was right. Maybe I don't belong on Hir. But I know I don't belong on Earth anymore either. All I know for sure, R'har . . . is that I belong with you."

His glowing eyes blinked at her.

"So that's why I'm kind of hoping the All Mother will step in here big time and break the curse. I mean—" Hope rambled. "I always pick losers but *you* picked *me* . . . okay, not this time but originally anyway. And Jenna explained the whole lifemating thing so that helps—" Hope put her hands on her hips. "Am I making any sense here?"

"I think you are choosing me as your mate," R'har said slowly. "Even though my claim to you is at an end."

"Yes." She glanced around at the other thunderstruck g'hir. "Why? Doesn't anybody ever do this?"

"No." R'har shook his head. "No g'hir female has *ever* abjured a mate who captured her and then later chosen him."

"Oh. Well—" Hope pointed at her forehead. "Human. And back on Earth there's a saying—'It's a lady's prerogative to change her mind' so—" She squared her shoulders. "I'm changing it."

Si'hala's face lit up. "I like this saying."

"I mean, I am so crazy desperately in love with you, R'har, that I'm actually willing to just close my eyes and jump—"

"This cannot be," R'har murmured.

She searched his face, starting to feel a little panicky. "Wait a sec—don't you still want me to be your lifemate? I thought—"

"Yes," he rumbled, stepping forward to cradle her cheek in his warm broad palm. "Little one—Yes."

Her shoulders fell in relief. "Oh, thank God— Goddess—*whoever*—but just so you know, I'm really, really scared right now and please don't break my heart.

And I don't care if you think you have a good reason—no more lies. Never."

"Never," he promised, his growl low, fervent, and brushed his nose to hers.

Then, as if the whole Yir clan and Mirak and his clanbrothers too were not even there, R'har's mouth was hot on hers and her arms wound around his neck to pull him closer.

"Okay, just checking here," she said when R'har drew away, both of them a little breathless. "Do I have to do anything else now? Get something for you to eat or drink or anything? You need to tell me 'cause I have no flipping idea."

"All that is needed is your choosing and my acceptance. I am yours for always," he rumbled. "And you are my future, my heart. My Hope."

Her vision blurred as she smiled up at him.

"You do not have to tell me this time." R'har smiled back and touched his ridged forehead to hers. "These are the happy tears . . ."

EPILOGUE

"Are you certain, Hope?" Si'hala looked over her ensemble in despair. "There is still time to change."

"I'm sure," Hope said—*again*—from her place before the dressing room mirror. "Where I come from, white is the traditional color for a bride."

"But it is so . . . plain."

Hope regarded her reflection as she smoothed the silky skirt of her wedding gown. The gown was magnificent; decorated with real pearls—not beads—and stones that sparkled like diamonds—it was a dream of a dress. Her red curls were done half up and half down, dressed with stones like the ones on the dress that caught the light with every movement of her head.

"It's not plain," Jenna protested from where she sat nursing her new daughter, Anna—named for Jenna's mother—as she shifted the baby to a more comfortable position. "It's elegant."

Hope smiled. "I think it's perfect."

"It is *not* a winter fabric. You should have something that *dazzles* for a wedding." Her clansister tsked and headed for the racks to pull down a plum-colored gown shimmering with the kind of gold beading a Las Vegas showgirl would sport. "Now *this*—"

Hope sent a pleading glance across the dressing room at Jenna.

"Really," Jenna said to Si'hala, "this is just the kind of gown human brides from our part of Earth wear. I mean in plenty of other places—*Ow!*" Jenna gave a startled look at the infant in her arms. "Jeez, are you cutting a fang already?"

"Pumping," Hope muttered under her breath, turning back to her reflection as Jenna freed herself from her baby's bite. "I am definitely going to be pumping."

"Very well," Si'hala said sulkily as she returned the plum dress to its place. "I will tell them it is a human custom that I cannot talk you out of, no matter how I tried."

Hope didn't think even one of the hundreds of warriors waiting downstairs in the Yir clanhall to bear witness to the wedding would care either way. "I'm sure—once you explain it—they'll understand."

"I will let them know you are ready," Si'hala mumbled dispiritedly as she left.

Jenna closed her top and stood. "Don't worry. Remember, she didn't like my wedding dress either."

"I'm glad you're here. Both of you." Hope lightly touched the sleeping baby's soft cheek, peering down at the cherubic little face. "She's beautiful."

Jenna beamed. "Yeah, she is. She's going to be very human looking—except for the glowing blue eyes, of course. And she'll probably be really tall, six feet or so."

"That's a little short for a g'hir woman." Hope grinned. "But perfect for a supermodel."

Jenna looked down at her baby. "I hope she gets to see Earth someday. I want her to know where her people come from. Where I grew up."

"Maybe she will," Hope offered and gave a laugh. "It's not like we could have predicted *this*, right?"

The dressing room door opened and Hope, yelping when she saw who it was, flew to hide behind Jenna.

R'har stopped in the doorway, staring. "Hope? What are you doing?"

"You can't be in here!" Hope cried, as the shorter southern girl did her best to shield Hope from his view.

His brow creased, his own wedding clothes a more formal version of a warrior's usual attire. "These are our quarters. I am here every day."

"I mean right now!" Hope exclaimed. "You aren't supposed to see the bride before the wedding. It's bad luck!"

R'har's frown deepened. "But I have already seen you." His glance went over her in a way that showed exactly how much he'd seen of her. "Many times. How would we have lifemated if we did not see each other first?"

"We would lifemate after the wedding," Hope said impatiently.

"But how would we know we wished to marry if we had not lifemated?"

"Are you trying to make *sure* we have bad luck here?" Hope demanded. "Please, R'har, wait for me downstairs!"

"But I will see you then too," he argued, baffled. "Am I to close my eyes?"

"It's okay if you see her *at* the wedding," Jenna said, laughter in her voice. "Just not right before. Don't worry, we'll be down in a minute."

Shaking his head, R'har left and after the door was safely shut behind him, Hope straightened. "Thanks, Redneck."

"Anytime, Townie," Jenna came back.

The two women grinned at each other, then Hope's smile faded.

"Look, Jenna, I've never told you how much I appreciate what you've done for me. Helping me learn about Hir and everything, I mean. Si'hala helps but she's—"

"Not human," Jenna finished with an understanding smile. "I still get homesick too sometimes, but it gets easier. You'll see. I'm really glad you're here, Hope."

"Yeah, well . . ." Hope shifted her feet. Jenna and Si'hala had become real friends, the truest she'd ever had. "I know I didn't make it easy, especially at first. I was so guarded. Maybe even kinda obnoxious."

Jenna raised her eyebrows. "'Kinda'?"

"Very," Hope admitted, her throat closing at how hard she'd pushed Jenna away, at how hard she'd been on R'har.

"Okay, seriously," Jenna said quickly and not entirely feigning panic. "Si'hala will snatch me baldheaded if you come downstairs with your eyes all red, so no crying!"

Hope laughed. "Sorry." She took a deep breath and gave a nod. "I'm okay."

"Good, 'cause it looks like R'har is all set to get married," Jenna said. "How about you?"

"Yes." Hope squared her shoulders. "I am."

"Then let's get to it, girl."

Jenna led the way out and smiled at her mate, Ra'kur, who waited at the bottom of the stairs.

"Can you take the baby?" Jenna asked. "I have to do the matron of honor thing now."

It hardly looked as if she needed to ask. Ra'kur, his face aglow with love for his mate and child, gently took the infant into his arms.

Ra'kur she knew, but the man who bore such a strong resemblance beside him she didn't recognize.

"Hi," she said. "I'm Hope MacGowan."

"Mata." The warrior bent his head respectfully. "I am Ke'lar, of the Erah enclosure."

"My brother," Ra'kur added.

"R'har is greatly blessed to have you as lifemate." Ke'lar was as handsome as his brother and had the same black hair and bright blue eyes as his kinsman. "I have never seen hair that color. You are utterly unique, Hope of the Yir."

"Oh." Hope gave a light laugh. "You'll see plenty like me on Earth."

His face instantly clouded. "I have not had the good fortune of being chosen to journey to your world."

"Oh," Hope said again, her face warming. "Maybe you'll get chosen next year."

"Perhaps," he said but the pain that flashed in his eyes said it all. His clan already had a human female and that knocked him to the bottom of a very long list. He gave a slight smile but even that seemed forced. "Spring will be here soon and I look forward to foresting this year." He bent his head to her again. "May the Goddess smile forever on your union."

"Thank you." Hope watched as he and Ra'kur, carrying the baby, joined the other guests. "That's too bad," she said to Jenna. "He seems really nice."

"Yeah," Jenna said with a glance at her brother-in-law. "There are a lot of good men like Ke'lar. They deserve better than a life alone."

Si'hala was looking her way anxiously and waving her forward, indicating that the time had come. Hope was suddenly hit with a stomach full of butterflies.

"It'll be okay," Jenna said quickly, accurately interpreting her expression. "I'm right behind you."

Hope was frozen in place but just then R'har turned and smiled and suddenly her feet were moving as if she were gliding across the Yir clanhall's ancient stones. Then his warm hand was enveloping hers and she made the vows expected of a g'hir pairing. He followed suit, his deep voice solemnly speaking the words to declare their marriage before the Yir and their guests.

"This is not part of a g'hir ceremony, my Hope," R'har rumbled, surprising her, as Lihr placed something into his palm. "But I would have it be part of ours."

He took her hand in his and Hope smiled through tears as R'har slid a ring onto her third finger, the band radiant with Hironian jewels.

Jenna McNally is tending to the heartrending task of clearing out her grandfather's cabin when she's knocked off her feet by the impact of a nearby plane crash. She races into the snowy North Carolina woods to help and discovers that this is no plane that's crashed.

Ra'kur's people have been brought to the brink of extinction by war. After years spent searching for a compatible mate to bond with, an enemy attack lands him on a backward, primitive planet and right to the very female he has been seeking. And a Hir warrior's first task in claiming a mate is to capture her . . .

Summer 2015
WARRIORS OF HIR SERIES
BOOK ONE

Willow Danes

STOLEN
WARRIORS OF HIR

Kidnapped from Earth by an alien warrior when she visits her uncle, Summer Mills is terrified she will never be able to return home. Her alien captors are using human females as breeding stock and her only chance to return to Earth is Ke'lar, the one Hir warrior willing to stand between her and his own kind.

Returning this human female home won't be easy and Ke'lar knows by this act of defiance he is throwing his own chances at a lifemate away. Both his family's enemies and his own clan have pledged to reclaim the woman he has stolen, the only woman he will ever love . . .

Acknowledgments

My deepest gratitude and thanks to my editor, Erin McCabe. Her support and encouragement make this book possible. Erin, you are the best!

Thanks to my cover designer Steven James Catizone for his talent and, as always, his patience.

Thank you to everyone who supported and encouraged me and, most of all, to my family.

Willow Danes

Willow Danes is the pen name of author Ariel MacArran. She loves all genres of Romance but especially Sci-fi, Paranormal and Historical.

Novels written as Willow Danes:

Science Fiction (Warriors of Hir Series)
> *Captured*
> *Taken*
> *Stolen*

Novels written as Ariel MacArran:

Historical
> *Another Man's Bride*

Science Fiction (Tellaran Series)
> *The Seer*
> *Stardancer*
> *The Consort*